OF VITAL INTEREST

BY

FRANK DEMITH

Ballast Books, LLC
www.ballastbooks.com

Copyright © 2023 by Frank Demith

ISBN: 978-1-962202-16-9

Printed in the United States of America

Published by Ballast Books
www.ballastbooks.com

For more information, bulk orders, appearances, or speaking requests,
please email: info@ballastbooks.com

This book is dedicated to my wife, The House Commander, whose support made this dream possible, and to the more than 1,500 men and women who chose to join the Army as interpreters/translators. You took this step with the clear understanding that your first assignment after initial active duty training would take you overseas to support units in the Global War on Terrorism. Thank you for your service.

Table of Contents

1

The call to prayers filled the streets of the small village as the two men made their way down the dusty road. They were moving toward the mosque to join the others in afternoon prayers.

"Are you sure you have everything you need?" the older man asked.

"Yes, I have packed everything. I am ready," the younger man replied. "There is nothing left to do."

"Good," the older man said as he began to walk faster. "We must hurry. We cannot be late for prayers."

The two men entered the mosque and took their place for prayers. They were not early, and they were not late. They were part of the middle, average, and relatively unnoticeable. That was good. That was what they wanted.

"OK, everyone, this should be a breeze," the bearded man in the dirty military uniform said to the small group of people around him. The man was the team leader, Sergeant First Class MacKenzie, who went by Mac. "All we have to do is put this into play the same way we practiced it."

The men stood around the small table and looked at the building that had been set up as a simulation of their objective. There were two floors to the building, but there was only one door on the ground floor. The building was in an old section of the village and close to other structures. A second team was to accompany them to provide security outside of the building as the operation took place inside.

"Piece of cake," one of the men said as he put his hand on the shoulder of a much smaller man standing next to him. "All we have to do is make sure Carson doesn't try to go through the door first again."

"I am sorry, Sergeant Joe," the smaller man said with a heavy accent, "but I just want to be part of the team. I am a soldier."

"Carson," the bearded team leader said with a smile on his face. "You are without a doubt the most squared away soldier on this team, but you are also our only terp. We can't afford to have you going through the door first every time we go on a mission."

"Hell yeah, Carson," one of the other men added. "We need you to tell us what those poor bastards are saying before we send them off to meet their maker."

"So how many virgins are we up to now, Carson?" Mac asked.

"Seventy-two, Sergeant Mac," Carson responded. "That is what has been said."

"Well," Sergeant Joe said, looking off into the distance. "Kind of makes you do a little thinking. That's a lot of women."

"Joe," Mac said, trying to keep a straight face. "I know you love your wife, but I've met her. Do you really want to have seventy-one more?"

"Good point," Joe replied. "Let's get back to work."

The decision was made to drive to the staging area for the operation. There were four vehicles carrying the twenty-eight soldiers to the designated location outside of the village. The plan was to have the two teams move by foot to the objective while the remainder of the force stayed with the vehicles. Once the operation was over, there would be a radio call to the personnel with the vehicles, and they would move to the objective to pick up the others.

The four vehicles worked their way around the village, staying on the roads that skirted the last of the buildings. As they neared the staging point, they turned off their lights and drove behind a large mound of sand. Everyone got out and set up a hasty perimeter, waiting to see if anyone was going to approach them from the village. After about thirty minutes, Mac gathered his team for some final instructions.

"I want everyone to do a quick equipment check," Mac said after all of his soldiers had arrived. "You have about ten minutes before we head out. We will trail the security force until we get to our rally point thirty meters from the objective. After that, it is all on us. Any questions?"

Everyone was quiet. They had all been through this before and knew what each of their roles was. There was always a chance Murphy would screw things up, but with any luck, this would be a clean op, and everyone would be back in their bunk before daylight.

The security team left the small perimeter and headed down the road toward the village. Intel and recon of the area had indicated that the threat was low, so the teams moved out with a purpose. Sergeant Mac's team was about twenty-five meters behind the security team. They expected it to take about forty-five minutes to get to the rally point.

It was a little over six kilometers to the rally point. Carson tried to focus on what was happening along the road as they continued to move forward, but his mind kept going back to his childhood in a village very similar to this one, no more than one hundred miles away. He had grown up in Iraq and immigrated to the United States with his parents when he was in secondary school. It was difficult for him to believe that had been less than four years ago.

So much had changed for his family and Iraq. His father had been a locally hired linguist supporting the US Army, and they were lucky to leave the country under a special visa program. His family now lived in Michigan as part of a large Arabic community. He remembered how surprised his parents had been when he'd decided to join the US Army. They had both attended his graduation from Advanced Individual Training, and though his father would never say it, he was very proud of his son.

"It is important that you go to help those who would be willing to give their lives for the future of our country," Carson's father had said at his graduation. "It is part of our debt to this country."

Carson's thoughts were brought back into focus when the team began to slow their rate of march as they neared the rally point and took positions near the security team. The rally point was a pair of burned-out hulls of two armored vehicles that sat next to the road. To the right of the vehicles was a partially destroyed mud wall. The vehicles and the wall provided cover for the security team while offering a clear view down the road and the back of the objective.

The team stayed for only a few minutes before moving on toward the building. There was no speaking or sound once they left the rally point. All instructions were given through hand and arm signals, with Mac being in the number two position followed closely by Carson as number three.

They had made it about halfway across the small road when Carson heard someone in the shadows saying "now" in Arabic. Before he could react, there was gunfire from both sides of the street in front of them. The lead for the team was hit first and went down after taking several rounds to his torso. As the security team opened up on the flashes from the enemy weapons, Sergeant Mac's team was caught out in the open. The air was thick with rounds being fired from both sides, and Carson thought it sounded like some type of bug zipping past his head.

Carson was lying in the dirt immediately behind Sergeant Mac when he saw two men moving toward them from the shadows to their right. He yelled out Sergeant Mac's name as he repositioned himself to the right of the team leader, firing two bursts from his weapon into the darkness. One of the men fell to the ground, but the other returned fire, hitting Carson in his right shoulder and upper arm.

It felt like getting hit with a burning hot pipe. Carson quickly began to lose consciousness, but before he passed out, he saw the other man fall to the ground as a member of the security team took him out. The last thing he saw was a third man moving back into the shadows.

The firefight was over in a matter of minutes, and the security team swept forward to secure the buildings and give initial first aid to their wounded comrades. The first man in Sergeant Mac's team had been mortally wounded, while Sergeant Mac, Carson, and two others from the security team had received less severe injuries.

The vehicles were brought forward, and Sergeant Mac, Carson, and the other wounded soldiers were hurried back to the staging point, which was now being used as a medical evacuation site. The other soldiers established a larger perimeter for the landing area, and within minutes, a Black Hawk helicopter landed to take the wounded back for further medical treatment. Sergeant Mac and Carson would need the most attention and were marked as priority patients. The latter was battling to remain conscious, but he had lost a lot of blood.

As the helicopter touched down outside of the medical facility, personnel were already standing by to get the wounded into the hospital. They were taken into an area to be prepped for surgery. Sergeant Mac and Carson were lying on gurneys as they waited.

"Hey, Carson," Sergeant Mac said. "Are you awake?"

"Yes, Sergeant Mac," Carson said, struggling to remain conscious.

"Just wanted to say thanks," Sergeant Mac replied as he tapped his chest with his right hand. "I owe you big time."

"No, Sergeant Mac," Carson said as he started to drift off again. "It is my job. I am Specialist Abdullah, and I am an American soldier."

2

The forty-three soldiers stood outside of the unit orderly room waiting for their first sergeant to arrive. This was a bittersweet day for many of them. The Army leadership had decided to disband their current Military Occupational Specialty (MOS), but some of the soldiers had scored high enough on their ASVAB test to be offered the opportunity to reclassify into another MOS. They were now just waiting to be told what MOSs they would be moving on to.

"So what do you think you will do?" a specialist named Bashir asked his squad leader, Sergeant Abdullah.

"Well, I think I'll just wait and see what comes up," Sergeant Abdullah replied. "It won't be easy to move on to another MOS, but at least we are getting a chance. The majority of our company is being released from active duty."

"That is right, but many of our people are moving on to better-paying civilian jobs as linguists," Bashir countered, trying to gauge the response from his squad leader's body language. "I think that Al Saadi is going to make almost twice what he made as a soldier."

"I am glad that he is going to do well," Sergeant Abdullah said with a visible level of angst. He had issues with Al Saadi as a soldier and was not really unhappy to see him go. "The good thing is that we will still be able to be soldiers and support the greatest country in the world. Hooah?"

"Hooah, Sergeant!" came the reply from the three soldiers standing nearby.

The first sergeant walked out of the door to the orderly room with a sheet of paper in his hand. He came over to the message board and pinned the paper to the corkboard wall.

"OK, soldiers," the first sergeant said as he turned to face the group. "Here are the new MOSs you have qualified for. Take a look and let me know in the next day or so if you have any issues or questions. If I don't hear anything from you by COB Friday, we will move forward with your out-processing and issue you travel orders to your follow-on training. Sergeant Abdullah, can I see you for a moment?"

"Yes, First Sergeant," Sergeant Abdullah responded.

"Let's go for a walk," the first sergeant suggested.

The pair walked down the hall to a small room that was used as a study area. When they stepped inside, the first sergeant asked Sergeant Abdullah to take a seat at the table with him and closed the door.

"Are you sure you want to go through with this?" the first sergeant asked.

"Of course, First Sergeant," Sergeant Abdullah replied. "There is nothing else I would rather do than stay in the Army as a soldier. Why do you ask?"

"I just think that all of you are getting a raw deal," the first sergeant said. "All of you joined the Army knowing that you would deploy as soon as you finished your training."

"Yes, but everyone knew that when they joined," Sergeant Abdullah said, not quite understanding the first sergeant's point.

"Most soldiers join the Army with a chance of deploying. It isn't a certainty," the first sergeant explained. "You shouldn't have to do this with all you have already done for this country. Nobody would question you if you decided to walk away."

"I choose to do this," Sergeant Abdullah stated firmly. "That is the best part. I can make that choice, and it is mine. That is why I will stay in the Army."

"You have served in combat three different tours and have earned three Army Commendation Medals, two Purple Hearts, and a Bronze Star," the first sergeant pressed with a serious look on his face. "You have earned the right to go out and make the big bucks as a linguist. It's just not right for the Army to be treating you like this."

"When my class graduated from individual training, an officer came down from the Pentagon and spoke to us," Sergeant Abdullah murmured as he tried to recall exactly what the officer had said. "He told us of the plans to make 09L a permanent occupational specialty, but he said that the program could only be what the Army would allow it to be. He told us all to be happy with the program because there were no promises of what might happen in the future."

"I know," the first sergeant sighed, as he had heard the same thing before he was assigned as one of the two active-duty 09L company first sergeants in the active Army. "Just because the Army can do things doesn't always make it right."

"This country and the Army do not owe me anything," Sergeant Abdullah insisted as he touched the patch above his left breast pocket that said *US Army*. "It is I who owes this country everything, and I am proud to be a soldier."

The two of them walked back out to where the list was posted. Sergeant Abdullah looked until he found his name. As he glanced across the different fields on the printout, he saw that he was going to be trained as a mechanic. He was hoping to be moving into the infantry, but if the Army needed him to be a mechanic, than he would be the best mechanic possible. Sergeant Abdullah knew that his father would be very happy for him.

"All right, let's get with it, ladies and gentlemen. Find a seat behind an information packet," the man on the stage said as the soldiers filed into the large theater. "Welcome to reclassification training for the wheeled vehicle mechanic's course. Because there are so many of you in this cycle, you will be going through the training with new soldiers attending Advanced Individual Training. We expect you to be outstanding role models and mentors."

Sergeant Abdullah looked down at the stack of papers in front of him. With a sigh, he reached down and took out a pen from his rucksack. He was not going to let anyone see his displeasure, but he would rather be almost anywhere else but here. It seemed like anything a person did in the Army required some type of paperwork to be filled out.

As he looked down at the first form, he chuckled to himself. Last name, first name, middle initial. The Army was still the same, no matter where he was.

The training was not difficult, but Sergeant Abdullah found that he had trouble when it came to the written exams. His English was not perfect, and he needed additional time to read through the test questions. Where he excelled was the hands-on training with the vehicles. He had helped his father who had owned an automotive repair shop in Iraq. Sergeant Abdullah had an uncanny ability to diagnose problems with the engines.

When the class did practical exercises on the vehicles, all the soldiers looked to Sergeant Abdullah for advice. One day, they were working with an old military version of an ambulance. The class was told the basics of the vehicle and instructed to try to determine why it would not start.

Everyone gathered around the engine compartment and began to go through the possible problems that would prevent the engine from starting. Sergeant Abdullah looked at the engine and knew what the problem was before the others had the diagnostic machine hooked up to it. One of the soldiers leaned over the compartment and tried to point out the same thing Sergeant Abdullah had noticed, but the other soldiers were too busy trying to hook up the machine to pay attention to what he was saying.

"Stupid pigs," the soldier muttered in Arabic as he backed away.

As the group of soldiers began to run diagnostics, Sergeant Abdullah walked over to the soldier who was still standing somewhat near the vehicle.

"Do you think they will find the loose wire?" Sergeant Abdullah asked the young soldier.

"Excuse me?" the soldier replied, looking a little shocked.

"I am guessing that you noticed the loose wire like I did, and that is why you are not crowding around the vehicle like the rest of them," Sergeant Abdullah clarified with a small grin.

"Uh, yes, Sergeant," the young soldier stammered. "I believe that is the problem, but I am not that good with engines."

"Well," Sergeant Abdullah said, "you would seem to have a keener eye than the others. Maybe you are just more inclined to notice things that seem out of place."

The soldier was considering how to respond when the instructor walked back to the area where the vehicle was sitting.

"OK, soldiers," the instructor said. "Let's wrap it up."

The soldiers stopped what they were doing and gathered once more around the front of the vehicle.

"So who can tell me what you found?" the instructor asked as he looked out over the group.

"Excuse me, Sergeant," the young soldier said to Sergeant Abdullah. "I need to get back to the group."

Sergeant Abdullah nodded as the soldier rejoined the others. They all stood and looked at the diagnostic machine, which was searching for an answer but not working very quickly.

"I believe a wire has become disconnected inside the engine compartment," Sergeant Abdullah stated as he walked closer to the vehicle and then pointed at the loose wire.

"All right, soldiers," the instructor called out as he looked at the group. "How many of you agree with Sergeant Abdullah?"

Several of the soldiers raised their hands, while the others still seemed puzzled and continued to look for an answer from the diagnostic machine.

"This is an important lesson," the instructor added. "The first step when trying to diagnose a problem is to do a thorough visual inspection of the vehicle. There are times when you can save a great deal of time and effort by simply looking closely at the vehicle. Good job, Sergeant Abdullah."

Sergeant Abdullah felt good knowing that he was going to be able to do his job well as a mechanic. Now all he had to do was figure out a way to study harder to do better on the written exams. Sergeant Abdullah never thought he would finish as the honor graduate of the class, but he wanted to do his best. He simply wanted to make it through the training so he could get back out to a unit and continue to serve as a soldier.

The only question left in his mind was why the young soldier he had met was speaking under his breath in Arabic. Maybe he was just having a bad day.

Time went by quickly, and before anyone could realize it, graduation day from AIT had arrived. It had been a difficult task for Sergeant Abdullah, but he had made it. He was happy that all of his hard work had paid off. Now he could be assigned to a new unit and return to the fight.

Graduation day could not have been nicer with the warm sun shining down on the soldiers in their dress uniforms. Everyone was standing in formation waiting for the distinguished visitors to arrive. The word was out that people from the Pentagon had flown down for the graduation ceremony. Most of the soldiers had originally thought it was just something running through the rumor mill until the company commander had confirmed it in a meeting a few days earlier.

The company commander, First Lieutenant Stevens, arrived with the battalion commander and four civilians. There were three men and a woman, all dressed in the normal business suit common to those who worked in the Pentagon. Sergeant Abdullah was familiar with the Pentagon staff types. There were people from the Pentagon who had shown up at his graduation from the interpreter/translator course several years ago. He thought it was a shame they had lost their interest and allowed the specialty to be disbanded.

The ceremony didn't last long, and it was difficult to figure out why the visitors from Washington had decided to attend. As the ceremony came to an end, the battalion commander stepped to the podium and asked everyone to rise for a special event. He called three of the soldiers forward to the front of the formation. Sergeant Abdullah recognized one of them as the young soldier who had spoken Arabic under his breath the day they had worked on the old ambulance.

"Soldiers," the battalion commander said as the four visitors got up from their seats and moved forward. "Today we have an opportunity to witness a very special ceremony. These three soldiers are part of a new program called Military Accessions Vital to National Interest, or MAVNI. Today they will become citizens of the United States of America."

"Please raise your right hand and repeat after me," one of the gentlemen from Washington said to the three soldiers.

"I hereby declare, on oath, that I absolutely and entirely renounce and abjure all allegiance and fidelity to any foreign prince, potentate, state, or sovereignty, of whom or which I have heretofore been a subject or citizen; that I will support and defend the Constitution and laws of the United States of America against all enemies, foreign and domestic; that I will bear true faith and allegiance to the same; that I will bear arms on behalf of the United States when required by the law; that I will perform noncombatant service in the Armed Forces of the

United States when required by the law; that I will perform work of national importance under civilian direction when required by the law; and that I take this obligation freely, without any mental reservation or purpose of evasion so help me God."

Sergeant Abdullah walked up to the three soldiers after the ceremony and congratulated them on their new citizenship status. He really only knew one of them. The other two, including the soldier he had met during the hands-on exercise with the old ambulance, had kept to themselves during AIT and hadn't socialized much with the others. Sergeant Abdullah just wrote it off as wanting to study more, but he had to admit that there was something a little odd with the way they acted.

"Congratulations, Specialist Al Khafaji," Sergeant Abdullah said to the younger soldier. "You must be very happy. It is a shame that your family could not attend."

"My family still lives in Iraq," the specialist replied without much emotion.

"Oh, well, they must be very proud of you," Sergeant Abdullah continued.

"Um, of course," Al Khafaji said, looking a little flustered. "I think I should go speak with the visitors before they have to depart."

"I understand," Sergeant Abdullah smiled. "I wish you all the best in your assignment."

"I would wish you the same good fortune, Sergeant," Specialist Al Khafaji replied, more out of decorum than genuine sincerity.

"Im sha allah," Sergeant Abdullah said as he walked away.

Specialist Al Khafaji was caught off guard by the other soldier's response in Arabic. He wondered how much Arabic the sergeant really understood and started to try to recall if there was anything he might have said during his training that would be considered a "red flag" to the noncommissioned officer. He didn't consider the possibility for long since he had not been approached by anyone to question his reasons for joining the United States Army.

The visitors from the Pentagon were very friendly. Al Khafaji thought they were maybe a little too friendly. They were all thrilled that the three soldiers had decided to join the Army and become US citizens. Al Khafaji was surprised at how gullible the Americans seemed to be. He imagined it would be easy for him to go to Washington and pay a special visit to their offices in the Pentagon, but he had a different mission and was excited to move on to his new assignment so he could help his unit in their deployment overseas. Maybe he could talk to his friends in Iraq about the possibility of visiting the Pentagon once he finished his deployment.

The next week was spent going through the business of out-processing and preparing for the move to their follow-on assignments. Everyone was excited to be leaving the training base, albeit a little hesitant to be moving on to a "real" unit. All, that is, except for those handful of soldiers who had gone through reclassification training. Sergeant Abdullah did his best to try to calm everyone's nerves and help them through their questions.

Sergeant Abdullah had learned he was to be assigned to Fort Bragg. He had been there before when he'd worked with the Special Forces. He wondered if anyone he had known would still be assigned there. Oh well—he would find out soon.

3

"Welcome to the Eighty-Second Airborne Division, Sergeant," the specialist at the reception center said. "Looks like you are being assigned to the maintenance company that supports the 1-319th Airborne Field Artillery Battalion."

"Thank you," Sergeant Abdullah replied. "It is good to be back at Fort Bragg."

"Your sponsor should be here shortly," the specialist said, looking up at the clock on the wall. "It is not like your unit to be late. You can have a seat, and I will let you know when they get here."

Sergeant Abdullah sat down in the waiting area and started to look at the division newsletter. He thought it was funny how much the units in the Army seemed to focus on the same things. There always was a newsletter or something in the in-processing center that talked about how good the unit was and all the interesting things happening on post. On the other side of the building was the out-processing point where the waiting area consisted of job notices and aids to help soldiers who were transitioning to civilian life.

After about ten minutes, the door opened, and a young-looking soldier came hustling in. "Sorry I am late," he apologized to the specialist at the desk. "I had a ton of stuff to take care of down at the unit."

"Sergeant," the specialist called out to Sergeant Abdullah. "Your sponsor is here now."

"Hey, Sarge," the younger soldier said as he reached out his hand. "Sergeant Maczrakolski, but you can just call me Mac."

"Thank you, Sergeant," Sergeant Abdullah said as he shook hands, "but if it is OK for you, could I call you another name instead? I have a good friend who I call Sergeant Mac."

"Sure, not a problem," Sergeant Maczrakolski agreed with a smile. "How about Ski?"

"That is very good, Ski," Sergeant Abdullah answered. "When I served in Iraq, everyone called me Carson."

"Carson," Sergeant Maczrakolski repeated, a little puzzled. "Not sure I understand that one, but if it works for you, it's good for me. Do you have a vehicle, or do you need a lift?"

"No, I have not bought a car yet," Sergeant Abdullah explained. "I just have my carry bag. Everything else is at the room."

"OK, well, let's go," Sergeant Maczrakolski said as he walked toward the door. "We'll take you by the unit and then get the in-processing in gear."

The pair walked out to the parking lot and got in Sergeant Maczrakolski's oversized pickup truck. It wasn't new, but Sergeant Abdullah could tell it was well taken care of. Sergeant Maczrakolski explained that he'd bought it from the "lemon lot" on post. That was where the soldiers put their used cars for sale, and Sergeant Abdullah made a point to discover where it was located.

The drive to the unit orderly room took only ten minutes. On the way, the two talked about the unit and the upcoming deployment to Iraq. Rumor had it that they would be heading back before the end of the year, even though it was not their turn in the rotation. They were not supposed to go until next year, but the current unit scheduled to deploy was having issues meeting their evaluation requirements. Sergeant Abdullah wondered if this had anything to do with his assignment. He decided not to talk about his old MOS. The only important thing now was to make sure he did a good job as a mechanic.

"Hey, Mac, where you been?" a soldier yelled out as they got out of the truck. "Big B has been looking all over for you. He seems pissed."

"He'll get over it," Sergeant Maczrakolski said. "Hell, he was the one who told me to go down to in-processing and sponsor the new guy. I think he is losing it. Hey, this is Sergeant Abdullah. He is going to be working with us."

"Great, we could use another pair of hands around here," the soldier said. "My name is Staff Sergeant Feister, but most of the folks just call me Uncle."

"Very good to meet you," Sergeant Abdullah responded. He wasn't entirely sure he had heard the sergeant's name correctly or why the other soldiers called him Uncle, but he didn't want to ask him to say it again, feeling a little self-conscious about his English skills. "In my other unit, people called me Carson."

"Carson?" Uncle said. "Can't say I really understand that one, but if it's something you are used to, I'll take note. Have a good one."

Sergeant Abdullah and Sergeant Maczrakolski walked into the orderly room where they came across Sergeant First Class Broadmoor. When Sergeant Abdullah saw him, he immediately thought he was the biggest individual he had ever seen. He had to have been well over six feet tall and every bit of two hundred and fifty pounds.

"Sergeant Mac, where in the hell have you been?" Sergeant First Class Broadmoor demanded in a deep voice that sounded like a rumble of thunder before a storm. "Why in the sweet name of Jesus am I answering phone calls from the in-processing center on why my man is a no-show? Do you not know that we have a ton of stuff to get done around here? What the hell have you been doing? Do you want to stay on my shit list forever? Well, come on. Let's try to put a couple words together and answer at least one of my questions just to make me feel better."

"Sergeant First Class Broadmoor, this is Sergeant Abdullah," Sergeant Maczrakolski said calmly. "He is the new guy you told me to sponsor."

"Sergeant Abdullah," Sergeant First Class Broadmoor greeted him as he reached out his hand. "Don't go thinking this is the way we do things around here. Mac is not one of our more motivated soldiers, but we accept his shortcomings in hopes that he will continue to try harder."

"Yes, Sergeant," Sergeant Abdullah said as he obligingly shook his hand. He was still amazed at the size of Sergeant First Class Broadmoor. Sergeant Abdullah's hand seemed to disappear inside of the much larger man's grasp.

"Mac," Sergeant First Class Broadmoor barked. "Take the FNG down to the shop and get him set up. We got a ton of work to get done just in case we have to fill in on the next trip to the sandbox."

"Will do," Sergeant Maczrakolski nodded.

"Try not to get lost," Sergeant First Class Broadmoor quipped as the two left the orderly room. "And make sure to bring him back to meet the first sergeant and commander when he is done with in-processing."

"Don't worry about Big B," Sergeant Maczrakolski said after he checked to make sure the orderly room door had completely closed behind them. "He is usually all smoke and no fire. You just have to get used to him."

"If you say so, Ski, but he is a very large man," Sergeant Abdullah observed, checking to see if his hand was all right.

"Yep, that he is," Sergeant Maczrakolski agreed with only half a smile. "You definitely don't want to get on his real shit list."

The two soldiers walked down to the motor pool. Sergeant Maczrakolski made sure to get Sergeant Abdullah a locker in the maintenance building and showed him around. Sergeant Abdullah was ready to get to work, but unfortunately, he still had several places to go to complete in-processing. It would take days to finish.

Specialist Al Khafaji received orders to Fort Campbell, Kentucky. He was being assigned to a Special Operations unit. The MAVNI program sent a portion of soldiers to Special Operations units to serve as linguists. He had been told this was the practice but was a little surprised when it actually happened. He did not believe the Americans would be so accepting of individuals who were volunteers from another country. But he forgot he was a citizen now.

When Specialist Al Khafaji arrived at the in-processing center, he was met at the door by a sergeant first class wearing a green beret.

"Good morning," the sergeant first class said in Arabic as he held the door open. "You must be our new linguist, Specialist Al Khafaji."

"Yes," Al Khafaji replied, trying to hide his amazement at the greeting. "I am Specialist Al Khafaji. I was told to report here for in-processing, Sergeant."

"You don't have to worry about it much," the sergeant first class said. "We will take care of most of it. You just need to sign in and give them a few copies of your orders."

"Yes, Sergeant," Al Khafaji replied.

"Relax," the sergeant first class said. "My name is Bill Hermanson. Everyone just calls me Herm."

"Yes, Sergeant." Then, Al Khafaji corrected himself. "I may have to take some time to get used to that."

"We'll work on it," Sergeant First Class Hermanson smiled. "And what should I call you?"

"My name is Samir," Al Khafaji replied.

They entered the in-processing center and walked up to the front desk. Sergeant First Class Hermanson told the specialist at the desk who he was and had Al Khafaji give her two copies of his orders. Sergeant First Class Hermanson then gave her his contact info and told her if they needed anything else from Al Khafaji to call him and he would take care of it. Finally, he asked if there was anything else she needed at the moment. The clerk shook her head without saying a word, not really prepared to respond outside of the normal routine she was used to. The entire process took only five minutes before the two men were heading back out to the parking lot.

"Follow me over to the unit," Sergeant First Class Hermanson instructed as he opened the door to his old Ford pick-up truck.

"Yes, Sergeant," Al Khafaji complied, forgetting about their agreement.

"Yep, we'll have to work on that," Sergeant First Class Hermanson muttered to himself as he closed the door and started the truck.

Sergeant First Class Hermanson waited to make sure that Al Khafaji was in his car and ready. As Al Khafaji backed out of his parking space, Sergeant First Class Hermanson pulled forward and stopped at the stop sign. He made sure to use his turning signal so it would be easier for the new linguist to follow him. As they pulled out onto the road, Sergeant First Class Hermanson wondered to himself what a new soldier was doing driving a brand-new car. He remembered that when he was a young soldier, all he could afford was the bus.

The two drove through a checkpoint and a gate that marked the entrance to the Special Forces admin area. The unit headquarters was a simple brick building with no outward indicators of anything different from the other buildings that Al Khafaji had seen. He noticed that Sergeant First Class Hermanson was backing into a parking space and found another one close by. He parked the car and grabbed his briefcase.

Sergeant First Class Hermanson saw the company commander and sergeant major standing near the door to the supply room. He told Al Khafaji to wait for him while he walked down to speak with them. The group talked for a few minutes, and then Sergeant First Class Hermanson motioned for Al Khafaji to come over.

"Sir, this is one of our new linguists, Specialist Al Khafaji," Sergeant First Class Hermanson said.

"Good to meet you, Specialist," the major greeted as he reached out to shake Al Khafaji's hand. "My name is Major Palmer, and this is Sergeant Major Wagner."

Sergeant Major Wagner shook hands with Al Khafaji as well but didn't say anything. He had a firm handshake.

"Glad to have you with us," the sergeant major finally said. "You have a lot of work to do. Better get him moving out, Herm."

"Roger that, Sergeant Major," Sergeant First Class Hermanson said as he moved out with Al Khafaji right behind him. "We need to check in here first," he added to Al Khafaji. "Once we are done, I'll take you down to the unit and try to introduce you to the other folks."

"Yes, Sergeant," Al Khafaji replied, once again forgetting to use first names.

The in-processing was easy. Just a couple more copies of his orders, and he was practically hand-carried through everything else. The support staff for the unit was extremely friendly and glad to do whatever they could to make the process simple and without issue. He wondered if this was normal. He didn't recall things being so easy when he went through Basic Training and AIT.

"OK," Sergeant First Class Hermanson said as he hung up the phone. "Time to go down and meet the boss."

The two soldiers left the building and walked down the sidewalk and around the corner to another row of brick buildings. They marched up to the door of the second building and went inside. There didn't seem to be anyone around, but Sergeant First Class Hermanson told Al Khafaji to have a seat, indicating he would be right back. Specialist Al Khafaji watched as Sergeant First Class Hermanson knocked on the second office door, waited, and then stalked inside, closing the door behind him.

"So what do you think?" the man sitting behind the desk asked as Sergeant First Class Hermanson stopped just before him.

"Well, Boss," Sergeant First Class Hermanson began. "This one is hard to read. He seems distant and not really focused on being here, but at the same time, he pays attention to what is going on around him. Might try to figure out where he is coming from and where he expects to be going. I also would try to dig a little into finances since he is driving a new car. Nice car, not flashy, but still a little more than I would expect on a specialist's pay."

"OK," nodded the other man in the room, who was standing to the side of the desk near the window. "What about his language skills?"

"Haven't had a chance to check much on that," Sergeant First Class Hermanson admitted. "I gave him a chance when we first met, but he chose not to respond. I think he would be good based on his background, but it would probably be smart to check with our other folks in country before sending him over on a mission."

"Sounds good," the man behind the desk said. "We'll give him plenty of chances to stand out during the train up. Anything else you picked up on?"

"Not really," Sergeant First Class Hermanson responded. "Just something I can't quite put my finger on. There is something more to him, but I just can't figure it out right now. I'll keep working on it while he finishes his in-processing."

"Let's show the young man in," the standing man suggested.

Sergeant First Class Hermanson opened the door and motioned to Al Khafaji to come in. When Al Khafaji entered the room, he had no idea who he would be meeting. He quickly looked at the two new soldiers and came to attention, raising his hand to salute the officer.

"My apologies, sir," Al Khafaji said as he held his salute.

"It's OK, Specialist," the captain said. "You aren't in AIT anymore, and unless you are directed to report to the commander, we are a little less formal."

"Yes, sir," Al Khafaji replied as he lowered his hand.

"My name is Captain Starn," the man behind the desk continued. "This is Master Sergeant Mandess. Most folks call me Boss."

"Yes, sir," Al Khafaji answered.

"Most soldiers call me Top," Master Sergeant Mandess said. "I am the company operations sergeant. As long as you are doing your job and not on my special person list, you can do the same."

"Yes, Sergeant," Al Khafaji said as he continued to stand at attention.

"Do you understand why you were assigned to this unit?" Captain Starn asked as he leaned forward a little bit in his seat.

"Sir, I believe I was recruited to use my language skills," Al Khafaji stated, wondering if he had answered the captain's question. "But I was trained as a wheeled vehicle mechanic."

"You will probably not be using your training as a mechanic with our unit," Captain Starn revealed with a smile. "You are here for your language skills and knowledge of Iraqi customs. When we deploy our teams, we send two of our linguists with them for support. You will be a busy soldier."

"Yes, sir," Al Khafaji said. "I understand."

"Good," Captain Starn responded as he stood up with his hand outstretched. "Welcome to the unit."

Al Khafaji reached out and shook the commander's hand. He stood still, not knowing if he was expected to salute or not.

"OK, Specialist," Master Sergeant Mandess said. "You can go wait outside a second. Sergeant First Class Hermanson will be out in a couple of minutes to get you back on track with your in-processing."

Al Khafaji left the room and closed the door behind him. Then, he went back over to the center of the room to wait for Sergeant First Class Hermanson. He wondered if he should make a point of his meeting with his family. Maybe he would just mention it in passing.

"I see what you mean, Herm," Captain Starn stated thoughtfully, taking out his notebook. "Top, make sure you get him with the other terps and let's see how things work out."

"Will do, Boss," Master Sergeant Mandess said as he walked toward the door with Sergeant First Class Hermanson. "Herm, finish up today and have him over to the Ops office by 0800 hours tomorrow."

"Dang, Top, 0800 hours," Sergeant First Class Hermanson whistled. "You're getting soft in your old age."

"Not really," Master Sergeant Mandess replied. "I just want to check on a few things in the morning before our new specialist gets there."

Sergeant First Class Hermanson walked back into the common area and had the new linguist follow him to the remaining points on his in-processing form. They were done before 1700 hours, so Sergeant First Class Hermanson told him to take care of whatever personal issues he had and be back at the headquarters building at 0745 hours the next day. He wanted to make sure the new soldier was on time.

Al Khafaji had a few things to do. First, he found the post library on his map and drove over. He went inside and asked the librarian if he could use a computer. After checking in a book, she wrote a number down on a slip of paper. Once Al Khafaji found the computer with the number that matched the sheet of paper, he sat down and turned it on. He had not checked his email in several days.

He had an account on a public email site under a different name. When his inbox came up, he saw that he had only received a few that were coded as unread. He looked them over quickly and determined they were not all that important. Then, he opened his junk mail folder and saw twenty-five messages that most people would just delete without giving them much thought.

To any other person in the United States, it would have looked like simple junk mail and email scams. Al Khafaji took particular caution to make sure that there was nobody near as he reviewed these messages. They were from his fellow fighters overseas. He looked closer and found that a phone number was coded into one of the messages, along with a date and time. The message identified his need to call the number before 1900 hours local time. He had about ninety minutes to make the call. Wasting no time, he quickly shut down the computer and left the library. He had to hurry.

Al Khafaji went back out to the parking lot and got in his car. Then, he headed off post toward the local Walmart. He was sure that

Walmart would have what he needed. Al Khafaji went into the store and bought a cell phone. The one he purchased was very basic and had a minimum number of minutes. He would be using it only once and then would destroy it. If necessary, he could always buy another phone later.

Al Khafaji returned to his car and drove to the nearest shopping center. He parked outside the store that seemed to have the largest number of shoppers. It was a discount clothes store, and it seemed like a perfect location. Clutching the phone, Al Khafaji entered the store and then punched in the number he'd found in the message. He let the phone ring five times before hanging up. He then redialed the number, and after two rings, the call was answered by a woman.

"I will tell him that you have called," the woman said without waiting to hear who had called. As soon as she finished her last word, she hung up.

It was just an attempt to determine if Al Khafaji was still able to communicate with them. He was certain there would be other information to follow, but he could only check his messages a few times a day. He didn't want to draw any special attention to himself.

"Achmed's Camel Shop," the voice on the other end of the line said.

"Steve, what the hell are you up to?" Master Sergeant Mandess asked, recognizing the voice on the other end.

"Bob, is that you, you old bastard?" the voice said, sounding a little more enthused. "How the hell is life back in the real world?"

"Same old shit, different day," Master Sergeant Mandess replied. "Hey, I hate to bother you, but I got a favor I need to ask from you."

"No, you cannot sleep with my wife. I don't know how many times we have to go through this," Steve joked.

"Well, that wasn't exactly the favor this time," Master Sergeant Mandess said. "This one is real world, and I could use your help."

"Well, you aren't laughing at my lame-ass jokes, so I guess it's something hot," Steve said, sounding a little more serious. "What can I do for you?"

"Nothing hot right now, Steve," Master Sergeant Mandess stated. "Just something that I would like you to take a look at for me. We got a new terp in, and he came out of your area of the sandbox. Just would feel a hell of a lot better if you could do some snooping and let me know if anything comes up."

"No problem," Steve replied. "I'd be happy to see what shakes out. What's this guy's name?"

"He goes by Samir Al Khafaji. According to his personnel file, he is twenty-three years old." Master Sergeant Mandess paused and then added, "Let me know if anything out of the ordinary shakes loose. Me and my guys are feeling a little unsettled with this guy."

"Will do. Anything else?"

"Nope, nothing for right now," Master Sergeant Mandess said. "I'd like to see if you can put a fire under this one. We may be heading out soon, and I might have to use this kid."

"I'll make sure to get it done as fast as possible," Steve replied without a hint of kidding. "I can't blame you for being concerned. Too much crazy shit going on over here now. Doesn't hurt to play it as safe as possible."

"You got that right, man. Take care," Master Sergeant Mandess replied, ending the call.

4

"Worthless piece of shit!" Staff Sergeant Feister yelled out as he looked into the engine compartment of the vehicle he was standing next to.

Sergeant Abdullah entered the maintenance building and paused to see if Staff Sergeant Feister had finished with his outburst. There was no more yelling at the vehicle, so Sergeant Abdullah walked toward a group of soldiers. He had finished his in-processing a few days earlier and was relieved to finally be getting back to work. He had noticed over the last week that his new unit seemed to be friendly with each other, but they were also tense about something. Maybe it was just the thought of having to deploy overseas again.

"Are you ready to give up yet?" Sergeant Maczrakolski asked as he walked over to the vehicle Staff Sergeant Feister was working on.

"No fricking way," Staff Sergeant Feister replied as he threw the hand towel he was using on the floor next to the vehicle. "This fucking hangar queen isn't going to beat me. I'm going to get it fixed or die trying."

"Is there anything I can do to help?" Sergeant Abdullah asked.

"Not right now," Staff Sergeant Feister said, sounding a little aggravated with the amount of help he was being offered. "If I can't get it up and running, I doubt I'll be looking for help from the FNG. I've been doing this stuff for five years now. Hell, this wasn't even your MOS."

"Come on, Uncle, give him a break," Sergeant Maczrakolski frowned. "He just wants to help."

"Mac, I don't really need any shit from the peanut gallery right now, and I still don't need any help," Staff Sergeant Feister groused as he stepped away from the vehicle. "I got to take a shit, and no, I don't need any help."

"Don't worry about him," Sergeant Maczrakolski said to Sergeant Abdullah as Staff Sergeant Feister walked down the hall toward the latrine. "He's just having a rough time with this vehicle. No matter what we do, it always seems to be back in the shop after a couple of weeks."

"It's OK, I understand," Sergeant Abdullah answered, although he honestly did not understand. "Ski, are we supposed to have a meeting with the first sergeant and commander?"

"Dang, that completely got away from me," Sergeant Maczrakolski said. "Big B is going to be pissed. I'll go by the orderly room and try to set it up for today. Thanks for reminding me."

Staff Sergeant Feister came back after a few minutes and started working on the vehicle again. He worked on it all morning. The yelling seemed to get louder and louder until it stopped around noon. The mechanics all paused what they were doing and watched as Staff Sergeant Feister hooked up the exhaust hose to the vehicle and started it up. The engine sputtered a few times and then started to run.

"Let's see how long it lasts this time," Staff Sergeant Feister called as he picked up the phone to let the unit know their vehicle was ready for pickup.

"No, I'm not kidding," Staff Sergeant Feister said into the phone. "It's done, and if it goes down again, just blow the piece of shit up."

Staff Sergeant Feister put the phone down, and all the mechanics started clapping. He gave them all a one-finger salute as he opened the bay door and pulled the vehicle out into the motor pool. There was plenty of fuel in the vehicle, so he decided to keep it running until the unit came over to pick it up. He didn't want to take a chance on shutting it down.

Sergeant Abdullah and the other mechanics finished up what they were working on and headed to the mess hall for lunch. A lot of the mechanics liked to go off post for lunch, but Sergeant Abdullah could not understand how they would rather spend money eating somewhere else instead of dining at the mess hall. He wanted to buy his own house someday, and the mess hall food didn't cost him anything, so it fit into his plan.

Master Sergeant Mandess arrived at the operations building a little after 0500 hours. He wanted to check his messages before getting in a little PT. When he opened his email account, he didn't see anything out of the ordinary. Nothing yet from Steve, but he would try to give him a call after PT just to make sure.

He hit the gym with a couple of the other guys and went out for a three-mile run. The other guys gave him a hard time for cutting his run short at three miles, but they all knew he was waiting for a call. He was finished before 0700 hours and headed back to the operations building.

Master Sergeant Mandess was just about to open his email when the phone rang.

"Operations, Master Sergeant Mandess speaking," he said as he continued to open his email.

"Damn, Bob, why so formal?" Steve quipped.

Master Sergeant Mandess smiled. "Well, if I knew it was you, I would have answered a little differently. So did you come up with anything?"

"We looked into a few places, but nothing really showed up," Steve said and then paused a second. "I do have one more source I am checking with, but I haven't heard anything yet."

"All right, I appreciate the effort. Just let me know as soon as possible if anything does come from the other source," Master Sergeant

Mandess said. "I'm going to throw this kid in with the other terps and see how he does in a couple of our exercises today."

"OK, I'll keep you posted," Steve replied. "I need to work on a few other things on my end today. We lost another couple local hires yesterday. I'm going to see if we can dig a little deeper into what is going on."

"You think there is anything more than just poor security?" Master Sergeant Mandess asked.

"Well, it's possible," Steve replied. "That's the eighth and ninth local hire we have lost in the last two weeks."

"OK, well, let me know what happens with that," Master Sergeant Mandess requested. "I got a funny feeling our rotation might get pushed up a bit, and I don't want to wait until I get there to find out the bad news."

"Will do, Bob. Have a good one," Steve said before hanging up the phone.

Al Khafaji got to the parking lot a little early and sat in his car just trying to see if anything was going on that he should make note of. He spotted a couple of other specialists standing near another vehicle but was surprised that he didn't notice anyone walking around inside the gate or near the operations building. He figured that most folks were probably already at work.

He was about to get out of his car when he saw Sergeant First Class Hermanson approach the other specialists and start talking with them. He put his passenger side window down a little to see if he could hear anything they were saying. They were too far away for Al Khafaji to hear them very well, but the one thing he was certain of was they were speaking Arabic. Sergeant First Class Hermanson's language skills were better than he had imagined. That was something he had not expected. He would definitely have to be more careful with these soldiers.

Sergeant First Class Hermanson noticed Al Khafaji sitting in his car and motioned for him to come over. As he was getting out, he accidentally pushed the panic button on his key fob instead of the door lock. He quickly hit the right button but saw Sergeant First Class

Hermanson and the others laughing. *Infidels! How dare they make a joke of me,* he thought to himself. *I will take pleasure in what is waiting for them once we get to Iraq.*

"I am sorry, Sergeant," Al Khafaji said as he walked up to the small group. "I am not used to all the new cars. I may have pushed the wrong button."

"No worries. It's all part of a learning experience," Sergeant First Class Hermanson smiled. "It makes for one heck of an intro song."

"What is an intro song, Sergeant?" one of the female specialists asked.

"It's a ritual when a player comes out onto the field," Sergeant First Class Hermanson explained.

"What field would this be?" the specialist inquired.

"It is not important," the male specialist responded as he pushed his way forward to meet the new interpreter. "My name is Wafiq. It is nice to meet you."

"My name is Samir," Al Khafaji replied as he nodded his head once, ignoring the outstretched hand that was presented to him.

"Hello, Samir. My name is Aisha," the talkative specialist said.

The last one in the group was an older woman. She was also a specialist but was not interested in making small talk. Al Khafaji did not press the issue.

"The quiet specialist over here is Sara," Sergeant First Class Hermanson said. "She isn't much for casual conversation, but she is an excellent interpreter."

"Thank you, Sergeant, you are very kind," Sara said without looking in Samir's direction.

"OK, now that we have all the introductions done," Sergeant First Class Hermanson said, "let's talk about what we have planned for today. Take a seat at the table over there and I'll get all of you up to speed."

The four specialists walked over to the wooden picnic table and sat down while Sergeant First Class Hermanson stood at the end of the table so everyone could easily hear him and see him.

"We will be bringing individuals through a mock interrogation, and the four of you will be providing written interpretations of what the individual is saying. Each interrogation will last roughly fifteen minutes. The interrogations will be recorded to assist in our evaluation of your skills. We will gather after every interrogation and go over what happened. Does anyone have any questions?" Sergeant First Class Hermanson looked at the four specialists. "Seems like everyone understands the game plan," he said after a short pause. "I need to go into the operations building to check on a few things. Just wait out here and I will be back shortly."

Sergeant First Class Hermanson walked up to the gate and entered the code to gain access to the operations building. Before entering, he took one more look at the specialists through the reflection in the glass. All four were still sitting at the table. He heard the click of the door as it unlocked and he went inside.

"So are we supposed to write our notes in English or Arabic for the interrogation exercise?" Aisha asked the group.

"Why didn't you ask the sergeant that?" Wafiq wondered aloud. "You don't seem to have any problem saying things."

"I just want to make sure I am doing things right," Aisha countered, trying not to show that she was upset.

"I think it would probably be good to write in English," Al Khafaji answered. "We are working as interpreters, so if the person answers in Arabic, we should write in English."

"What if he was answering the questions in English?" Aisha asked.

"Well, if he was being interrogated and was answering in English, they probably would not need interpreters," Wafiq replied and started to laugh.

Sergeant Abdullah finished lunch and walked back to the maintenance building. He noticed that the building was empty except for three people in the office. He recognized Sergeant First Class Broad-moor, but he did not know the other two. One was a first sergeant, and the other was a captain. They seemed to be looking at the large monthly calendar on the wall and writing notes on it. He walked over to the large scheduling board near the lockers to check if his name had been assigned to any work. Nothing yet, but he did notice that he was marked in the standby section. This meant that if anyone needed extra help, he was available. That was a good start.

In a few minutes, the other mechanics started to return from lunch. He heard them talking about a new fast-food place that had just opened. They all seemed happy with it, except Sergeant Maczra-kolski. He seemed to be upset with something.

"Ski, is everything OK?" Sergeant Abdullah asked.

"He'll be fine," Staff Sergeant Feister said with a smile, holding a five-dollar bill in his hand. "Isn't that the prettiest thing you have ever seen?"

"Uncle, you cheated, and you know it," Sergeant Maczrakolski accused, pushing Staff Sergeant Feister in the back as he walked by.

"Cheated? Why, I wouldn't think of it, Mac," Staff Sergeant Feister chortled, ignoring the push. "I just used my head instead of counting on luck and look what I got. The prettiest five dollars I have ever seen."

"You suck, Uncle," Sergeant Maczrakolski retorted with a smile.

Sergeant Abdullah walked with Sergeant Maczrakolski over to the lockers. Staff Sergeant Feister was still busy showing everyone the five dollars he had won. Everyone was laughing, and nobody noticed the three people in the office.

"Hey, quit jacking around," Sergeant First Class Broadmoor called as he opened the door to the office. "We have a ton of shit to do, and we can't even hear ourselves think. Knock it off and get to work."

Sergeant Maczrakolski was going to say something but saw the first sergeant and captain in the office. Without another word, he went back to his locker and put on his coveralls. Testing Sergeant First Class Broadmoor in front of the chain of command was a definite no go.

"So what has happened with the five dollars?" Sergeant Abdullah asked.

"Well, it's not really a big deal, but I still say Uncle cheated," Sergeant Maczrakolski said as he began to tell the story. "When we were going to lunch, I heard Uncle call the unit to let them know that their vehicle was ready. Uncle said something about being the best mechanic in the unit, so I told him that I would bet him five dollars that it wouldn't even start when the unit showed up."

"Yes, but you saw that he had fixed it," Sergeant Abdullah said. He did not understand why Sergeant Maczrakolski would wager on the vehicle that he saw had been fixed.

"Normally I wouldn't have bet, but that vehicle is always broken," Sergeant Maczrakolski reasoned. "Well, Uncle didn't want to take any chances, so he sat here in the motor pool with the vehicle running and waited for the unit to show up. That's cheating."

"Ah, I see your point," Sergeant Abdullah conceded.

"Honestly, between you and me, I'm fine with it," Sergeant Maczrakolski said as he started to smile. "Uncle needed something to get his mind off things, and giving up five bucks was worth it. He's really not a bad guy."

"You are a good person, Ski, and I am happy to know you," Sergeant Abdullah said.

The mechanics were standing near the work schedule board trying to see if any of their requirements had changed. The door to the office opened, and the first sergeant and commander left the building. Sergeant First Class Broadmoor came out and walked over to the center of the bays.

"Listen up, everyone," Sergeant First Class Broadmoor began. "Top and the CO want to have a meeting today at the company headquarters at 1600 hours—that's four o'clock for all of you civilian types. Don't miss it and don't be late."

"What if Uncle's hangar queen comes back?" Sergeant Maczrakolski yelled out.

"Blow it up and get to the meeting!" Sergeant First Class Broadmoor replied with a smile as he walked back to the office.

⸺

Sergeant First Class Hermanson made his way to Master Sergeant Mandess's office and looked inside. Master Sergeant Mandess was on the phone but saw Sergeant First Class Hermanson and waved for him to come in. Sergeant First Class Hermanson opened the door and stood near the small conference table, waiting for the phone call to end.

"Top, I figure you might want me to swing by first before taking the terps over to the interrogation exercise," Sergeant First Class Hermanson said as Master Sergeant Mandess hung up the phone. "We find anything out on Al Khafaji?"

"Nope. Steve is still planning to do a little more checking, but nothing has popped up yet," Master Sergeant Mandess explained as he motioned for Sergeant First Class Hermanson to sit down. "Herm, I want you to be particularly careful with this guy," he continued. "I don't know what it is, but something just makes the hair that used to be on the back of my neck stand up."

"Yep, Top, I get it," Sergeant First Class Hermanson replied. "He is kind of standoffish with the other terps. I'll let you know if anything comes out of the drills today. Sure hope we can get all this sorted out before we head back over. It would really suck to take him with us if we still feel odd about this kid."

"Don't worry, Herm," Master Sergeant Mandess said, trying to alleviate any of Sergeant First Class Hermanson's concerns. "He isn't going anywhere if we don't feel like he can be a team player. Sounds like there are enough issues already with the local hires. Steve said they had quite a few killed recently."

"Sounds like things may be heating up again," Sergeant First Class Hermanson stated. "Got anything else for me, Top?"

"Nope, not right now," Master Sergeant Mandess said. "I'll let you know if Steve comes up with any more info from his end."

"Roger that, Top," Sergeant First Class Hermanson responded as he headed back to round up the interpreters. He was interested in seeing how the interrogation exercise would go. Every once in a while, the role players being interrogated would have a couple of tricks up their sleeves for the interpreters.

On the way out, Sergeant First Class Hermanson picked up four notebooks and four pens. He was running short on time and didn't want to take a chance that one of the interpreters may not have brought a notebook or pen with them. He also wanted to make sure they used pens so he could see what their first take was on the interpretations. They needed to be good, and they needed to be good the first time around, especially if things were getting hot again overseas. If there was a shortage of local hire interpreters, these folks might have a much larger workload than normal.

"All right, folks," Sergeant First Class Hermanson called out as he approached the gate. "Pick up your stuff and head over this way. We'll be going down to the building next to the operations building."

The four specialists gathered up the things they had brought with them and started walking toward the gate. Al Khafaji looked at the things Aisha had brought with her and wanted to laugh out loud. It was almost as if she were planning to spend the night. Sara, on the other hand, carried only a small camouflaged covered binder in her hand.

"Before we head down, do any of you need a notebook or pen?" Sergeant First Class Hermanson asked, hoping no hands would go up.

"I do," Aisha said as she raised her hand.

What a surprise, Al Khafaji thought to himself.

"OK, here you go," Sergeant First Class Hermanson said without a hint of surprise.

The little group walked behind Sergeant First Class Hermanson down the path toward the smaller building. When they got to the door, Sergeant First Class Hermanson stopped and turned to face the interpreters.

"The exercise begins once we walk through this door," Sergeant First Class Hermanson warned, observing the group's reactions. "Once inside, you need to take note of what happens. Be very alert to what is being said and what is happening and don't forget that I am expecting all of you to provide written interpretations of the interrogations. Are there any questions?"

"No, Sergeant," the four said almost in unison. The other three looked at Aisha just to make sure.

"OK then. Let's get started," Sergeant First Class Hermanson said, opening the door.

The interpreters were met by a staff sergeant who was standing just beyond the threshold. He didn't look like a typical Special Forces soldier. He was no taller than Aisha, who was only five foot three inches tall. He had thick glasses and was practically bald except for hair along the sides of his head.

"Soldiers, my name is Staff Sergeant Hall," the man said to them. "I will be working as the interrogator during this exercise. Since this exercise focuses on your ability to provide written interpretations, there will be no communicating among yourselves or with the individual being interrogated. We will have the video cameras on to aid us in your critique at the conclusion of each interrogation. Follow me to the interrogation room, and once you are seated, stay seated."

"Art, do you want me inside or in the control room?" Sergeant First Class Hermanson asked as they walked across the open area toward the interrogation room.

"Whatever works for you is fine by me, Herm," Staff Sergeant Hall replied.

"Thanks. I think I'll just stay in the room with you," Sergeant First Class Hermanson said. He wanted to stay close to make sure he could focus on Al Khafaji.

Staff Sergeant Hall opened the door, and the room was empty. There was a table in the center of the room with three chairs around it. Along the wall were also three chairs on each side. Staff Sergeant Hall directed the specialists to sit in the chairs behind him, so Sergeant First Class Hermanson moved one of the chairs at the table to where they would be sitting. When the four specialists were seated, Sergeant First Class Hermanson moved to the other side of the room and sat down.

Al Khafaji looked around the room and noticed that there were cameras in every corner. He had expected the room to be much worse. There were supposed to be mad dogs and loud music playing with pictures of homosexuals and posters denouncing his religion.

"Bring the detainee in," Staff Sergeant Hall said out loud to an unseen person.

The door opened, and a young man near Al Khafaji's age walked in and was seated at the table. Staff Sergeant Hall began the questioning, and the four specialists immediately got busy writing down everything that was said. Sara was the only one who was paying attention to the detainee while trying to keep up with the interpretation.

The questions were very basic and seemed silly to Al Khafaji. He was sure that he would have everything written down exactly as it was said. What is your name? How old are you? Where do you live? Who lives in the house with you? Have you ever assisted the enemy? Are you a Muslim? Would you like to kill Americans? Al Khafaji was especially surprised at how bad the detainee's Arabic was. He could never be mistaken as a true Iraqi, not to mention being jihadi. Al Khafaji wanted to laugh out loud at this exercise.

The detainee was dismissed, and when he had left the room, Staff Sergeant Hall collected all the work from the specialists. Sergeant First Class Hermanson moved up to the table, and both sergeants looked over the work for about ten minutes, each one making notes and sharing with each other. When they were done, they turned their chairs toward the specialists.

"Interpretation is more than just capturing what is being said," Staff Sergeant Hall stated. "The environment, the body language, the tone of a person's voice can all be important. Most of the good interrogators will pick up on those things but never take it for granted. Sara, can you share what you noticed besides the detainee's answers?"

"Yes, Sergeant," Sara replied as she thought for a moment. "The person answered all of the questions in short responses without adding anything beyond simple answers. He had no emotion during the interrogation and was neither upset nor angry. His Arabic was not that of a native speaker, and at one point, he seemed to utter something that I could not hear."

"Very good," Staff Sergeant Hall told her and looked at the others. "Did any of you have the same impressions?"

None of the specialists raised their hand or commented. Al Khafaji decided to remain silent to blend in with the other three, even though he knew the individual was not a native speaker of Arabic. He would do better in the next interrogations.

"Sara, have you worked as an interpreter before?" Staff Sergeant Hall asked.

"Yes, Sergeant," Sara replied without trying to explain any further. "I have worked with the Army in Iraq as a linguist."

"OK, that's good to know," Sergeant First Class Hermanson said, wondering why this had not been mentioned before. "Why didn't you say anything about that earlier?"

"I am sorry, Sergeant," Sara began. "There are some Iraqis who do not believe we should have helped the Americans. It is something I would rather not share with others that I do not know."

That's right . . . because you are a traitor to our people, Al Khafaji said to himself. He was boiling over inside but managed to maintain his composure. *You and your family will all be punished for your actions, and I will help make sure of it.*

"OK," Staff Sergeant Hall said again to the unseen person. "Can we play back the interrogation? Set it at regular speed first."

The group watched as the interrogation was played on the big flat-screen monitor attached to the wall. The other specialists noticed what Sara had said in her comments, and it all became much clearer. Right after Staff Sergeant Hall asked the question of whether the detainee would like to kill Americans, the prisoner answered and then turned his head slightly.

"Stop it there, and rewind to the beginning of that question," Staff Sergeant Hall commanded. "Replay at a slower speed and raise the volume."

The tape was brought back to where the question began and replayed. It sounded strange, but at the slower speed, it was easy to see that the detainee had said something when he turned his head. With the volume turned up, Al Khafaji could recognize the word *infidel*.

"Nice work, Sara," Staff Sergeant Hall praised her in almost perfect Arabic.

"Thank you, Sergeant," Sara replied in Arabic.

The next two interrogations were relatively easy, and there were no surprises. The specialists were doing much better at watching for additional points of interest besides capturing only what was said out loud.

The only one that didn't seem to be catching on very well was Aisha. She had missed a few phrases and was beginning to get frustrated. During the third interrogation, she did happen to notice a very expensive ring on the detainee's hand, which earned her a word of praise from Staff Sergeant Hall during the post-interrogation review. This helped provide her with some much-needed confidence.

The fourth detainee was brought in wearing handcuffs and an ankle chain with two armed guards. All the specialists were taken off guard by these actions, but at least it was more along the lines of what Al Khafaji had expected. When the detainee would not sit down, one of the guards struck him in his back with his hand. He finally sat, all the while uttering insults at everyone in the room.

"What is your name?" Staff Sergeant Hall asked the man.

"I am a warrior sent here to purge this country of all infidels," the man growled, beginning to stand again. The guard pushed him down into the seat once more. "Take your hands off me, you dog!"

"What is your name?" Staff Sergeant Hall calmly repeated.

"I am a true believer of the one and only," the man yelled, spewing spittle as he did.

"What is your name?" Staff Sergeant Hall asked one more time.

"You are all traitors to the prophet," the man screamed out as he looked at the specialists. Al Khafaji wanted to jump up and proclaim his devotion but stayed in his seat. He looked and saw that Sara was the only one still making notes. Aisha and Wafiq were staring at the prisoner and had stopped writing.

"God is most great," the detainee exclaimed as he rose again from his seat. This time, his hands were no longer restrained by the handcuffs. The guard tried to make him sit back down but hadn't noticed that his hands were free. The detainee grabbed the guard and pushed him across the table into Staff Sergeant Hall. The other guard approached him, and the two men started to wrestle for control of the pistol the guard had in his holster.

Sara started to get up from her seat. Al Khafaji thought she was crazy.

"Sara, no!" Sergeant First Class Hermanson cried as he walked over to the two men. "That's enough, guys. Let's call it a day."

"OK," Staff Sergeant Hall said to the specialists. "Let me see your work."

All the specialists turned in what they had done, but it wasn't much. Aisha and Wafiq had both stopped once the detainee had spoken to them directly. Only Al Khafaji and Sara had anything close to what happened after that. Sergeant First Class Hermanson and Staff Sergeant Hall took much less time to gather their thoughts. The detainee and the guards remained in the room, but they were now sitting against the wall opposite the specialists.

"Well, I don't think you performed any worse than others we have put in this situation," Staff Sergeant Hall stated as he looked at the four specialists. "It isn't easy to remember how important your job is when things don't exactly go as planned. What you need to remember is how important your work is to us. It is critical that you maintain your focus. Whether we are working with a detainee or doing a tactical mission, we count on your language skills and familiarity with the culture from a native speaker's perspective," Staff Sergeant Hall continued. "We can't really afford for you to be jumping into the fray; however, as soldiers, we expect you to be able to use your firearms when the time comes."

"Sara," Sergeant First Class Hermanson said, "what exactly were you planning to do once you got out of your chair?"

"Well, Sergeant . . . " Sara cleared her throat. "If the man had threatened me or harmed someone else, I would assist to detain him or kill him."

This elicited a little chuckle from the two guards and the detainee. Al Khafaji and the other specialists looked at her in disbelief. Sergeant First Class Hermanson just nodded his head.

"You know what, Sara?" he said. "I believe you."

Sara slowly opened her right hand and held it out in front of her. In her hand was the pen she had been using to take notes.

"Damn," the detainee said and then smiled. "The power of the pen."

The company headquarters wasn't far from the motor pool. Sergeant Abdullah walked up to the building with Sergeant Maczrakolski. It took under ten minutes to get there, and by the time they arrived, most of the company was already gathered around the outside of the building. Sergeant First Class Broadmoor stood near the door directing everyone to head to the training room.

"Come on. Let's go. The meeting is inside, not out here," Sergeant First Class Broadmoor snapped as the soldiers slowly made their way into the building. "You all move like pond water. Move out with a purpose!"

Sergeant Abdullah followed the rest of the soldiers down the hall to the training room. There weren't many seats left, but Sergeant Maczrakolski managed to grab two and called Sergeant Abdullah over.

The front of the room had a large table set up, and the company commander and first sergeant were standing next to three other people whom Sergeant Abdullah did not recognize. After a few minutes, when the room seemed to be full, the first sergeant motioned to the others to have a seat at the table. He leaned over and said something to the company commander and then turned toward the crowded room.

"I am sure many of you have probably already guessed what this meeting is for," the first sergeant said as he scanned the room. "Our deployment to Iraq is going to be pushed forward. We will be supporting the artillery battalion, and we have Captain Freeman, the operations officer from the Field Artillery Battalion, here to tell us about what will happen next."

"Thank you, First Sergeant," Captain Freeman said, shuffling some papers in front of him. "The other unit that was scheduled to deploy cannot meet their pre-deployment requirements, so we are going to take their place. We will be deploying to Iraq in roughly six weeks in support of a maneuver brigade. Unfortunately, this means we will not have time to do the regular train up at the National Training Center, so we are scheduling a series of shorter exercises here on post over the next three weeks."

Many of the soldiers were frustrated with the news; the training exercises would mean less time to spend with their families before deploying. Several hands shot up to ask questions as the captain continued to talk. The first sergeant saw the hands fly up and shook his head, but the hands remained in the air.

"Excuse me, sir," the first sergeant said as he interrupted Captain Freeman. "All right, folks, put your paws down until the captain is done speaking. I know you have a shitload of questions but just sit tight. Sorry, sir."

"No worries, First Sergeant. Thanks," Captain Freeman said. "I will be providing the exercise information to the unit as soon as we get confirmation from post range control on the training areas we have requested. I expect to hear something today or tomorrow morning. Once the exercises are completed, we will begin the Soldier Readiness Processing in week four. Are there any questions?"

"Sir," the first soldier said as he stood up. "My wife is pregnant and is going to have our baby in a couple of months. Is it possible to deploy after the child is born?"

"I think that is a question for your company leadership," the captain responded, looking in the direction of the first sergeant and company commander.

"Roberts," the first sergeant called. "Since when did you get married?"

"Well, we are planning to get married first, Sergeant," Sergeant Roberts replied.

"Sit down," the first sergeant commanded as some of the soldiers started to laugh.

"Sir," Sergeant First Class Broadmoor said as he stood up to ask his question. "During the exercises, I would like to suggest allowing us to set up contact teams here in the garrison area to support any vehicle maintenance issues. I can have the personnel on call, and they will move out to your location if anything breaks down. We still have a good number of vehicles here in the motor pool that we need to finish up."

"I think that would work," said the captain as he wrote a note in his notebook.

"Big B, my man," Sergeant Maczrakolski said to Sergeant Abdullah as some of the other soldiers gave a short round of applause that was quickly ended by the first sergeant smacking the table with his fist. A few of the raised hands went down with the first sergeant's table smack, but there were still two hands raised.

"Where are we going this time, sir?" asked a specialist who was standing near the back wall.

"Iraq," the first sergeant responded before the captain could answer. "Next!"

The final raised hand dropped without asking a question. The captain looked around the room to see if any other questions were going to be asked. When he didn't see any additional hands go up, he turned to the company commander, and they spoke for a few minutes.

"Cut them loose, Top," the company commander said to the first sergeant.

"All right, folks, I want to talk with the section sergeants in my office," the first sergeant said as the company commander and the remainder of the group at the front table got up and started to walk out. "The rest of you are dismissed."

The soldiers in the company waited for the company commander and the other three officers to leave the training room before they started to exit. Once they got outside, there was a lot of talk going on among the soldiers. The soldiers who had not deployed were excited while the ones who were going back for a second, third, or fourth time were pissed because they were returning before their projected deployment date.

As they walked to the parking lot, one of the sergeants started a cadence call: "Here we go again!" All the soldiers, including Sergeant Abdullah, responded with, "Same old shit again." It was a little louder than they had wanted, and the first sergeant heard them, but to everyone's surprise, he had nothing to say. He knew that the soldiers needed a way to express their frustration, and if it happened through a simple cadence call, he was fine with that. He just knew that was where it had to stop. He didn't like going back to Iraq earlier than planned either, but that was just the way things worked sometimes. Suck it up and drive on.

Sergeant Abdullah had no misgivings about going back to Iraq. When he'd joined the Army, he'd known that was where he would be going—in fact, the recruiter had told him that the occupational specialty he was enlisting for was the only one that included a guaranteed deployment to Iraq following AIT. He had joined because he wanted to help the people of Iraq, and nothing had changed. There were still very bad things happening in Iraq, and according to the news, a strong terrorist cell had emerged since his deployment with the Special Forces.

He really enjoyed working with the Green Berets; they were very professional in what they did, and they seemed to care about the Iraqi people. The individuals in his new unit were good at their jobs, but the soldiers were focused on their own roles with little awareness of what others were doing. That could not happen in the Special Forces. Every individual in the team played an important part, and the team members counted on each other. He missed that sense of togetherness and unity the most.

"Top, are you busy?" Sergeant First Class Hermanson asked as he stood in the doorway of Master Sergeant Mandess's office.

"Nope, come on in," Master Sergeant Mandess replied, motioning him to have a seat. "So tell me about the Arabic ninja with the killer pen."

"I guess I should have run up here instead of walking," Sergeant First Class Hermanson smiled.

"Well, Staff Sergeant Hall and Staff Sergeant Pederson seem to have enjoyed it," Master Sergeant Mandess replied, forcing himself to keep a straight face. "Don't bother trying to explain it to the commander either. He already heard and got a good laugh out of it."

"To tell you the truth, it wasn't all that funny when it happened," Sergeant First Class Hermanson admitted without a smile. "Sara was really fired up in there. She has a lot of guts, and when she opened her hand and held the pen out, Staff Sergeant Pederson was a little shocked. I don't know about anyone else, but I know I am glad she is on our team."

"So you wouldn't have any issues with her being on your team?" Master Sergeant Mandess wasn't really looking for a reply. "That's good you got it. What about the other three?"

"Might sound a little odd, but between the other three, Al Khafaji seems to be the next choice," Sergeant First Class Hermanson admitted, scratching his head. "I still don't know what to make of him when it comes to reactions or emotions, but he is a quick learner, and when it comes to interpretation, he is much better than Wafiq and Aisha."

"Do you think any of them should not deploy?" Master Sergeant Mandess asked, and this time, he waited for the response.

"Well, Top, I would say no," Sergeant First Class Hermanson said after giving it some thought. "I am sure that there will be plenty of things for all four of them to do, but I'm not sure I would recommend taking Aisha on an actual mission."

"OK, I respect your judgment," Master Sergeant Mandess replied with all sincerity; after all, Sergeant First Class Hermanson had made some great calls the last time they were in Iraq. "Let's continue with their training but send Aisha and Wafiq to work with Staff Sergeant Hall on interpretation skills. I got a bad feeling that we are not going to have a lot of time before we are deploying."

"Sure thing, Top," Sergeant First Class Hermanson answered. "Is there anything else?"

"Just make sure the ninja doesn't try to take anyone out in the building entry drills," Master Sergeant Mandess quipped as the phone rang. "Operations, Master Sergeant Mandess speaking."

Sergeant First Class Hermanson turned around and began to walk out the door. He tried to close it behind him without making too much noise so he wouldn't disturb Master Sergeant Mandess. No sooner had he gotten out the door and taken three steps down the hall when he heard Master Sergeant Mandess yell out, "Herm."

"Yes, Top?" Sergeant First Class Hermanson responded, walking back into the room.

"We have three weeks until it's go time," Master Sergeant Mandess said solemnly.

5

The four specialists met Sergeant First Class Hermanson at the gate to begin the training for the afternoon. Sergeant First Class Hermanson explained to them that they would be split into two groups for the afternoon but did not go into detail about what each group would be doing or why they were in separate groups. He had them follow him down to the building where the interrogation exercises had been held earlier in the day.

"OK, Sara and Samir, wait out here for me," Sergeant First Class Hermanson instructed as he waited for the door to unlock. "Aisha and Wafiq, you can follow me inside."

"Hey, Herm," Staff Sergeant Hall said. "Back so soon?"

"Art, Top said to bring these folks by for some introductory interpreter training," Sergeant First Class Hermanson replied as the two specialists stood by his side. "I'll be taking the other two to the mock-up site."

"OK," Staff Sergeant Hall nodded. "I would have thought Top would want all of them to get a little more training, but I just work here. Come on, folks, follow me and we'll find a nice quiet place to go over a couple things."

"Thanks, Art," Sergeant First Class Hermanson said as he turned to go back outside. "I'll be back to gather everybody up in about two or three hours."

"All right, you two, follow me," Sergeant First Class Hermanson said when he got outside. He turned and started to walk quickly down the gravel path toward another area that looked like a collection of walls and stairs. "We are going to meet up with some other members of the team and go over some ways that we do things to see how well you might fit in."

Neither Sara nor Al Khafaji had any idea what Sergeant First Class Hermanson was talking about, and they were a little apprehensive about what might lie ahead of them, especially after the interrogation exercises earlier. Al Khafaji looked at the training area and thought some of the structures looked like houses or commercial buildings with a second floor. They were built much differently than what he was used to in Iraq, but he thought it made sense that the infidels would always try to be better than anyone else.

Sara was the first to notice the three men from earlier in the day. The two guards and detainee were now all dressed in their military uniforms. She was a little embarrassed at how the interrogation exercise had ended. When they saw her coming, they all put their hands in the air, and that made her smile.

"So, I don't think any introductions are needed," Sergeant First Class Hermanson said as the men put their hands down. "What we want to do for the next few hours is go over the procedures we use when we are going into a building or a room and there might be combatants present. First, we want both of you to just stand back and observe how we work together. Later, we will walk you through the process and see how you are able to adjust to our team."

Sergeant First Class Hermanson went over to the three men and talked through what he wanted to do. He then had them go through a room breach at normal speed. Both specialists were impressed at how well the team worked together; it was clear that they had a lot of experience in this kind of operation. Al Khafaji knew too well the skills the American soldiers possessed when it came to hunting down and killing true believers.

"Each man in the team has a position and a responsibility when conducting a breaching operation," Sergeant First Class Hermanson explained as he walked up to the three men. "Number one is the lead;

he sets the pace and direction of the other two. If the number one man enters the room and goes to the right, the second man enters and goes to the left and vice versa. The number three man watches the other two and determines if he needs to focus right or left depending upon what is happening. If the entryway is off-center to the right, like it is here, then the third man will try to move to the left where there is more room. If the door were in the center of the room, the third man would stay toward the center while observing the number one and number two man's situation to determine whether they were still in the fight. We would never want either of you to be in the number one or number two position.

"Next, we are going to show you a four-person breach of a closed door," Sergeant First Class Hermanson continued as he walked over and picked up a sledgehammer. He took up a position at the end of the file. The number one man checked to see whether the other three were ready and then moved forward. When they got next to the door, the number one man called for the hammer, and Sergeant First Class Hermanson moved forward. When the number one man nodded, Sergeant First Class Hermanson struck the door with the sledgehammer, knocking it open. Sergeant First Class Hermanson then moved to the other side of the door and shouldered his rifle as the other three entered the room.

After completing the breach, the four soldiers exited the room and stood near the specialists. Sergeant First Class Hermanson laid the sledgehammer down near the door and looked at Sara and Al Khafaji. He hoped that they would never have to join them in a breaching operation in Iraq, but he knew that it was a possibility.

"There are other ways to do a breach, but I want you to become familiar with these," Sergeant First Class Hermanson clarified. "Do you have any questions?"

"Sergeant," Al Khafaji asked. "Is it usual for there to be four soldiers?"

"Good question, Samir, and it really depends on the mission and the environment," Sergeant First Class Hermanson explained. "Four soldiers provide the base to work from. There are times when it could be less or more depending on what is happening. If we are looking for a person and believe that person is alone, a four-person breach may be sufficient, but if we are going into a building with multiple floors or rooms, a larger force may be required. There are times when it may be necessary for a single soldier to clear an area or a room, but that would not be the optimal method."

"Sergeant," Sara began as she considered what Sergeant First Class Hermanson had explained. "What are the other methods you talked about?"

"Well, you probably aren't going to see any of them, but again, they are all dependent upon the operational environment," Sergeant First Class Hermanson stated as he began to describe the different options to Sara. "Instead of going through a door, you may choose to go through a wall, or the situation might dictate entering through a hole in the ceiling or maybe even just driving an armored personnel carrier through the door. It just depends on what you think you may be facing on the other side."

"I understand," Sara said, nodding her head. "Thank you, Sergeant."

"Are there any other questions you have right now?" Sergeant First Class Hermanson asked the two specialists before waiting expectantly for a response. When he didn't see a hand or notice a questioning look from them, he continued. "OK, if you don't have any questions, let's try a slow walk-through with one of you as number two in the stack. Samir, why don't you give it a try?"

Al Khafaji walked over to number two who, in turn, gave him his rifle. Then, number one checked to see that the others were ready and started moving toward the open doorway. They slowed down and stopped momentarily when they reached the doorframe. When number one moved through the doorway and to the right, Al

Khafaji hesitated and then moved through the doorway and to the left. Number three came in right after him and occupied the center.

"OK, not bad," Sergeant First Class Hermanson said, moving closer to them. "Samir, there are a couple things you need to focus on. The first is your place in the stack. If you are number two, you need to be right on number one's back. You don't want to have a lot of space between the two of you. You must keep it tight. Secondly, you do not want to hesitate once you commit to moving. The number three is reacting to your initial decision, and you don't want to be stepping on each other once you move through the doorway. Anyone have something else to add?" Sergeant First Class Hermanson asked as he looked over the three-man team.

"All good, Herm," Staff Sergeant Pederson answered for the group. "You were spot on."

"OK, let's change it up," Sergeant First Class Hermanson pronounced. "Sara, let's try you out in the number two position."

Sara got up and changed places with Al Khafaji who moved to the side to watch. Al Khafaji would take pleasure in witnessing Sara try to keep up with the team. He would do everything possible to not laugh when Sara fell on her face.

Sara adjusted her helmet and held a firm grip on the rifle. She made sure to keep the muzzle up until they prepared to enter. When the team moved toward the doorway, she kept her left elbow on the number one man's right shoulder blade. She felt comfortable working with the team, and to her surprise, she wasn't a bit nervous.

The team slowed down when they approached the doorway, and the number one man looked back. He then went through the doorway and headed to the right. Sara quickly made it around to the left with her rifle up, scanning for targets, but she didn't see any movement. Next, the number three man came through the doorway and stayed in the center, sweeping from left to right with the muzzle of his rifle. Finally, the team moved back through the doorway for their critique.

"Really good work, Sara," Sergeant First Class Hermanson noted and looked at Al Khafaji. "Did you notice how Sara stayed close to the number one man as they approached the doorway?"

"Yes, Sergeant," Al Khafaji replied, trying not to show his anger at being second to a woman. This was just one more thing that he would remember in the future when the time came for him to settle the score. "I know that I can do better next time."

"Well, that's the right attitude. We are going to keep working on it," Sergeant First Class Hermanson said.

They continued to focus on breaching techniques for the next two hours. They moved from two- to three- to four-person breaches using other tools like a pry bar and a shotgun to open closed doors. Sara and Al Khafaji moved from one position to another but never set up as the number one man. Al Khafaji was wondering how long they would be doing this when Sergeant First Class Hermanson looked at his watch.

"OK, folks, I have a couple other things to take care of today, so let's run through the four-person breach of a closed-door room one more time." Sergeant First Class Hermanson glanced at Al Khafaji and said, "Samir, why don't you fall into the number two position on this one?"

"Yes, Sergeant," Al Khafaji replied as he moved into position.

The team moved out quickly toward the door. The number one man called for the hammer, and one of the sergeants moved forward and struck the door. When the it swung open, the number one man went in and immediately went down. Al Khafaji was moving forward as he had in many other drills, but when he saw the number one man on the ground, he froze in the doorway, not sure what to do next.

"OK, cease work," Sergeant First Class Hermanson called. "Everyone on me. This is an important lesson that we need to talk about." Sergeant First Class Hermanson waited until the team had reassembled outside of the door. "Remember when I said everyone on the team has a job to do? Well, one of the things everyone on the team needs to do is be able to do the jobs of everyone else on the team. If someone goes down, the next person in the stack has to move forward and assume the person's role. So, if you are number two and number one goes down, you are now the number one man."

"Yes, Sergeant," the two specialists said.

"It's OK. We will get it down eventually," Sergeant First Class Hermanson said as he looked at his watch again. "You both did well today, and you are off to a great start. We will have you working in the stack in no time. Let's head out and call it a day. Tomorrow, there is much more to learn. Do either of you have any questions?"

"No, Sergeant," the specialists replied in unison.

"OK, I'll walk you out to the gate and see you at 0800 hours tomorrow morning," Sergeant First Class Hermanson commanded as he turned to escort the specialists back to the gate.

"You need anything else from us, Herm?" Staff Sergeant Pederson asked.

"Nope, I'll catch all of you in the morning at PT," Sergeant First Class Hermanson replied as he kept moving toward the gate.

Sergeant First Class Hermanson stopped by the interrogation site on the way out to see if Aisha and Wafiq were done yet. One of the other NCOs opened the door and said that Staff Sergeant Hall was working with the other two down the hall. Sergeant First Class Hermanson walked to the room that was being used for training and opened the door.

Staff Sergeant Hall had the two specialists working on visual recognition by playing a series of videos of people and stopping along the way to have the specialists describe what was going on. They seemed to be doing well from what he could tell, but Staff Sergeant Hall appeared a little more excited than usual about something.

"Art, how is it going?" Sergeant First Class Hermanson asked.

"Well, I think we have gone as far as we are going to go for today," Staff Sergeant Hall replied. "I'm going to step outside for a second with Sergeant First Class Hermanson. The two of you can get your stuff together and get ready to leave. We'll work on things again tomorrow."

"Yes, Sergeant," Wafiq responded while Aisha just continued to gather her stuff.

The two sergeants stepped outside the door, and Staff Sergeant Hall started to explain what was bothering him.

"Herm, I'm not sure the female is going to be much help to you," Staff Sergeant Hall began, keeping his back to the door to avoid displaying any emotion to the two specialists through the glass pane. "She has not been in in Iraq for years and was mainly raised in Egypt. She has very little knowledge of local culture, and her Arabic is not anywhere near what you would need outside of the compound. If you have to take her, I would recommend keeping her within the compound to work with the locals. Just my two cents for what it's worth."

"Thanks, Art. That's good to know," Sergeant First Class Hermanson said as he considered his options. "How about Wafiq. Is he better?"

"I think he will be fine, but his interpretation skills are going to need some work," Staff Sergeant Hall replied. "Any idea how long you have before you deploy?"

"Looks like we have less than a month," Sergeant First Class Hermanson answered as he looked over Staff Sergeant Hall's shoulder at the two specialists. They were standing near the table they had been working at, waiting quietly. "Looks like they are ready to move out."

"OK, I'll do the best I can to get him ready," Staff Sergeant Hall said. "If you decide you need to take the female, I'll continue working with her as well. Just say the word."

"Why don't we do that, Art," Sergeant First Class Hermanson decided. "Not sure how hard it is going to be to get any local hires;

the news is things are getting hot again. I may need her regardless of her shortcomings."

"You got it, Herm," Staff Sergeant Hall agreed. "We better head them out. I don't want them getting skittish on me. They have a ways to go."

Staff Sergeant Hall turned toward the door and motioned for the two specialists to come over.

"All right, Herm," Staff Sergeant Hall said as the two exited the room. "We'll see you all again in the morning. Good work today, you two."

"Thank you, Sergeant," the two specialists replied, Aisha using a much less excited tone. Wafiq was more confident than before and seemed proud of the compliment from Staff Sergeant Hall. Sergeant First Class Hermanson was happy to see it. He had thought that Wafiq was at a tipping point, and he could have slipped off into a difficult position, which would have made him much harder to work with. He had seen it before on a previous rotation, and it was not good for anyone on the team.

"So how did the two of you like your training?" Sergeant First Class Hermanson asked Aisha and Wafiq as he and the four specialists walked toward the gate.

"It was very interesting, Sergeant," Wafiq replied without giving Aisha a chance to answer first. "I did not realize that interpretation was so interesting. I believed we were just here to tell the soldiers what people were saying."

"Interpretation is a different skill, and trained interpreters are very important to our work," Sergeant First Class Hermanson explained to Wafiq and the others. "Sometimes how people act and what is happening around us is just as important as what is said. Aisha, what do you think?"

"Yes, Sergeant, that is what Staff Sergeant Hall told us, but—" Aisha stopped mid-sentence, not wanting to share what was really on her mind. She thought it might be a bad thing to say, so she decided to just let it go and try harder.

"Yes, but what?" Sergeant First Class Hermanson prompted. He wanted her to open up and let her frustrations out. "It's OK to say what you think. I would like to know."

"Well, Sergeant," Aisha began, carefully choosing her words. "I do not understand why it is so important to know that an old man has more than one phone, or a child is playing with a ball, or a woman stands near a table of fruit for a long time, or a shop owner closes his door and windows."

"When we are in Iraq, all of those things could be very important," Sergeant First Class Hermanson explained, stopping the group. "You are all native speakers in Arabic, but your cultural expertise is also very important to us. How many of you came to the United States as a student?"

Aisha, Wafiq, and Al Khafaji raised their hands. They looked at Sara, but she did not join them.

"Sara, and you?" Sergeant First Class Hermanson inquired.

"I was allowed to immigrate with a visa for my work as a linguist when my family was killed," Sara replied quietly. "That is why I joined the Army."

"OK, thank you," Sergeant First Class Hermanson said. That was one of the more important things he had learned that day. "You all still have a great asset that you carry with you, and that is the knowledge of everyday life in Iraq. That is what you need to also share with us when you are providing interpretation work. All those things that Aisha mentioned may just be what happens during a regular day, but is it common for an elderly man to have two phones? Why would a shop owner close his windows and door during the middle of the day? If there were children chasing a ball, and the ball was kicked across the street and none of them went to get it, is that a problem?"

"Yes, Sergeant," Wafiq piped up with a smile from ear to ear. "It is important to recognize the environment to be a good interpreter."

"That is correct, Wafiq," Sergeant First Class Hermanson answered, smiling. "That is why we need to do more training and become even better."

The four specialists exited through the gate and went off in different directions to head back to the hotels they were staying at. Al Khafaji made a stop at the public library on the way back. He tried to check his email every day that he could. There was a business center in the hotel he stayed at, but the computers were always taken or not working. He could always count on a computer being available at the library.

"Hello, young man," the lady at the front desk smiled as Al Khafaji entered the library. "Back again, I see."

"Yes, I would like to check my email messages," Al Khafaji stated as he walked up to the counter.

"Of course," the librarian responded as she looked at a page posted in front of her and wrote down a number on a piece of paper. She handed the paper to Al Khafaji and said, "I think this one should be open. Please do not stay on the computer for longer than thirty minutes."

"Yes, I understand. Thank you," Al Khafaji said, clutching the scrap of paper as he walked to the back of the library where the computers were set up on a long table with partitions between each one for some level of privacy.

He found the computer with the number five on it and sat down. It took him only about two minutes to log in and check his email. There were no new messages, so he decided to check some news items before leaving. He scanned one or two news stories, but there was nothing of interest. It seemed that almost every day, there were stories of murders in the United States. There were times when he thought the Americans would all kill each other before he returned to Iraq.

Al Khafaji looked at his watch and decided it was time to go, so he shut down the computer and went back up to the counter. The lady was helping someone else, so he just laid the paper on the counter and walked out.

The sky was clear, and he could see many stars sparkling down from above. When he was young and before the Americans came to Iraq, he could remember standing outside at night, and there were so many stars, it looked like they lit up the world. The invaders changed all that, and he would make sure they paid with their blood.

6

Sergeant Abdullah was a little surprised about the way things went over the next couple of weeks. It was almost like nobody had heard that they were going to deploy to Iraq. Nothing seemed to have changed at work. Everyone was still focused on the same things with little mention of deploying. He wondered if it was because most of the people had already been there before or if they were so nervous that they didn't feel like they could talk about it. Whatever the reason was, Sergeant Abdullah knew that ignoring it wouldn't change anything. In four weeks, they would be on a plane heading to Iraq and away from their families for a year.

There were some good things happening for Sergeant Abdullah. He was no longer the "new guy." The company had just had another specialist report to their unit. He was originally supposed to be sent to another unit, but since Sergeant Abdullah's unit was short on personnel and scheduled for deployment, the specialist was sent to them instead.

Sergeant Abdullah was also finally able to meet the company commander and first sergeant. The company commander, Captain Pickett, was very young and did not seem very sure of himself. He let the first sergeant do most of the talking during their meeting. First Sergeant Holman, on the other hand, was a hard-core soldier who had no time for excuses or failure. He was not interested in making friends; he was interested in making soldiers, and he was very good at it. Sergeant Abdullah respected him and the position he held.

Sergeant Abdullah liked being just another one of the mechanics, even though he still had not seen his name on the work board with a vehicle assigned to it. He did have a few chances to work with others on their assigned vehicles and had begun to develop a good reputation among the others. Some of the mechanics were even at the point that they would come find Sergeant Abdullah to get his opinion on what was wrong with a certain vehicle. He still had a knack for being able to look and listen to engines and find what was wrong. Things were so good that many of the other mechanics were now calling him by his old nickname of Carson, even though, just like Sergeant Maczrakolski, they could not really understand why.

When Sergeant Abdullah came into the building on Monday of the third week, he checked the work board the way he had every day since he had arrived at the unit. He mainly just checked as part of his routine and didn't really expect anything more than maybe helping someone else again as he had been doing. However, when he looked, he was amazed to see his name on the board. He was so happy to finally have a vehicle to work on that he didn't really pay attention to what vehicle it was. He put on his coveralls and went over to start his inspection. As he walked around the vehicle, looking for any obvious issues, Sergeant Maczrakolski came into the building.

"Well, look at that," Sergeant Maczrakolski smirked. "Uncle's hangar queen is back again. Carson, what are you doing?" he asked as he noticed Sergeant Abdullah walking around the vehicle. "Where is Uncle? I want to rub this one in his face as much as I can."

"He has not been in yet," Sergeant Abdullah responded, suddenly realizing which vehicle he had been assigned to work on.

"Why are you in coveralls inspecting his vehicle?" Sergeant Maczrakolski asked, puzzled about what was happening.

"My name is on this vehicle, Ski," Sergeant Abdullah replied as he pointed at the work board with a smile.

Sergeant Maczrakolski strained to see the board, and when he could finally make it out, he said, "Oh no, that's not good. It has to be some kind of a mistake. Uncle will flip out if he comes in and sees someone else working on this vehicle. It's probably better to just see if anyone else needs help and leave this thing alone."

Sergeant Abdullah thought that Sergeant Maczrakolski was probably right, so he walked over to his locker and started to change out of his coveralls. Sergeant First Class Broadmoor opened the door to the office and saw what Sergeant Abdullah was doing.

"Carson," Sergeant First Class Broadmoor called out in his normal booming voice. "What are you doing, soldier?"

"I was going to see if anyone needed help with their vehicle, Sergeant," Sergeant Abdullah replied.

"Now why would you want to do that?" Sergeant First Class Broadmoor asked, then continued without waiting for an answer. "I think your name is listed with that vehicle right there."

"Yes, Sergeant," Sergeant Abdullah began, "but that is Uncle's queen."

"I don't give a rat's ass if it is Staff Sergeant Feister's princess," Sergeant First Class Broadmoor replied. "Do you know whose board that is?"

"It's the . . ." Sergeant Abdullah didn't bother finishing his sentence.

"That's *my* board," Sergeant First Class Broadmoor declared. "I'm the one who fills it out, and I'm the one who is responsible for all that work getting done."

"Yes, Sergeant," Sergeant Abdullah replied.

"Now get those coveralls back on and do your job," Sergeant First Class Broadmoor commanded with a grin. "I don't want to see anyone else but you crawling around that vehicle trying to get it back on the road. If Staff Sergeant Feister finally makes it into work and has a problem, he can come and see me. Is that clear?"

"Yes, Sergeant," Sergeant Abdullah yelled out with a smile.

"Dang, this is going to be good," Sergeant Maczrakolski muttered to himself as he pulled his coveralls out of his locker.

Sergeant Abdullah went over every inch of the engine, trying to determine what was making the vehicle stall. He replaced the fuel filter, but it still did not run right. Sergeant Abdullah asked another mechanic to come over and step on the gas pedal. When he did, Sergeant Abdullah noticed a spray of fuel under the vehicle. He had the other mechanic turn off the engine. When Sergeant Abdullah crawled under the vehicle, he found a tear in the fuel line that was not allowing more fuel to be sent to the engine once the accelerator was pressed. Sergeant Abdullah replaced the fuel line and the vehicle started right up. He was going to park it out in the motor pool when Staff Sergeant Feister walked in.

"What the hell is going on with that piece of shit?" Staff Sergeant Feister asked nobody in particular. Then, he saw Sergeant Abdullah in the cab of the vehicle. "What are you doing in my hangar queen? Nobody touches that thing but me! Do you understand?"

"I am sorry, but I was told to fix it because you were not here," Sergeant Abdullah explained. "The fuel line was bad, so I had to replace it. The repairs you had done before still look very good. You are a very good mechanic."

"Thanks, Carson," Staff Sergeant Feister replied. How could he be angry with someone who had such a keen eye for good work? "How did you know the fuel line was bad?"

"Well, Sergeant, it sprayed me with fuel when I looked at it," Sergeant Abdullah said.

"That's one way to figure it out," Staff Sergeant Feister admitted, laughing. "You're OK in my book, Carson. Thanks for taking care of the queen for me."

"It was good to have a vehicle to work on," Sergeant Abdullah confided.

"Well, in another sixty days, you might have a different set of wishes," Staff Sergeant Feister warned as he motioned to the vehicle. "Did you let Big B and the unit know it's ready?"

"No, Sergeant, I had just finished when you came in," Sergeant Abdullah answered. "I was going to pull the vehicle into the motor pool."

"Why don't you go tell Big B and call the unit, and I'll move the vehicle," Staff Sergeant Feister suggested as he got into the driver's seat.

"Thank you, Sergeant," Sergeant Abdullah said. "I will do that right now."

"Call me Uncle, Carson. You earned it," Staff Sergeant Feister said as he started the vehicle.

"Yes, Uncle," Sergeant Abdullah said, feeling very good about being accepted as a real member of the unit.

The rest of the week, the four specialists stayed in the same two-person groups. Aisha and Wafiq continued to work on interpretation skills, while Sara and Al Khafaji did countless types of breaching exercises every day. First, they would watch the team go through it at full speed. Then, they would walk through it at a slower pace, and the specialists would be placed in different positions in the stack. It did not make any sense to Al Khafaji. They did these exercises so many times that he could do them with his eyes closed. He was beginning to think all of this was a big waste of time.

On the last day of the first week, Sara and Al Khafaji were given goggles and protective vests to wear over their uniforms, along with magazines loaded with blank rounds. When it came time for the specialists to join the stack, they were told that they would be encountering resistance as they did the breach. Neither one of them really understood what that meant until they started the exercise.

The number one man went through the doorway, and as Al Khafaji moved to do the same, he felt a thud against his protective vest and paint splattered up on his goggles. He stopped to adjust his view, and two more paint balls exploded on his equipment.

"Cease fire!" Sergeant First Class Hermanson yelled out. He walked over to Al Khafaji to see if he was OK.

"That's another reason why you don't hesitate in the doorway, Samir," the number one man said as he looked at Al Khafaji's paint-splattered vest and goggles.

"Samir," Sergeant First Class Hermanson said, trying to focus Al Khafaji on what had happened. "If the number one man goes into a room and rounds start going off, you have to be ready to go in shooting. The doorway is what we call a fatal funnel. The enemy knows that if one person comes through the door, others are probably going to follow. You have to get in there as fast as possible while returning fire. Remember, the number three man is coming in to cover the middle. You need all three of you in the room to neutralize the enemy."

"Yes, Sergeant," Al Khafaji replied as he looked at the splatters on his vest. For a moment, he thought about what would have happened if this were a real situation. The thought was very sobering.

"Are you ready, Sara?" Sergeant First Class Hermanson asked, but it was more a directive than a question.

Sara walked over and took Al Khafaji's place in the stack that had reassembled twenty yards from the doorway. Everyone did a quick equipment check and then began to move toward the doorway. When they reached the wall, they slowed their approach and cautiously made it to the doorway. The number one man looked back to check one last time and then moved through the doorway and to the right while rifle fire began.

Sara was right behind him. She checked quickly to make sure the number one man had turned to the right. Then, she turned the muzzle of her rifle into the opening and began to fire while quickly moving through the doorway and to the left, all while maintaining a steady rate of fire. She felt something graze her shoulder but continued to fire her rifle. She heard one beeping sound and then a second going off. The number three man came through the doorway right after her and was also firing toward the opposite wall when a third beeping sound started.

"Cease fire!" Sergeant First Class Hermanson yelled out. He didn't have to look to know what had happened. The beeping let him know that all three enemy role players had been eliminated. "Excellent work, folks."

"Herm, could you please turn off these damn beepers?" one of the role players shouted as the beeping continued.

Sergeant First Class Hermanson went over to the three people with the paintball guns and used his controller to turn off the beeping vests. He came back to check the breach team and was amazed to find only a small spot of paint on Sara's right shoulder.

"OK, everyone, that's about it for today," Sergeant First Class Hermanson said. "Tomorrow, we will all be down at the interrogation building for some work on interpretation with Staff Sergeant Hall and some more mock interrogations."

"Mock interrogations, Sara," Staff Sergeant Pederson added. "No pen killings allowed."

Sara simply nodded her head. She was still embarrassed over what had happened, but everyone else seemed to be fine with how she had acted. She thought that maybe she was not the first one to become excited about the interrogations.

Time seemed to just drag on throughout the third week for Sergeant Abdullah. The atmosphere in the unit had changed, and everyone was more edgy than usual. He imagined the pending deployment must have been a difficult issue to deal with for the soldiers with families. Their entire world was about to be flipped upside down once again. For once, he was glad that he had not met the right woman yet. He would not want someone he cared for to be left at home worrying about him or to have his children concerned for his safety. He had always wanted to buy a home and have a family, but maybe it would be better to wait until he was no longer a soldier.

He had seen so many of the soldiers preparing to deploy while trying to make sure that things were in order with their families. Staff Sergeant Feister was even having a difficult time. He was married but did not have any children, yet he was very concerned about his two dogs. He even had pictures of them in his locker and always made sure to show them to other people. Sergeant Abdullah thought that maybe the dogs were like his children; it seemed like many Americans were funny that way.

The only things remaining for the unit to do before deploying was to continue working on any vehicles, qualify with their weapons, and complete the Soldier Readiness Processing, which was to begin on Monday of the fourth week. Sergeant Abdullah had gone through the process many times, and he wondered how many soldiers would have issues.

There were already two soldiers who would not be deploying with them. One of them was a female soldier who was an administrative specialist. She'd learned a few days ago that she was almost two months pregnant. The other soldier was a specialist who'd wrecked his car in an accident and broken his leg. He would require surgery to fix it. None of the soldiers seemed unhappy that he was not going with, as they did not believe he was a very good mechanic. First Sergeant Holman thought the soldier had hurt himself on purpose and wanted to initiate a Line of Duty investigation, but Captain Pickett was happy to just not have him deploying with them.

The entire process had been much easier when he'd deployed with the Special Operations units. If the individuals there had been nervous or apprehensive, they never showed it. Maybe it had to do with the different missions the units had. Special Operations soldiers were highly trained warriors in Sergeant Abdullah's eyes, while here he was working with support people who may not have much combat experience. The soldiers in this unit were all very good mechanics, but they just didn't have the same mindset about things. He was very interested to see how things went on the rifle range. He hoped the soldiers were as good at hitting targets as they were at fixing vehicles.

When Sergeant Abdullah returned from lunch on Thursday of the third week, he heard two of the mechanics arguing with each other. There were many others standing near them watching, but nobody was trying to stop them. Sergeant Abdullah was just about to try to separate them when he heard Sergeant First Class Broadmoor coming out of his office.

"All right, what the hell is going on in my maintenance building?" Sergeant First Class Broadmoor yelled out. The crowd of mechanics moved away to leave the two mechanics standing alone near the vehicle they were working on together.

"I'm going to knock the snot out of this idiot," one mechanic said. "He is a total fuckup."

"Kiss my ass," the other mechanic said as they grabbed each other's coveralls again.

"Ain't gonna be any fighting in my maintenance building, soldiers!" Sergeant First Class Broadmoor boomed as he walked over to the two soldiers. He separated them like they were two small kids on a playground. "So do you two want to settle this by fighting?" Sergeant First Class Broadmoor asked, looking down at them.

"Hell yeah," the first mechanic said. "I'm going to kick his ass."

"Bring it on, shithead," the other retorted.

"OK, change out of your coveralls," Sergeant First Class Broadmoor commanded. "We're going to the gym. Just let me get my stuff."

"What stuff?" the first mechanic asked.

"Well, whichever one of you idiots beats the snot out of the other is going to have to go a couple of rounds with me next," Sergeant First Class Broadmoor said as he threw a couple punches into the air. "This ought to be fun for everyone."

The two mechanics looked at Big B and walked back over to their vehicle.

"What are you two doing?" Sergeant First Class Broadmoor asked.

"We ain't crazy," the second mechanic said.

"Hell, Big B, the only one that would have any fun with that would be you," the first mechanic added.

"You got that right," Sergeant First Class Broadmoor growled. "Why don't you two knuckleheads try to remember that next time? Save all this macho fighting bullshit for the enemy. You'll get to take it out on the right folks soon enough. Now get back to work, everyone. The show's over."

All the mechanics moved back to their work areas, including the two combatants who no longer had a desire to kill each other. Sergeant Abdullah had a great deal of respect for Sergeant First Class Broadmoor. He thought he was a very good leader. There were times when a good leader understood it was a time to fight and other times when it was time to be angry but still be a team.

Al Khafaji was not very happy to be going back to the interrogation building. He wondered if they would have to work with any other crazy people again. It was difficult for him to even look at Staff Sergeant Pederson without thinking of his wild eyes looking at him and calling him a traitor to the one true god. He was just another infidel trying to mock him.

When Al Khafaji saw Wafiq and Aisha walking toward the gated entrance, he got out of his car. He sauntered toward the other two and saw Sara getting out of a vehicle on the other side of the parking lot. The four specialists waited together for Sergeant First Class Hermanson to get them.

"So how did you like your training, Samir?" Wafiq asked.

"It was challenging for me," Al Khafaji admitted, "but Sara seemed to do very well."

"I was just fortunate that Samir went through the exercises first," Sara said, trying to be modest. "When Sergeant First Class Hermanson made points of what to do better, I just did what he said."

"Our training was not as interesting," Aisha sighed. "Too much for me to focus on. Wafiq did well."

"Yes," Wafiq said with pride. "I believe it was very good training. The interpretation work is very interesting to me. I think when I leave the Army, I will find one of the high-paying civilian positions and buy a big house in Michigan."

"Did Staff Sergeant Hall say anything to you about what we would be doing this week?" Al Khafaji asked.

"No, not really," Wafiq said after thinking for a minute. "All he said was it was very important that we would be on a very busy schedule for the next two weeks."

Al Khafaji made note of the two-week time frame and wondered what that meant. He would pay particular attention to see if there was anything else said about their schedule. He would need to let the leader know when he found out when his team would be deploying to Iraq.

"So how is everybody doing today?" Sergeant First Class Hermanson asked as he walked toward the gate. "Is everybody ready for some more good training?"

"Yes, Sergeant," the four specialists replied.

"OK, let's head on down to the interrogation building for a good day of interpretation lessons," Sergeant First Class Hermanson said as he opened the gate and watched the four specialists file in.

"Will we be doing the interrogation exercises again, Sergeant?" Aisha asked, hoping the answer was no.

"Well, we will not be doing that today," Sergeant First Class Hermanson replied. "I am not exactly sure what the rest of the schedule looks like. We can ask Staff Sergeant Hall that question later."

"Yes, Sergeant," Aisha answered.

Sergeant First Class Hermanson and the four specialists finished the short walk down to the building, and Staff Sergeant Hall met them at the door.

"Good morning, everyone," Staff Sergeant Hall said in Arabic.

"Good morning to you as well, Sergeant," Wafiq replied, impatient to learn more about interpretation.

"Wafiq, can you please take everyone down to the training room we used last week?" Staff Sergeant Hall asked. "I will be there shortly."

"Yes, Sergeant," Wafiq replied with a smile. "This way, please."

"I think I may have been a little too quick to judge Aisha," Staff Sergeant Hall said to Sergeant First Class Hermanson when the four specialists entered the training room. "She did much better as the week progressed. I think it may just have been a confidence issue. She should be fine."

"Thanks, Art. That's good to know," Sergeant First Class Hermanson said. "Are you planning to run them through any more interrogation work this week?"

"I doubt it," Staff Sergeant Hall replied. "The contract support will be working with the teams, so we will be a little shorthanded. Why, what's up?"

"Well, I think the specialists are a little concerned after the last go around," Sergeant First Class Hermanson explained. "If we can get by without it, I think it might be a good call. I want them to head out of here on a strong note and not doubt their abilities. What do you think?"

"Sounds like a plan, Herm," Staff Sergeant Hall agreed. "There is more than enough to keep us busy, and a week isn't nearly enough time to get them much more proficient in interpretation. We're just scratching the surface."

"Thanks, Art," Sergeant First Class Hermanson said as he turned to exit the building. "I need to take care of some other stuff. When do you want me to head back this way?"

"How about 1600 hours?" Staff Sergeant Hall suggested.

"Works for me," Sergeant First Class Hermanson said. "See you then."

Sergeant First Class Hermanson headed over to the operations building. He wanted to check in with Master Sergeant Mandess to see if there was any additional information available on Al Khafaji. It was getting to be down to the last minute to make a decision on whether or not to take Al Khafaji with them on the deployment. He was not wild about taking him, but the fact that local-hire linguists might be more difficult to come by might mean that Al Khafaji would need to go. Sergeant First Class Hermanson figured if there was a need, he could just keep Al Khafaji close at hand.

Sergeant First Class Hermanson went by the office, but Master Sergeant Mandess was not there. He checked a couple of other places but still could not find him. When he saw one of the other team members, he stopped by his desk.

"Hey, Phil, any idea where Top is?" Sergeant First Class Hermanson asked.

"I think he had a meeting to go to with the boss," the other team member said without looking up from his computer. "Do you want me to tell him you were looking for him?"

"Nope, nothing important," Sergeant First Class Hermanson said. "I'll try to check back in with him later today."

Sergeant First Class Hermanson left the operations building and headed over to the arms room. He needed to talk with the armorer about rifles for the four specialists. If they were going to deploy, they needed their own rifles. Since they were not actually members of the unit, they didn't have assigned weapons. At this point, he might have to settle for whatever was available.

The arms room was located in the headquarters building. Sergeant First Class Hermanson entered and headed down the hall to the arms room. He knew the armorer was in because the top of the door was open.

"Hey, Tim, are you in there?" Sergeant First Class Hermanson asked, glancing inside of the room. "I need to talk to you about the four linguist specialists."

"Yep, just a second," the armorer replied. "Top said you would be coming by."

"Looks like I may be taking all four of the specialists with me, so I need to make sure they have some bullet launchers," Sergeant First Class Hermanson explained, once again amazed at Top's ability to always be one step ahead of him.

"Looking for anything in particular or will four standard carbines work?" the armorer asked as he put down the handgun he was working on.

"The carbines will be fine," Sergeant First Class Hermanson replied.

"I'll get four of them set aside," the armorer stated as he looked at a calendar on his desk. "Looks like we have a team going out to the range on Thursday. You want me to give them a call and see if you can piggyback off them?"

"That would be great, Tim. Thanks," Sergeant First Class Hermanson said. That would be one less thing he had to worry about. "I'll bring them by tomorrow to sign for the rifles."

"No need," the armorer said. "I'll be heading out with the team, so I'll just bring them out there with me. We are scheduled for the range between 0800 hours and 1000 hours. Just come out when you can."

"Roger that," Sergeant First Class Hermanson said. "We'll be there before 0900 hours. That will give the team time to get their stuff out of the way before we get there."

Sergeant First Class Hermanson had a few other things to take care of before getting back to the interrogation building to get the specialists for lunch. He decided to put off trying to find Master Sergeant Mandess until the workday was done. It would be much easier to find him then since he usually stayed late taking care of things at the end of the day when it was quiet.

Right now, he wanted to head over to the post exchange and pick up a nice anniversary card and gift for his wife. Their anniversary was not for another couple of months, but they had both agreed to celebrate before he deployed again. They had been married for six years and had a four-year-old boy. This was going to be his third deployment during that time. Following his first deployment, they decided to celebrate birthdays and anniversaries prior to deploying. That was when Sergeant First Class Hermanson received his first Purple Heart while he was deployed during their marriage.

Staff Sergeant Hall had the specialists working on interpretation preparation exercises. He provided them with a list of people that he would meet in three separate interviews. He told them the individual's name, age, and occupation. Staff Sergeant Hall told them to develop lists of possible questions for the interviewee and a list of vocabulary words for each specific interview. When thirty minutes were up, he asked everyone to share their questions and lists with the group.

The first time they did this exercise, the questions and vocabulary lists were rudimentary at best. The questions were very basic and resembled what was asked during the interrogation exercises, and the list of vocabulary words was no more than a couple words for each interview.

"Folks, this is also what distinguishes interpretation from simple knowledge of a language," Staff Sergeant Hall began. "If you are lucky enough to know what the interpretation requirement entails, you need to focus on technical terms that might apply to the subject. So, if you are providing interpretation for a medical person, you might want to become familiar with some medical terms beforehand. The same thing goes for an accountant, lawyer, or engineer. All of these people may have technical terms that apply to their profession, and an individual who is conducting the interview or interrogation may ask questions concerning their profession."

Wafiq's hand shot up into the air, and he waved it to catch Staff Sergeant Hall's attention.

"Yes, Wafiq," Staff Sergeant Hall said. "Do you have a question?"

"Yes, Sergeant," Wafiq responded. "How can we find these technical words?"

"Well," Staff Sergeant Hall started before launching into the point he was trying to make. "A good interpreter will try to meet with the person conducting the interview or interrogation beforehand. If the person in charge does not provide specific words or phrases, the interpreter should ask for a list of topics or words that might come up. Once they have those phrases or words, it's a simple matter of looking them up to become familiar with them."

"Ah, I see," Wafiq said. "So there will be a computer that can be used to do this."

"Yes," Staff Sergeant Hall replied. "Now I would like all of you to try again to provide questions and terms that may be useful for each of the three people I told you about earlier. You can use the laptops near the front of the room to look up any information you may need."

"Are there any specific words you would like us to find?" Al Khafaji asked Staff Sergeant Hall, trying to show that he had been paying attention to what had been said.

"Good question, Samir," Staff Sergeant Hall said, pleased with the progress Al Khafaji showed. "Always be sure to try to ask this question to the person in charge, folks. There is a small list next to each computer, but you can add words that you think may be important. I will give you an hour to complete all three."

The specialists walked over and sat down in front of the computers. They looked at the lists and started their computer searches. Staff Sergeant Hall was not surprised to see Aisha working much slower than the other three. She still had a long way to go, but she was trying to be better, and that was all Staff Sergeant Hall was looking for at this point.

When ninety minutes were up, Staff Sergeant Hall saw that Aisha and Al Khafaji were still working on the computers, so he decided to give them a few more minutes. Ten minutes later, it looked like everyone was done, so he walked over and had them all go through their new and improved lists. Each one of them had thought of three or four additional terms, and the questions they had developed were more in line with what he wanted to see. Progress was a good thing. He just hoped they would remember some of what they were learning.

"All right, that was much better," Staff Sergeant Hall told them. "You can start getting your things together. It's about time for lunch."

They gathered their notebooks and papers and trailed Staff Sergeant Hall to the door. Staff Sergeant Hall opened the door and followed them out. Then, they stood outside and waited for Sergeant First Class Hermanson.

"How are all my interpretation warriors doing today, Staff Sergeant Hall?" Sergeant First Class Hermanson called out as he walked down the sidewalk toward the building.

"Outstanding!" Staff Sergeant Hall exclaimed. "All of them are doing amazing work."

"Great to hear," Sergeant First Class Hermanson smiled. "I had to set up some time with Tim on Thursday morning, but they are all yours the remainder of the week."

"OK," Staff Sergeant Hall agreed. "I'll take a look at the schedule and move some stuff around. No problem."

Sergeant First Class Hermanson walked the four specialists out. He was surprised that nobody had any questions today. They all just walked to the gate, waited for him to open it, and went to their cars, almost as if they were on autopilot. He didn't feel a need to tell them to be back by 1300 hours; somehow, he figured they would all be standing there waiting when he walked up to the gate.

7

"**N**ext," the administrative specialist said as Sergeant Abdullah approached the table. "Name?"

"Abdullah," he replied as the specialist searched the roster for his name. When she found it, she handed him a packet of papers.

"You can go to station one, Sergeant."

Sergeant Abdullah walked over to the next table and waited in line. There were several different stations set up in the gym. Each one focused on a different readiness requirement, including personnel records, medical, dental, and legal. All the soldiers had to complete the readiness processing in order to deploy.

There was also a section that reviewed an individual's elections for insurance and wills. It was a very necessary thing in Sergeant Abdullah's mind even though he did not have a family. He had known many soldiers who were killed during the war who had thought it was not necessary. There was no front line in this war. Everyone who was deployed was a combatant regardless of MOS or what unit they were assigned to.

Sergeant Abdullah didn't have any issues during the readiness processing. All his paperwork and physical exams were up to date. He needed new immunizations, as did most every soldier in his unit. The physician's assistant asked him if he had any issues with his previous wounds. When Sergeant Abdullah said no, the soldier signed off on his paperwork, and he moved on to the psychiatrist. Sergeant Abdullah said he had no issues with post-traumatic stress, and once again, the doctor signed off on his paperwork, and he moved on. He finished the entire process in about three hours and headed back to his unit.

"How did it go, Carson?" Sergeant First Class Broadmoor asked when he walked into the maintenance building.

"Very well, Sergeant," Sergeant Abdullah replied.

"No need for you to be around here," Sergeant First Class Broadmoor commented. "You can take an early lunch if you want. The only people who are going to be working in here this week will be the ones working on pacing items. I can keep you on standby if you want, but if you need to do anything to get ready to deploy, now is the best time to do it."

"I would be happy to be on standby," Sergeant Abdullah said. "I am always happy to help."

"OK, I'll put you on the list," Sergeant First Class Broadmoor stated as he walked over to the work board. "If you change your mind or have something to do, just let me know."

"Will do, Sergeant," Sergeant Abdullah smiled. "But I don't think you will have to change it."

Sergeant Abdullah decided to take Sergeant First Class Broadmoor's advice. He left for lunch early and then went to the post exchange to get some things he might need for the deployment. He bought several packages of baby wipes, ibuprofen, powdered drink mix, multivitamins, lip balm, travel-size toothpaste, foot powder, boot insoles, antibiotic cream, eye drops, facial tissue, and body glide. He would go back to the exchange again before he deployed once he knew what the unit would supply to the soldiers. He thought there would probably be plenty of free time now that he had finished the readiness processing.

The specialists were all waiting at the gate at 1300 hours, just as Sergeant First Class Hermanson had expected. Sara and Wafiq were discussing some aspects of the training from the morning while Aisha was scrolling through messages on her phone. Al Khafaji stood with the group but didn't join in their conversation. Sergeant First Class Hermanson had become used to their way of acting and didn't expect anything else. He was most surprised with the change in Wafiq's attitude since starting the interpretation training. It was a marked improvement.

"I think the point Staff Sergeant Hall was making was the technical differences between each profession," Wafiq explained to Sara. "Arabic is Arabic."

"Yes, I agree," Sara replied while trying to stress her point. "What I mean is that professional people have more formal discussions than many others."

"Very true," Aisha added, tearing her focus from her phone for a second. "My father is a doctor—well, a surgeon—and he has a terrible time understanding what some of the young people are talking about. He is just an old person stuck in the past."

Al Khafaji wanted to correct her for showing disrespect toward her father. He thought to himself that if they were in Iraq, she would be harshly punished for being so insolent. It bothered him to see how America corrupted the young.

"OK, folks, let's get back down to Staff Sergeant Hall," Sergeant First Class Hermanson instructed as he opened the gate and watched the four of them pass by. "I'm sure there is plenty of good stuff yet to be learned."

"Will we be doing this training all week?" Aisha asked.

"Every day but Thursday," Sergeant First Class Hermanson replied. "On Thursday, we are going to get you to the rifle range."

"But I thought we were going to work as language specialists," Aisha countered, sounding a little disappointed.

"You will be working with your language and culture skills," Sergeant First Class Hermanson explained. "Every soldier in the Army needs to be able to qualify with a rifle regardless of what their occupational specialty is. Soldier first."

"Yes, Sergeant," Aisha said without much enthusiasm.

Staff Sergeant Hall worked with the specialists for the remainder of the day. He gave them many different scenarios and walked them through the correct way to approach each situation. He decided that the best way to utilize the rest of the week would be to coach them through different approaches instead of having each of them try to complete a task, correcting their action, and having them attempt the same task again. He just didn't have the time to complete the training any other way. He was already trying to finish months of training in a week. The marksmanship training was causing him to restructure the training schedule, but he knew how critical it was for the deployment. The teams were not very large, and every person needed to be able to pull their weight, even a linguist. If shit hit the fan, every member of the team had to be capable of returning fire.

The afternoon went well, and the specialists seemed to be getting better with their understanding of interpretation. Staff Sergeant Hall would never be able to think of them as trained interpreters, but they would at least have a working knowledge of what interpretation entailed when he was done with them. Sergeant First Class Hermanson understood what they needed to practice after they deployed, so that made Staff Sergeant Hall feel better about what he was doing.

"OK, folks, let's wrap it up for today," Staff Sergeant Hall said to the specialists. "We'll work on it again in the morning. Until then, be thinking about how the physical environment of an interview can impact your job as an interpreter. We'll go into that in more detail tomorrow."

"Yes, Sergeant," the specialists responded. They all seemed to be getting more involved in the training. Staff Sergeant Hall thought his change in training methodology might be helping them.

The specialists gathered their stuff and followed Staff Sergeant Hall to the door. It was odd to not see Sergeant First Class Hermanson waiting for them. Staff Sergeant Hall opened the door and stood outside with the specialists. They waited for Sergeant First Class Hermanson for more than ten minutes, and Staff Sergeant Hall was about to bring them all back inside when they finally saw him walking quickly down the sidewalk.

"Sorry, Art, I had a couple things I had to get done," Sergeant First Class Hermanson apologized as he reached the end of the sidewalk. "Everything going OK?"

"No worries, Herm," Staff Sergeant Hall replied. He knew there had to be a good reason for Sergeant First Class Hermanson to be late. "See you all tomorrow."

Sergeant First Class Hermanson escorted the four specialists down to the gate at a quicker pace than normal. He still wanted to go by and give Master Sergeant Mandess an update and see if there was any additional news on the situation overseas. He watched the four specialists go through the gate but didn't wait for them to get into their cars before he headed off toward the operations building.

Al Khafaji watched as Sergeant First Class Hermanson moved quickly down the sidewalk. He had a feeling something was going on but had no idea what it could be. He wondered if it would be suspicious to ask Sergeant First Class Hermanson about it tomorrow but decided to just leave it for now. The last thing he wanted to do before going to Iraq was raise any suspicions.

All in good time, Al Khafaji thought to himself. *Soon the infidels will pay for their actions against my brothers.*

Sergeant First Class Hermanson's hunch was right. When he got to the office, Master Sergeant Mandess was right where he thought he would be. He looked frustrated over something.

"Hey, Herm, come on in," Master Sergeant Mandess called when he looked up and saw Sergeant First Class Hermanson in the doorway. "Damn meetings. I don't know how they expect us to get anything done around here with all the meetings they want us to go to. Drives me up a freaking wall sometimes."

"If you are busy, I can stop by tomorrow, Top," Sergeant First Class Hermanson offered.

"Nope. What do you got?" Master Sergeant Mandess inquired, turning his chair away from the computer.

"I wanted to check in to see if there was anything new on Al Khafaji," Sergeant First Class Hermanson began. "I also wanted to let you know the specialists all seem good to go now. Art and I both think they will be ready to deploy with the team."

"That's good to hear," Master Sergeant Mandess said. "I just read through a message from Steve, and he lost another four local hires. Something is definitely heating up over there, and they are having issues finding local hires to replace the losses. We could be in a real bind for linguists once we get there."

"Do they still have any contract linguists?" Sergeant First Class Hermanson asked.

"Sure," Master Sergeant Mandess answered. "But you're going to have a hard time getting them to go outside the wire. If things start getting worse, we may have a hard time just keeping the contract linguists, period."

"Makes you kind of wish we still had those uniformed interpreters," Sergeant First Class Hermanson said wistfully, as he remembered having used them before in an earlier deployment. "They were right there with us, and we never had to worry about their background for the most part."

"Yep, I liked having them too," Master Sergeant Mandess agreed. "But somebody decided these new folks would be good enough. Another big Army decision. What could possibly go wrong?"

Both of them smiled as they continued talking about preparations for deployment. Master Sergeant Mandess wanted to hear updates on several members of the team. Sergeant First Class Hermanson went through the list of team members and assured him that everyone was ready to go, but he knew more than a couple of them were still recovering from the last rotation. Master Sergeant

Mandess knew it as well, but he trusted Sergeant First Class Hermanson's judgment.

Sergeant Abdullah spent most of the next few days checking in with other mechanics to see whether they needed any help. There were only a couple of mechanics still working on vehicles. Everything else had been wrapped up, and since most of the unit was going to be deploying, any repairs were being sent to another unit. The maintenance building looked almost empty. Most of the mechanics only showed up for morning formation, then went about what they needed to do with their families before deploying. The only thing to do as a unit was the weapons qualification and a deployment ceremony, which was scheduled for next Wednesday.

The weapons qualification was on Friday, and everyone was instructed to be in at 0700 hours to draw their weapons from the arms room. Sergeant Abdullah pulled into the parking lot at 0645 hours and saw only five other cars. For a second, he wondered if he had the day wrong, but then cars started to pull in, and it didn't take long for the parking lot to be full. All the late arrivals would have to park in another lot and walk over to the company headquarters.

Sergeant Abdullah exited his car and joined the other soldiers in line. Everyone was talking about how well they were going to shoot, and some of them were even taking bets on who would be the best shot. Sergeant Maczrakolski got in line shortly after Sergeant Abdullah and moved up behind him.

"So how do you think you'll do today, Carson?" Sergeant Maczrakolski asked as he adjusted his web gear. "This stuff never fits right."

"Here, Ski, let me help you," Sergeant Abdullah offered, adjusting Sergeant Maczrakolski's gear for him. He loosened the web belt and moved the canteen onto Sergeant Maczrakolski's hip.

"That's better. Thanks, Carson," Sergeant Maczrakolski said as he moved from side to side, testing the fit. "Not used to my canteen being so far back."

"If you have to move into a prone firing position, you don't want to have to worry about laying on top of your canteen, do you?" Sergeant Abdullah explained with a smile.

"No, I guess not. Thanks." Sergeant Maczrakolski figured he would get used to it, and after all, what Sergeant Abdullah said made a lot of sense.

The line moved quickly, and Sergeant Abdullah was soon standing in front of the door to the arms room. The armorer came back to the front and looked at Sergeant Abdullah. He did not recognize him.

"Name?" the armorer asked.

"Abdullah," Sergeant Abdullah answered.

"Oh, you must be one of the new guys," the armorer said, not waiting for an answer. "I got a rifle over here for you. Have you ever used a grenade launcher before?"

"Yes, a few times," Sergeant Abdullah replied.

"Good. Here you go," the armorer said, handing the rifle to Sergeant Abdullah. "We'll have range time with the grenade launcher next week. I'll let you know when it will be. Next!"

Sergeant Abdullah took the rifle and examined it. He moved outside and did a function check near the discharge barrel. Everything seemed to be in working order, so he moved out into the parking lot and waited for formation.

"Just go get on the trucks once you have your rifles," First Sergeant Holman told everyone. "Sergeant First Class Broadmoor will give you a safety briefing once you are at the range."

There were five two-and-a-half-ton trucks parked along the side of the road. Sergeant Abdullah and Sergeant Maczrakolski were able to get into the first one. Once the vehicle was full, the driver put the truck in gear and headed down the road. The second truck filled up slowly and was far behind them.

"Good timing," Sergeant Maczrakolski called to Sergeant Abdullah over the noise of the truck engine. "We can get there, knock it out, and be back in time for lunch."

Sergeant Abdullah didn't try to say anything. He just nodded his head, but he was not certain it would be quite that easy for all the soldiers in the unit.

The drive to the range took only about twenty minutes. Most of the drive was over paved roads with only the last mile or so on a dirt road. When the truck came to a stop, two soldiers near the back of the truck removed the chains from the tailgate, which dropped down to allow the men inside to get out. Sergeant First Class Broadmoor was standing near the bleachers. Sergeant Abdullah recognized the range as a zero range, which was used prior to trying to qualify with a rifle, and it allowed a shooter to adjust the sights on his rifle if necessary.

"All right, get your asses over here so I can give you your safety briefing," Sergeant First Class Broadmoor called out, gesturing toward the bleachers.

The soldiers moved into the bleachers and took a seat. Sergeant First Class Broadmoor read the safety briefing to them from a sheet of paper he had on his clipboard. When he was finished, he asked if there were any questions. Nobody raised their hand.

"We have twenty firing positions and twenty targets," Sergeant First Class Broadmoor said as he pointed out toward the range. "Go on down and find a spot. Take up a good firing position but don't do anything else until I tell you."

Sergeant Abdullah and Sergeant Maczrakolski walked down the firing line and stopped at their spot. Sergeant Abdullah had position thirteen, and Sergeant Maczrakolski had position fourteen. There were three magazines at each firing position that held three rounds each. All the firers took up a good prone firing position and put in the first magazine when Sergeant First Class Broadmoor said to do so from the control tower. They were instructed to fire three rounds, and once they were done, they walked down to check their shot groupings and accuracy. Each soldier evaluated where the rounds impacted and determined how to adjust their sights. Then, they walked back up to their positions and made the necessary adjustments. Sergeant Abdullah's rounds were very close to each other but low and to the right of the center.

The soldiers went through the same routine again and went down to check their targets. Sergeant Abdullah was happy with the changes he had made. He was just slightly off-center. Sergeant Maczrakolski was still having an issue with his shot groups. They were not very close together, which made it difficult to know what adjustments needed to be made to correctly zero the rifle.

"You should try to focus more on your breathing before you pull the trigger, Ski," Sergeant Abdullah suggested, trying not to offend his friend. He reached down and pulled the paper target from the backing.

"Why?" Sergeant Maczrakolski asked, smiling. "This is all just for fun. When we go out on exercises, I always carry the hog."

The hog was the squad automatic weapon. It was a belt-fed machine gun. Sergeant Abdullah now understood why Sergeant Maczrakolski was not overly concerned with his poor shot groups. The hog was a much heavier weapon, and most people did not want to be the one carrying it. Sergeant Maczrakolski was likely very safe in assuming he would still have the honor of carrying the hog.

Sergeant Abdullah waited in the bleachers to see if there was anyone else ready to qualify with their weapon. When the third and final magazine had been fired, there were five other soldiers who had finished. The remainder were given three more magazines with three rounds and sent back to the firing line. Sergeant Abdullah thought that some of them could be out there all day, judging from their targets.

The other trucks started to pull into the range when Sergeant Abdullah headed to the qualification range. Sergeant Maczrakolski was still on the firing line. Sergeant Abdullah was amazed that it could take so long to zero a rifle. When he was given a firing point by the officer in charge, Sergeant Abdullah moved down to his position on the qualification range. When it was all over, he had qualified as an expert, missing only one target. He went back to the bleachers and waited for there to be enough qualified soldiers to go back to the company area. It took another forty-five minutes before there was a truck on its way back.

Sergeant Abdullah cleaned his rifle when he got back and returned it to the armorer, who told him the grenade launcher familiarization would be the following Monday and that he should be at the arms room by 1300 hours. Sergeant Abdullah went over to the maintenance building before he went to lunch to check the work board. Nothing had changed.

The four specialists were all standing at the gate at 0730 hours, but this time, Sergeant First Class Hermanson was already there. He came out instead of letting them in, and they walked over to his old truck, which thankfully had a back seat. There was no need to take a military vehicle since the firearms were being transported by the armorer.

They were headed to a weapons familiarization range. Since the specialists had only been in the military for less than a year, they still had valid weapons qualifications in their records. Master Sergeant Mandess didn't want to take any chances on one of them having an issue with qualifying. He would be surprised if they all fired experts, but he wouldn't be surprised if at least one of them could not fire well enough to qualify.

Everyone was fairly quiet during the ride out to the range. Sergeant First Class Hermanson decided he didn't want to test anyone's musical choices, so he left the radio off. He passed the time by thinking about the upcoming deployment and trying to visualize how each of the specialists would react to contact once they got to Iraq. For some reason, he still had a hard time reading Al Khafaji, but the others he thought were easy. Aisha would not get off a round, Wafiq would put up a good fight, and Sara would kill everything in sight even without a rifle.

As they pulled into the range parking lot, they could hear rounds going off. It was about 0815 hours, so Sergeant First Class Hermanson figured the team had another thirty minutes or so of firing left. That worked out well because after the specialists picked up their rifles from the armorer, Sergeant First Class Hermanson wanted to take them through some dry fire drills. That way, he could at least get a rough idea of which of the four might have issues on the range.

The armorer was sitting in the back of an open-bed truck with a rifle rack. He motioned to Sergeant First Class Hermanson to come over to the truck when he saw him.

"Ready whenever you are, Herm," the armorer said as he unlocked the rifle rack. "All I need is name and rank and a signature. How many rounds do you need for each?"

"What magazines did you bring with you?" Sergeant First Class Hermanson asked.

"I have a box of twenties and a box of thirties," the armorer replied. "Your pick."

"Let's do three of the twenties each," Sergeant First Class Hermanson decided. "That way, we can go through a few different firing positions."

"Sure thing," the armorer said, pulling twelve loaded magazines from the box. "OK, folks, I'm going to need you to print your name and rank and then sign for each rifle. When you bring them back, you will sign again as you turn them in."

"What about cleaning kits?" Sergeant First Class Hermanson asked.

"Got four of them right here, but don't have them spend a lot of time on them," the armorer said. "I am planning to go over everything one more time to make sure they are all ready to go."

"Thanks, Tim. Much appreciated," Sergeant First Class Hermanson responded, knowing that the armorer was doing him a favor. Usually, things had to be spotless to be turned in.

The specialists filed up to the back of the truck. The armorer handed them each a rifle and called out the serial number. When the specialist verified the serial number, they would sign the paperwork from the armorer. Sergeant First Class Hermanson took the twelve magazines and put them inside his helmet bag. He told the specialists to put the cleaning kit in the cargo pocket of their uniforms. Then, they all moved to the bleachers to wait for the team members to finish shooting. It took only about ten minutes before they were ready to move onto the firing line.

"Before we start shooting, I want you all to go through a few dry fire exercises," Sergeant First Class Hermanson said to the specialists. "Spread out in a good prone position next to this first firing point."

Sergeant First Class Hermanson watched as the specialists laid down on the ground with their rifles pointing downrange. When it looked like they were all settled, he placed a washer on the barrel of their rifle and told them to pull the trigger. The washer fell off all of their barrels except for Sara's.

Sergeant First Class Hermanson had each of them pull the charging handle back on their rifle, and he went down the line, watching each one of them pull the trigger on their rifle. Aisha seemed to be just nervous, while Wafiq and Al Khafaji were jerking the trigger. He corrected each one of them and placed the washer on the barrel again. Wafiq was still jerking the trigger a little, but Aisha and Al Khafaji were much better.

The specialists moved to their individual firing positions and were each given the first magazine. Sergeant First Class Hermanson explained to them that the targets would be brought up and they should fire one round. The targets were set at fifty, seventy-five, and one hundred meters. He told them the targets would be brought up one at a time to start.

He gestured for the tower to bring up the first target. The target came up, and all four specialists fired their rifles with all four targets going down.

Not a bad start, Sergeant First Class Hermanson thought to himself even though it was very difficult to miss a target at fifty meters.

Sergeant First Class Hermanson motioned to the tower again, and the seventy-five-meter target came up. Once again, all four specialists fired a round, but this time, only three targets went down. The target in Wafiq's lane was still standing and had to be brought down by the tower.

Sergeant First Class Hermanson motioned again, and the one-hundred-meter target came up. The specialists fired, and all four targets went down again. Maybe the miss by Wafiq was just a fluke. Sergeant First Class Hermanson turned and gave a thumbs-up to the tower. The targets no longer came up in order but instead came up randomly. Sara and Al Khafaji hit all of the remaining targets while Aisha missed only two and Wafiq missed three.

Sergeant First Class Hermanson talked with the specialists and told them that the targets would now come up as pairs. They were to fire one round at each target but would only have five seconds to engage both targets. He also told them to remain in the prone position. Sergeant First Class Hermanson waited for the specialists to get into position, then turned and gave a thumbs-up to the tower. When the firing was completed, Al Khafaji hit all targets, and Sara missed one, while Wafiq and Aisha both missed two.

Sergeant First Class Hermanson walked over to them once again and said that the last targets were to be engaged in the standing position. He used Wafiq as an example and coached him into the proper firing position. When the specialists were ready, he told them the targets would come up in pairs randomly again, and they would have five seconds to engage both targets.

One last time, Sergeant First Class Hermanson gave the tower a thumbs-up, and the specialists engaged the first set of targets. They fired at nine more sets until they were out of ammunition. The results didn't really surprise Sergeant First Class Hermanson. Sara and Al Khafaji hit all of the targets, while Wafiq missed three and Aisha missed four. He had expected the standing firing position to be the most difficult for Aisha, who was not a very large person. She had difficulties keeping her rifle on target. Wafiq just seemed to not be a very good shot, but he was still proficient enough to be called upon if needed.

"Not bad, folks, not bad at all," Sergeant First Class Hermanson said to the specialists as they picked up the brass from around their firing positions. Sergeant First Class Hermanson had them clear their rifles as he walked them off the range. "Let's head over to the bleachers, and you can do a quick cleaning of your rifles before turning them in."

"No need to take the bolt apart. Just wipe down as much of the carbon as you can and run a cleaning rod down the barrel a few times," the armorer instructed as they neared the bleachers.

The specialists cleaned their rifles as directed and were ready to turn them in ten minutes later. The armorer took each of the rifles and secured them in the rifle rack. Sergeant First Class Hermanson walked them to the truck, and they headed back to the headquarters building. The ride back in was a little more vocal, and the specialists seemed happy with the range experience.

"I didn't think it would be so hard to fire the rifle while standing," Aisha admitted. Nobody was surprised that she was the first one to speak. Al Khafaji thought she was the perfect example of what happened to his people when they spent too much time with Americans.

"It is, but that may be a very important firing position for you to master," Sergeant First Class Hermanson said. "We will work on it."

"Yes, Sergeant," Aisha answered.

"What did the rest of you think about the range?" Sergeant First Class Hermanson asked, encouraging everyone to participate in the discussion.

"It was good practice," Wafiq said, not wanting to say too much, as he knew he had not done very well.

"Yes, it was good practice," Al Khafaji acknowledged. He really thought it was senseless that Americans judged their shooting skills by shooting at paper and plastic pop-up targets. If they wanted to prove their skills, he thought that only shots to the head should count. They even counted hits if the bullet struck in front of the target and made the target go down.

"Sara, you shot well," Sergeant First Class Hermanson observed. "Where did you learn how to shoot?"

"My father made sure my entire family was able to fire a rifle," Sara replied. "We lived in the north and had to protect ourselves and our home."

Kurdish dog! Al Khafaji thought to himself. *I will kill her first for being a traitor to my country and true believers.*

When Sergeant First Class Hermanson pulled into the parking lot near the headquarters building, he looked at his watch.

"OK, folks, why don't you head out to lunch," he suggested to the specialists as they got out of the truck. "Be back at 1300 hours so we can see what Staff Sergeant Hall has for you to do."

"Yes, Sergeant," the specialists replied.

8

When Sergeant Abdullah returned from lunch, he noticed that most of the soldiers had returned from the range; however, many of them still had their rifles. He thought that they must have returned a short while ago and not had a chance to clean their rifles yet. Sergeant Abdullah did not understand how some of the soldiers could spend so much time on the range. He saw Sergeant Maczrakolski and some of the others looking at something posted on the window of the headquarters building. When the group of soldiers saw him coming, they all started clapping.

"Great shooting, Carson," Sergeant Maczrakolski called. "Maybe we should call you Deadeye instead."

"Thank you, Ski," Sergeant Abdullah said, somewhat embarrassed by all the attention. "I had a good day."

"Good day?" Sergeant First Class Broadmoor laughed. "Best damn shot in the company. Good day. Hell of a job, Carson. Congratulations."

"But I missed a target," Sergeant Abdullah pointed out. "How could I be the best in the company?"

Everyone gathered around the results looked at Sergeant Abdullah and then started laughing.

"Come on over and take a look," Sergeant Maczrakolski invited, making an opening for Sergeant Abdullah to look at the scores.

There were only two other soldiers who scored close to Sergeant Abdullah. Most of the others in the company were well behind, and three had failed to qualify at all. Sergeant Abdullah could not understand how this could be, but the results were right in front of him.

"All right, folks," Sergeant First Class Broadmoor called out. "Get your rifles cleaned up and turned in. Once you're done, you're dismissed for the day. I want to see all of you back here on time on Monday morning, no excuses."

Sergeant Abdullah waited to see if anyone needed any help, but there was nothing left to do. He checked the work board, but it was wiped clean since all the pacing items were now repaired. Sergeant Abdullah had not heard anything about items that would be provided by the unit for the deployment, so he decided to make one more stop at the post exchange before heading home. He was not even listed as standby for maintenance requirements any longer, so he would have the entire weekend to himself.

Staff Sergeant Hall worked with the specialists that afternoon and again on Friday. He wasn't sure if what he had done would be enough, but it was all he could do. Master Sergeant Mandess had told him to not work the specialists over the weekend unless it was absolutely necessary, and in all honesty, there wasn't enough time to get them much further than they already were with understanding the basics of interpretation. It was more important for them to function as part of the team for the remainder of the time, even if it was only a matter of going through the soldier readiness checks.

All the specialists seemed to be markedly better than when they'd first started. Staff Sergeant Hall was still very pleased with the progress Wafiq had made, while Aisha had also shown improvement over the last two weeks. Al Khafaji seemed indifferent to learning interpretation, and Sara was already beyond what he had taught the other two. He would make sure to help Sergeant First Class Hermanson out with some exercises to be used during deployment if possible.

Staff Sergeant Hall would not be going with them this time. He would be leaving the service in the next two months as a promise to his wife and family. He didn't really want to go through with it, but he felt it was the best thing for his family. A very large company had already offered him a position managing their contract linguist program at a salary that was more than double what he was currently making as a staff sergeant. As much as he liked the Army, his family had to come first this time.

At the end of the day on Friday, Staff Sergeant Hall walked the specialists to the door. He thanked each one of them in Arabic and wished them well. He got the feeling they were hiding something from him as their answers were all very short and emotionless. For some reason, he had been expecting something more. He opened the door to let the specialists out and was surprised to see Sergeant First Class Hermanson standing there with a cake and a balloon that had *Thank You* written on it.

"Surprise!" Sergeant First Class Hermanson yelled before handing Staff Sergeant Hall the cake and balloon. "The specialists insisted that they give you something for all the things you taught them about being an interpreter."

"Thank you, Staff Sergeant Hall!" the specialists cried as they clapped.

Staff Sergeant Hall was stunned. He was completely surprised and had trouble finding the right words to say.

"Well, Art," Sergeant First Class Hermanson said. "In all the years I have known you, this is probably the first time I have seen you at a loss for words. Do you need me to call a medic?"

"Nope, but thanks for the concern," Staff Sergeant Hall replied as he looked at the specialists. "I truly appreciate your act of kindness. If you couldn't tell, it was a total surprise to me. I hope you can all join me in enjoying the cake."

The specialists all glanced at Sergeant First Class Hermanson to see if it was all right. He just nodded his head.

"I just happen to have some forks and plates right here," Sergeant First Class Hermanson revealed as he held up a plastic bag. "There's always time for cake."

They walked back to a room that the cadre used as a break area. Sergeant First Class Hermanson bought drinks from a vending machine, and they all sat around a table to enjoy the cake. It was a nice way to end the week and was one of the last official tasks for Staff Sergeant Hall before he left the Army. The two months ahead of him would be mostly out-processing and appointments.

"We will all miss you, Art," Sergeant First Class Hermanson said sincerely as they cleaned off the table.

"Thanks, Herm. I really appreciate that," Staff Sergeant Hall replied.

Sergeant First Class Hermanson had no way of knowing that this would be the last time he would spend with his friend. That's just how things went sometimes in the Army. People moved on, and someone else would report in to take their place. Staff Sergeant Hall had not told anyone but Master Sergeant Mandess about his decision to leave the Army. That's how he wanted it, so people knew only that he was not deploying with them. The why didn't really matter. They knew it must be for a good reason, and that's all that mattered.

Sergeant Abdullah spent most of the weekend getting prepared for the deployment. He made sure that his dress uniform was ready for the deployment ceremony and that his dress shoes were shined. He made another trip to the post exchange to get some other items to pack in his bag and decided what he would leave behind in his vehicle since he would not have any other place to store his items. Luckily, he did not have much besides his military items and some civilian clothes. Anything else he needed to store would easily fit into the trunk of his car. The one he'd purchased at the lemon lot on post had a nice-sized trunk and would be perfect.

He also wanted to spend time with his parents before he deployed, so he set up a call on the computer. He didn't tell them that he was deploying again, but he could tell that they knew something was happening. His mother was especially concerned, as she had heard from people in Iraq that things were getting to be very dangerous again. The militants were active, and the people were scared of confrontations with the Americans. So many innocent people had already died. It was difficult for Sergeant Abdullah to not say anything to them, but he would contact them again when he had been in Iraq for a few months. They would understand. They both told him that they would keep him in their prayers.

Sergeant Abdullah also decided to download six new books to his computer. He still had the computer he had been given during interpreter/translator training. The laptop had been very helpful to him in his other deployments, but now it just provided a way to relax when he was not on duty. He still had items on his computer that he had used as an interpreter, but he thought maybe it was time to delete them since that was not his job any longer. He checked his files and decided it would be OK to just leave them for now. There was plenty of space available to store the new books.

The weekend went by quickly. He was anxious to finish everything and get back to Iraq. The thought of not going on patrols was something new to him, but from what he knew of previous deployments, there would be no shortage of vehicles to repair. Between poor operator maintenance, the sandstorms, and improvised explosive devices, there would always be a need for a mechanic. He thought about how different it would be working in a maintenance building instead of kicking down doors. Then, he started to recall all the people he had known who had been killed or injured at a base, and it reminded him that there were no front lines in Iraq. It wasn't like other wars; everyone had to be prepared to fight, regardless of where they were located.

꩜

Al Khafaji checked his email again on Friday night. The usual librarian was not there, but the process was still the same. The librarian was a middle-aged man who gave Al Khafaji a piece of paper with the computer number on it. Number three this time. He also asked Al Khafaji to not stay on the computer longer than a half hour.

When Al Khafaji opened his email, he found two messages with code. It was looking for verification of deployment in the next two weeks. Al Khafaji sensed they would be deploying soon, but none of them had been notified yet. He would have to try to find out. The second message was just a communications check. Al Khafaji shut down the computer and dropped off the slip of paper with the librarian.

Al Khafaji drove down the street to the nearest shopping center and parked outside a restaurant that seemed busy. He took out his phone and dialed the number. He waited for the fifth ring and was about to hang up when someone answered. Al Khafaji didn't know what to do, so he quickly ended the call. He had no idea what had happened. He checked the number, and everything seemed correct. Nonplussed, he called it again and waited for the second ring. He was about to hang up when a man answered.

"Never hang up on me again," the man said in a calm, cold tone.

"I have not heard anything," Al Khafaji murmured, still not quite sure what was happening.

"Find out," the voice commanded. "Check your messages closely." Then, the man hung up.

Al Khafaji was certain he had seen all his messages. He couldn't go back to the library, as it was nearing closing time. He would have to wait until the next day. Al Khafaji thought that the man's voice sounded very familiar, but he just could not place it with a name.

The next day, Al Khafaji went to the library shortly after it had opened. The regular librarian was at the counter.

"I would like to use a computer," Al Khafaji said to the woman, hoping she did not want to start a conversation.

"Of course," the librarian nodded as she handed him a piece of paper without even checking her book. "You are here awfully early. I hope there isn't anything wrong."

"No," Al Khafaji began, scrambling to come up with a quick response that would not cause any concern. "I just want to see if my mother has sent me a message to tell me she received my last letter."

"That's very nice of you," the librarian commented. "I wouldn't think many people your age would be sending their parents letters."

"Yes, my mother enjoys reading them," Al Khafaji said.

"Well, you have a good day," the librarian smiled.

"Yes, and you as well," Al Khafaji replied as he turned to walk to the computers.

Al Khafaji sat down and started the computer. When he logged into his email, he went to the junk mail and couldn't find anything that fit what he was looking for. He decided to look at his regular messages even though that was not the normal method of receiving messages from the leader. At first, he saw nothing that meant anything to him. It was all just regular mail, but then he saw a message from a cousin whom he had not seen in several years. He opened it and started to read. Inside the message was the code that required him to call. It was then that he recognized the voice on the phone as that of his cousin.

It still made no sense to Al Khafaji. His cousin had never mentioned any desire to join the Jihad. He was very smart but did not strike Al Khafaji as a warrior. Something must have happened in Iraq. At some point, he would try to find out what had occurred. For now, he just needed to do what he was told and try to find out more information about the deployment.

Al Khafaji met the other specialists at the gate at 0800 hours. Aisha and Wafiq were talking about a new movie they had seen over the weekend. Sara was quiet as usual as she stood near the fence. Sergeant First Class Hermanson surprised them by approaching from the parking lot. He opened the gate and let the specialists in.

"We will be doing readiness processing this morning," he said to the specialists. "I don't believe there will be much for you to do, but I need you all to follow me down to the processing center."

"Can we all go in the same vehicle?" Aisha asked.

"Not this time," Sergeant First Class Hermanson replied. "I need each one of you to follow me in your car."

The specialists got in their vehicles and followed Sergeant First Class Hermanson to the gym. When he pulled into the gym parking lot, they all followed and parked their vehicles.

"Make sure you bring your ID and personnel files with you if you have them," Sergeant First Class Hermanson instructed. "OK, follow me."

They walked up the sidewalk to the front doors of the gym where they were met by a personnel specialist who checked their names against a roster.

"The four of you recently in-processed to the post, so you only have to go to the medical station," the specialist said to the group. "Sergeant First Class Hermanson, looks like you also need to check in at legal, along with medical."

"OK, folks," Sergeant First Class Hermanson said to the specialists. "I want you to do the medical check and then go back to your hotels and check out. Bring all your stuff with you and meet me at the gate by 1000 hours."

"Where will we be staying?" Aisha wondered.

"I'll go over that with you when you return," Sergeant First Class Hermanson replied. "No time for any more questions. Let's move out and make it happen."

"Yes, Sergeant," they chorused as they moved out toward the medical screening station.

The medical screening went quickly for all of them. Their medical records were not very big, and all they needed were additional immunizations.

"What are these shots for?" Aisha nervously asked the medical specialist.

"Just normal immunizations," the specialist replied. "Everyone going overseas has to have them."

That was all Al Khafaji had to hear. He would have to try to contact his cousin in Iraq when he went back to his hotel to check out. Al Khafaji also received immunizations and had to answer some questions with a doctor on childhood diseases, which he had no knowledge of. When he was finished, he looked at his watch. He had less than ninety minutes to check out and return to the post. He took his paperwork and walked quickly to his car.

Al Khafaji drove to his hotel and ran down the hall to his room. He didn't have much to pack, so he had time to make his call. He went through the same call process, and when a woman answered on the second ring, he felt relieved.

"How soon?" she asked, but it didn't sound like the same woman as before.

"This week, maybe two or three days," Al Khafaji replied, wondering what had happened to the other woman and his cousin.

"Call when you are home," the woman commanded and hung up the phone.

9

Al Khafaji didn't have time to get a new phone, so he kept the one he had and put it inside his duffel bag between several pairs of socks and T-shirts. He hoped that would provide enough cushion for the flight. If the phone broke, he could try to find a replacement once he arrived in Iraq. For now, he had to put his things in the trunk of his car and get back to the base.

He went to the front desk and checked out of his hotel room. The lady at the counter wished him luck and gave him his receipt. Al Khafaji thought this was probably normal for hotels near the base, and people likely checked out with little notice on a regular basis.

Al Khafaji pulled into the parking lot and saw the other three specialists standing near the gate with Sergeant First Class Hermanson. He raced over to the group as Sergeant First Class Hermanson was opening the gate.

"You are late," Sergeant First Class Hermanson said coldly. "Don't make this a habit. It's not a good thing."

"Yes, Sergeant," Al Khafaji replied breathlessly.

"We are going to have the four of you staying in the training room at the operations building," Sergeant First Class Hermanson explained. "You can go back out to your vehicles in a while to get your bags. In case you have not figured it out, we are getting prepared to deploy to Iraq."

"Sergeant, may I ask a question?" Aisha piped up as they walked down the sidewalk.

"It would be best if you waited until we are inside the building," Sergeant First Class Hermanson replied as he continued walking.

The four specialists noticed that Sergeant First Class Hermanson was moving at a faster pace than usual. They wondered if there was something wrong. As they continued to walk, they saw that a soldier was standing outside the operations building. He opened the door as they approached. Sergeant First Class Hermanson took them down the hall and into the training room. The specialists noticed that there were several cots set up where the desks used to be.

"Grab a cot," Sergeant First Class Hermanson said to them. "I'll be right back and then we can go over any questions you might have."

"Yes, Sergeant," the specialists answered as Sergeant First Class Hermanson left the room.

Sergeant First Class Hermanson walked down the hall to Master Sergeant Mandess's office. He wanted to speak with him before he went into any details with the four specialists. He also hoped there might be additional information on Al Khafaji.

"Top, they are all here," Sergeant First Class Hermanson stated as he stood in the doorway of Master Sergeant Mandess's office. "I got them in the training room."

"Any problems?" Master Sergeant Mandess asked.

"Nope," Sergeant First Class Hermanson replied. "We are all good."

"OK, I guess it's time to go down and tell them a thing or two," Master Sergeant Mandess said as he got up from behind his desk.

They walked down to the training room and found the four specialists sitting on the cots. Wafiq jumped to his feet when he saw Master Sergeant Mandess. The others also stood up.

"Have a seat, soldiers. We are going to have a talk," Master Sergeant Mandess said to them as he waited for them to sit back down. "We are going to be leaving for deployment in the morning. I want you to draw your equipment from the supply room this afternoon. You will be getting your rifles from the armorer tomorrow morning.

Make sure you get whatever you need from your vehicles and make sure the doors are locked. Your cars will be safe in the parking lot. There will be concertina wire put up after we leave to keep people out of the area. You can leave your keys here, and we will tag them and put them in the lockbox. If everything goes as planned, you should be back in about six months. What questions do you have?"

Everyone was quiet. Not even Aisha raised her hand. The fact that they were actually going to Iraq was still setting in with them. They had been told when they enlisted that the chances were very high that they would deploy to Iraq, but now it was an actuality.

"OK, if you don't have any questions, I'll turn you back over to Sergeant First Class Hermanson," Master Sergeant Mandess said before turning and heading back down the hall.

"Time to head over to see the supply sergeant," Sergeant First Class Hermanson declared. "Follow me."

They marched down the hallway and turned left. About halfway down the hall, there was another door with the top half open. Sergeant First Class Hermanson poked his head inside and looked around.

"Hey, Sergeant Prentiss. Are you in there?" Sergeant First Class Hermanson called out.

"Just a second," a voice hollered from the back. A burly sergeant with huge arms came up to the counter. "Hey, Herm. What can I do for you?"

"Top says we need to suit these four warriors up for deployment," Sergeant First Class Hermanson replied, pointing to the four specialists.

"Oh yeah," Sergeant Prentiss said as he looked the four over. "I remember Top said you would be coming by."

"You know, I kind of thought you were going to say that," Sergeant First Class Hermanson joked as he let the specialists move closer to the door.

Sergeant Prentiss opened the bottom half of the door to let the specialists in. He told them to wait by the counter and went off to the back of the room with a handcart. They could hear him putting things on the cart and moving it around. When he came back, there were four piles of equipment on the cart. He pointed at each of the specialists and then to a specific pile. Then, he gave each of the specialists a rucksack and a duffel bag and told them to put all the stuff into the two bags. When they were done, he brought them up one at a time to sign for their gear. The specialists signed the paperwork but had no idea what they were signing for.

"Thanks," Sergeant First Class Hermanson said to the supply sergeant. "OK, soldiers, take your gear back to your cots and leave it there. Next, I want you to go out to your car and figure out what you need to bring and lock the rest in your trunk. Then, come back inside, and we will start packing up all your gear."

The four specialists carried and dragged their gear back to the cots and then went out to the gate. Sergeant First Class Hermanson let them out and then closed the gate behind them. None of them looked very motivated now. If this was tiring them out, he was afraid of what would happen when they got to Iraq. It would be interesting.

After about ten minutes, they started to head back toward the gate once more. It looked like they had all been able to fit everything they wanted to take into their rucksack. Aisha was struggling a bit, but everyone else seemed to be doing just fine. Sergeant First Class Hermanson opened the gate for them when they were near the sidewalk.

When they finally made it back to their cots, Sergeant First Class Hermanson gave them pointers on what to put in the rucksack and what to put in the duffel bag. As he walked them through how he packed his bags, he explained why items were put in the duffel bag or the rucksack. The specialists watched him closely and followed along. When Sergeant First Class Hermanson had finished, Aisha slowly raised her hand.

"What bag would women's items be packed in, Sergeant?" Aisha asked in a quiet voice.

"If you currently need them, it would be best to pack some on the outside pocket of your rucksack," Sergeant First Class Hermanson replied in an equally quiet voice.

None of the other specialists had a question, so Sergeant First Class Hermanson let them go about their business. He would check back with them later to see how they were doing. Sergeant First Class Hermanson decided to walk down to the operations center to see if there was an updated situation report on activity in Iraq. He put his common access card into the reader on the door to the secure area and opened the door. When he walked in, it looked like there was a briefing going on. Captain Starn and Master Sergeant Mandess were standing near the map and briefing the others sitting around the conference table. The only two others he recognized were Major Palmer and Sergeant Major Wagner. He also noticed that there were eight straphangers sitting in chairs along the wall. Sergeant First Class Hermanson figured it must have been a high-ranking individual to have so many staffers accompanying him. Whoever it was, he didn't need to be there.

Sergeant First Class Hermanson decided to exit the room and head back to see how the specialists were coming along. He was definitely not interested in entertaining a bunch of senior officers. It pained him to see his leadership doing the dog and pony show, but better them than him, Sergeant First Class Hermanson figured. That's why Top and the boss got paid the big bucks.

The specialists were still working on their packing when he got back. Sara was almost done, and her duffel bag looked like it had room to spare, while Aisha still had clothes on her cot and would be lucky to get her duffel bag closed. Wafiq and Al Khafaji were still packing, but neither one seemed to be having a problem with space. Wafiq and Al Khafaji were having a discussion about computers and cell phones.

"What seems to be the issue?" Sergeant First Class Hermanson asked the two of them.

"Is it OK to bring a computer or cell phone, Sergeant?" Wafiq asked.

"It is OK for watching movies or working on, but you have to use a unit laptop for sending emails," Sergeant First Class Hermanson explained. "You may not be able to call on your cell phone, but you can make a call with the unit computer."

"What should we do with our phones?" Wafiq asked, trying to get some clarification as to whether they could bring the phones with them.

"Probably best to lock them in your vehicle," Sergeant First Class Hermanson replied.

"Can we go out to our cars to lock up the phones?" Aisha asked.

"We can do that when we come back from lunch," Sergeant First Class Hermanson said as he glanced at his watch. "Speaking of lunch, are you all about ready to go? You can finish packing when we get back if you are not done."

"Yes, Sergeant," the specialists said.

Sergeant First Class Hermanson took them over to the dining facility where they ate lunch and talked about what they had learned. He shared some stories of people he had known and met on his previous deployments, although he made sure not to speak of any of the terrible things he had seen or the many firefights he had been involved in. There was an extremely high probability that all of these specialists would be engaged with the enemy during their deployment, and he didn't want to go there with them right now.

When they were done, they walked back to the headquarters building and stopped by their vehicles before going back through the gate. Al Khafaji decided to leave his phone in his car. He thought that he could easily get another phone from a vendor once he was in Iraq. There were always people selling items in the streets.

The specialists spent the remainder of the day in a few pre-deployment training classes. There was an hour-long medical training class for first aid and an operational security class that stressed the importance of the specialists identifying things that were written, heard, or seen. The instructor said that they were a combat multiplier because of their language and cultural experience. Al Khafaji did not believe what they said. When there were so many soldiers who already knew Arabic and had been to Iraq several times, why did they need any more? They even paid Iraqi civilians like Sara to work for them in Iraq. The infidels were liars, and he would prove it to everyone when they got back to Iraq.

Sergeant First Class Hermanson took the specialists back to the dining facility around 1600 hours for an early meal. He said that he wanted all of them to be in their cots and asleep before 2100 hours, as they would be getting up before 0500 hours to draw their rifles. He also told them to get a piece of fruit and a protein bar to bring back to the building, as there may not be time for breakfast in the morning.

Sergeant First Class Hermanson left after he got them to the operations building. It was a little after 1700 hours when he headed home. His wife had dinner ready and had left their child with a neighbor for a few hours. Sergeant First Class Hermanson was amazed. He thought he had the best wife in the world and was so happy he had met her. He was asleep before 2100 hours. His wife slept with their child as she had done on every deployment for the last six years. He didn't want to wake them up as he prepared to leave in the morning. Sergeant First Class Hermanson would be up by 0315 hours and would be heading back to the operations building.

Sergeant Abdullah came into work at 0630 hours on Monday to go to the gym. He lifted some weights and then went for a thirty-minute run. He even had enough time to get a quick breakfast at the dining facility before heading to the maintenance building. When he got there, it was a little after 0800 hours, and the place was empty. He went over to look at the work board, and it had been wiped clean. He walked over to the company headquarters, and there were a few soldiers in the orderly room, but everything was quiet. Sergeant Abdullah saw the armorer standing near the desk for the unit administrative specialist.

"Sergeant Abdullah," the armorer said when he saw him. "I got word that the familiarization for the grenade launcher has been canceled. Sorry I couldn't tell you sooner, but I just found out this morning."

"Thank you," Sergeant Abdullah replied, not knowing what else to do with his time. "Is there anything you need help with?"

"I could use a hand cleaning all the rifles if you have the time," the armorer answered, not really expecting any assistance.

"I have the entire day now," Sergeant Abdullah smiled. "I would be happy to have something to do."

"Great! I really appreciate it," the armorer said as he walked with Sergeant Abdullah back to the arms room.

It took several hours to clean the rifles and get them ready for issue to the soldiers for deployment. The armorer and Sergeant Abdullah worked until it was almost lunchtime. They talked about a lot of things and listened to the country music station on the radio.

Sergeant Abdullah was surprised to learn that the armorer had been in college when he'd decided to join the Army. He felt that he needed to do something to be a part of the fight against the terrorists who invaded America and killed so many innocent people. He was originally from Texas and had been around firearms since he was a young boy. Working in supply and being an armorer was a perfect fit for him.

"I think it's about time for lunch," the armorer said.

"What time would you like to start after lunch?" Sergeant Abdullah asked.

"No need," the armorer replied. "I can take care of the rest; I just appreciate all the help. It would have been a late day if you had not come along."

"I was glad to have something to do," Sergeant Abdullah said, wiping off his hands and putting the cleaning kit away. "It seems like everyone is just waiting for the week to end so we can be on our way."

"Yep, hurry up and wait." The armorer smiled. "That's the Army way."

Sergeant Abdullah left the company headquarters and went to the dining facility for lunch. He felt good that he had done something. After he finished lunch, he went back to his room and went through his bags again to make sure there wasn't anything he had forgotten. He knew that he hadn't forgotten anything, but it was always good to check.

～

Sergeant First Class Hermanson was up before his alarm went off; that's just the way he was. He could go to sleep and tell himself what time he needed to wake up, and he would always be within a few minutes of that time, with or without an alarm clock. He figured part of it was being anxious about getting on the way, and the rest was just a personal quirk.

He got showered and dressed and poked his head into the other bedroom to check on his family. They were still asleep. He wanted to go over and give them both a kiss but decided not to wake them up. He closed the door and started down the hall, not hearing his wife say, "Love you, baby."

Sergeant First Class Hermanson loved this time of the morning. Everything was still quiet, and there was very little traffic on the road. He made it to the parking lot a little earlier than he had planned, so he sat in his car and finished his cup of coffee. When he started to see other cars pulling into the parking lot, he grabbed his bags and headed to the gate, which had a soldier standing next to it. He went in and continued down the sidewalk to the operations building where the lights were already on. When he walked into the training room, he saw that the specialists were already up and getting their bags together.

"You can leave that for now," Sergeant First Class Hermanson said as he dropped his own bags on the floor. "Time to go get our rifles."

The four specialists followed Sergeant First Class Hermanson over to the arms room where there was a short line already waiting. The line moved quickly, and Sergeant First Class Hermanson drew his rifle first and waited for the specialists. When everyone had their rifle, they headed back to the operations building.

"Finish up with your bags," Sergeant First Class Hermanson told them. "When you are done, we need to head out to the trucks."

It didn't take long for the specialists to get ready. Sergeant First Class Hermanson had them pick up their gear and follow him outside. There was a line of two-and-a-half-ton trucks waiting out in the road. Sergeant First Class Hermanson checked their duffel bags to make sure names were visible and they were secured. He then told them to put their duffel bags in the first truck and get in the second truck. The second truck already had soldiers in it, so Sergeant First Class Hermanson had them move to the third truck, which was not full. The specialists all got in and took a seat with Sergeant First Class Hermanson sitting right next to them.

It was a thirty-minute drive to the airfield where there was a military cargo plane waiting for them. They all boarded the plane and waited for the rest of the soldiers to arrive. When the plane was full, it taxied down the runway and took off. Things went so fast the specialists barely realized that they were actually on their way to Iraq. Sergeant First Class Hermanson thought that was a good thing.

10

Sergeant Abdullah took his dress uniform out of the plastic covering from the dry cleaner and started to get it ready for the deployment ceremony. One more thing and one more day closer to deployment. He was more than ready to go.

The deployment ceremony was scheduled for 1000 hours on the parade field. There was to be a picnic lunch following the ceremony. Sergeant Abdullah wondered what the unit would be doing once the picnic was done. They were not scheduled to depart until Thursday afternoon and would be taking a large commercial plane that was chartered by the government.

Sergeant Abdullah checked his uniform in the mirror once he had finished putting on all his awards. Everything looked good, so he finished getting dressed. He hung his coat up behind the driver's seat and left for the post. He was told to drive directly to the parade field to meet up with the unit.

He was early as usual. He sat in his car wondering about the deployment. This would be his fourth trip to Iraq in the Army. So far, he had only one injury that he thought was severe, and he had healed well from that, but maybe he was pressing his luck too much. He remembered that Sergeant Mac had told him that if someone goes back to Iraq enough times, there is a bullet that has their name on it. Maybe since he had already been shot, the bullet with his name on it had already been used.

He started to see some of the people from his unit getting out of their vehicles but decided to wait a little longer. There was still almost forty-five minutes until the ceremony was to begin. He saw Sergeant

Maczrakolski pull into the parking lot about ten minutes later and decided to get out of his car and say hello. Sergeant Abdullah walked across the parking lot to meet his friend while other members of his unit started to walk out onto the parade field.

"Hello, Ski," Sergeant Abdullah greeted him as Sergeant Maczrakolski was getting out of his car.

"Hey, Carson," Sergeant Maczrakolski said as he turned to see Sergeant Abdullah. "Dang, where the heck did you get all those medals?"

"They are from my other deployments to Iraq," Sergeant Abdullah replied, feeling a little self-conscious. He really did not like to be recognized for what he had done. Sergeant Abdullah always thought that everyone would do the same thing if they had been in his place.

"What's that one?" Sergeant Maczrakolski asked as he pointed to Sergeant Abdullah's Bronze Star medal.

"That's a Bronze Star with a V device," Sergeant First Class Broadmoor said as he stopped to see what the two soldiers were doing. "That means our young sergeant here was in some shit and threw a lot back. Combat Infantryman Badge, two Purple Hearts, three Army Commendation Medals, two Army Achievement Medals, Airborne Wings, and a Special Forces combat patch. Dang, I guess that explains a lot. Good stuff, Carson. Now you two need to get on out to the parade field."

"Yes, Sergeant," Sergeant Abdullah said as they complied.

"Dang, my buddy is a Special Ops guy," Sergeant Maczrakolski crowed with a huge smile. "That's pretty cool."

"Was," Sergeant Abdullah said to correct his friend. "I was working with the Special Forces. Now I am a mechanic like everyone else."

They moved into the back of the formation. It didn't really matter where they stood. The first sergeant would reorganize them by size once everyone had joined. By the time the first sergeant was done,

Sergeant Abdullah was in the second row while Sergeant Maczrakolski was somewhere behind him.

The ceremony started with a hand salute from the units for the playing of the national anthem. When the national anthem was done, the post chaplain asked for God's blessing on the soldiers. The division commander spoke next and encouraged everyone to perform their missions in keeping with the grand history of the organization. He reminded everyone of all the history that was made by the division and said he expected nothing less of this brigade. Then, the brigade commander spoke and thanked the division commander for the great honor of representing the division in battle. He made sure to identify each of the units that were deploying, and as each unit was called out, the unit commander called the unit to attention, and the unit responded with a loud "HOOAH!" The band played as the units marched by the division staff. Each commander saluted as his unit passed by the division commander while the soldiers did an "eyes right" to show respect.

When the ceremony was over, all the units gathered at the far end of the parade field where tents had been set up with tables, chairs, and food. Carolina BBQ and plenty of it. If anyone left hungry, it was their own fault.

Many of the soldiers in the maintenance company wanted to ask Sergeant Abdullah about his awards and patches. They were not used to seeing someone with so many. Those soldiers were usually in the infantry or armor units, and most of them were more senior soldiers. Most had earned their awards from the First Gulf War, and that was more than a decade before many of them had even joined the Army. Sergeant Abdullah had three combat stripes on his uniform, so this would be his fourth deployment.

Sergeant Abdullah didn't really want to talk about it, but he did. He explained to them that he had deployed three times before joining their unit. His first and third deployments had been with the Special Forces, while his second deployment had been with a brigade headquarters. He did not go into what his previous occupational specialty had been. Sergeant Maczrakolski finally stepped in and saved him from any more questions.

"Hey, that's enough questions for my battle buddy," Sergeant Maczrakolski declared as he put his arm around Sergeant Abdullah's shoulder. "You got a whole year to hear him tell stories. Give him some space."

"Thank you, Ski," Sergeant Abdullah muttered once he finally had a little space to breathe. "I just am not very interested in talking about what happened before. I am more interested about what we are going to do this time."

"Well, I'm pretty sure it won't be anywhere near as exciting," Sergeant Maczrakolski speculated. "But I guess time will tell. How about we get some of that BBQ? I'm hungry."

It was a great party, and the soldiers and their families were having a wonderful time. The food was excellent, and there were games and an inflatable bounce house for the kids. Everyone was finishing up when the first sergeant asked for their attention.

"I hope all of you had a good time today," First Sergeant Holman said as he looked out over the soldiers and their families. "I just want you all to know that I am proud of every one of you and couldn't have a finer bunch of people to deploy with. I was also just informed that we will be on a flight tomorrow afternoon, so I need you to be at the company headquarters by 0900 hours tomorrow morning. Now get out of here and enjoy the rest of the day with your family."

"HOOAH, First Sergeant!" came the response from the soldiers.

The crowd thinned out quickly after the first sergeant's speech. The families wanted to spend as much time together as possible, and the single soldiers just wanted to get out of their dress uniforms and relax. Sergeant Abdullah decided to make one more trip to the post exchange before going back to the hotel. He needed to let the front desk know that he would be checking out in the morning.

Sergeant Abdullah didn't even need his alarm to go off the next morning. He was already up when the buzzer sounded. All he had to do was put his bags into his car and turn in his key. He left his hotel by 0730 hours so he could stop by the dining facility for breakfast. He wasn't sure if there would be time for lunch or not.

When Sergeant Abdullah arrived at the company headquarters, he was told to park his car inside a large area that had been surrounded by concertina wire. He turned his keys in to the orderly room, and they marked them with his name. He noticed that there were two large commercial buses parked on the road.

"All right, folks, let's get in formation so we can get accountability, draw our rifles, and get on the bus," Sergeant First Class Broadmoor called out to the soldiers gathered around the unit headquarters.

The soldiers all lined up for formation, and First Sergeant Holman took accountability reports from the different sections. Then, Captain Pickett came out and took the formation. He told them a little about their mission and then called First Sergeant Holman back to release the soldiers. Once they were released, they moved out in a single file to the arms room, where they drew their rifles and returned to formation. Once they were all back in formation, the first sergeant came out once again.

"You have all done everything that the commander and I have asked of you," First Sergeant Holman began. "Now we are going to ask you for one more thing. Be your best and do your best."

"HOOAH, First Sergeant!" the formation cried.

The first sergeant released the soldiers to board the buses. They picked up their gear, stowed it under the bus, and then got on the bus for the drive to the airport. Some families were there with banners and small US flags as the buses departed.

Sergeant Abdullah was surprised to find out that they were going to be taking a charter flight to Kuwait. All his unit needed to do was drive through the access gate at the airport and drive out to where the plane sat. They dropped their duffel bags near a luggage-loading ramp and got on the plane with their packs and rifles. The first sergeant had them all clear their rifles multiple times before arriving at the airfield. He didn't want any surprises.

There were only a handful of units who were bringing their own vehicles. Most units would be signing for equipment from large storage sites in Kuwait and would convoy into Iraq with their vehicles on flatbeds or driving them. Sergeant Abdullah thought his unit would be driving the majority of the vehicles from Kuwait into Iraq.

"Settle in, folks," First Sergeant Holman said. "We have a long flight ahead of us."

11

Al Khafaji looked at the soldiers in the seats on the opposite side of the plane. They were all smiling as they checked to make sure the belts on their jump seats were still firmly secured. One of them gave Al Khafaji a thumbs-up. Before Al Khafaji could return the gesture, the plane went into a hard banking turn while also descending. This continued for what seemed like several minutes until the plane evened out and hit hard on the runway.

"Welcome to Iraq," Staff Sergeant Pederson yelled out while he pointed at Wafiq, who seemed to have had too much for lunch, and Aisha.

"Wafiq! I cannot believe this," Aisha shouted as she tried to clean some of the puke from her arm.

"I am very sorry, Aish . . . " He wretched again before he could finish his apology, but there wasn't anything left in his stomach other than spittle that dripped down on his boots.

The airplane came to a stop, and the Air Force loadmaster lowered the ramp.

"Get off my aircraft," he said to the specialists.

"Sorry about that, brother," Staff Sergeant Pederson said as he and the other team members exited the plane.

"If I knew which one of these duffel bags was his, I'd piss all over it," the loadmaster replied.

The air crew unloaded the pallet of duffel bags, and the soldiers picked up their gear and walked toward a building next to the ramp where the planes were parked. Sergeant First Class Hermanson watched the specialists as they made their way to the building. Aisha was still having the most difficult time, but she was moving forward, and that was all that counted to Sergeant First Class Hermanson. She wasn't quitting.

"Why don't the two of you take another uniform out of your rucksack and change?" Sergeant First Class Hermanson suggested to Aisha and Wafiq, handing them both a large plastic bag. "Put your uniforms in this and tie it shut. We can get them cleaned later."

"Yes, Sergeant," the two replied as they walked toward the bathroom.

"I'm sorry, Aisha," Wafiq said apologetically.

"Shut up, Wafiq! Just shut up," Aisha responded emphatically.

Master Sergeant Mandess called Sergeant First Class Hermanson over to where he was.

"Herm, we got birds coming in to get us in about twenty minutes," Master Sergeant Mandess said as he leaned closer to Sergeant First Class Hermanson. "Did you tell the specialists anything about how we were getting to the forward operating base?"

"Nope, but I'm hoping it's a little less exciting," Sergeant First Class Hermanson commented with a smile.

Aisha and Wafiq came back from the bathrooms after a few minutes and rejoined the group. Sergeant First Class Hermanson directed them to pick up their gear and head outside. They followed the rest of the soldiers to an area that was about one hundred yards from the building and away from the planes. Sergeant First Class Hermanson covered a few points about riding in the helicopter and stressed how important it was to keep their rifles pointed down at all times.

There were twenty-nine soldiers in the group, including two twelve-man teams, the four specialists, and an intelligence specialist from the company headquarters. The remainder of the company headquarters would be staying near the airfield so they could provide support to the teams if needed.

A soldier near the helicopter landing zone had the twenty-nine personnel break into two groups of eleven and a smaller group of only seven. Master Sergeant Mandess, Staff Sergeant Pederson, Sergeant First Class Hermanson, and the four specialists made up the smaller group. They heard the Black Hawk helicopters coming in a few minutes later. They landed in a row about twenty yards from the three groups.

The crew chief from each helicopter got out and motioned each group to come to the open doors. The soldiers moved forward with their gear and duffel bags and got into the helicopters. Sergeant First Class Hermanson made sure to follow Aisha to the waiting helicopter. When they got near the door, he helped her with her duffel bag as she got in. The crew chief made sure everyone had their safety belts fastened and then said something into the microphone on his helmet.

The helicopters rose from the landing strip and headed southwest. It would only be a short flight to get to the forward operating base. The helicopters gained altitude to stay out of small arms fire and covered the distance in about twenty-five minutes. The door gunner fired off a few bursts from the machine gun as they flew, but the specialists had no idea why. None of the other people on the helicopter seemed alarmed.

The helicopters began their descent as they neared the forward operating base, and once again, the door gunner fired several bursts from the machine gun. They landed near the outpost, and the group formed a hasty perimeter twenty yards from the helicopters. A small group from the outpost came out to meet them and was waiting nearby to help provide cover if needed. The helicopters lifted off the ground and headed back toward the airport.

"About time you folks finally showed up," Master Sergeant Barker called out as he caught sight of Master Sergeant Mandess.

"Well, according to my calendar, we are a month or so early, Steve," Master Sergeant Mandess replied as the group moved toward the front gate of the outpost.

Al Khafaji wondered why there wasn't anyone firing at the helicopters or the group of soldiers. He thought they would have made perfect targets. He was very anxious to get into the fight for his country.

Master Sergeant Barker showed Master Sergeant Mandess the area that his team would occupy and then went back to the operations building. He told Master Sergeant Mandess to come over when everyone was settled, and he would go over a situation report with them. Master Sergeant Mandess made sure that his team and the other team got all their gear stowed and told Sergeant First Class Hermanson to stay with the four specialists for now. He would be sharing a hooch with Sergeant First Class Hermanson, so he could fill him in later on what was going on.

Sergeant First Class Hermanson found a couple hooches near where he and Master Sergeant Mandess would be and had the specialists move into them. They all resembled small prefab metal buildings. It was almost like staying inside a shipping container. They had small, wooden-frame beds that were just big enough for one person. Once Sergeant First Class Hermanson had the specialists in their hooches, he moved over to his own and dropped his bags and Master Sergeant Mandess's duffel bag. Master Sergeant Mandess came in about thirty minutes later.

"According to Steve, it looks like this place is near the center of a shitstorm," Master Sergeant Mandess said to Sergeant First Class Hermanson as he grounded his rucksack and set his rifle down. "He also told me why we are here earlier than planned. Seems like somebody has been inside the wire. They are not sure who it is, but both teams have walked into an ambush over the last three weeks. The folks that escorted us in are what's left of the two teams, not counting the walking wounded who stayed inside the walls."

"Kind of figured something like that, Top, when we got the deployment order," Sergeant First Class Hermanson said. "Anyone we know in a bad way?"

"They had three killed in action. One of them died on the way to the medical unit," Master Sergeant Mandess began. "Two more were choppered out with serious wounds, and six walking wounded."

"Damn, that's about one entire team out of action," Sergeant First Class Hermanson lamented as he counted up the casualties.

"That's why we are here," Master Sergeant Mandess said. "I want you to have the specialists working around the local hires and any other locals we have around. See if they can pick up on anything. It's probably a long shot, but it's worth a try. They'll have two or three days to poke around. Steve is going to take us out on a route recon over the next few days to give us the lay of the land."

"Will do, Top," Sergeant First Class Hermanson replied. Then, he went back to pick up the specialists and walk them around the outpost. The first thing he showed them were the bunkers. He noticed that Aisha was very quiet and wanted to try to calm her nerves, so he took them inside of one of the bunkers and showed them how well they were constructed. He also was quick to make a point of the fact that the enemy didn't have any weapons that could destroy it.

"Can we just stay in here?" Aisha asked. Sergeant First Class Hermanson was glad to see her asking a question.

"I don't think that would be the best thing to do. You will be fine in your rooms most of the time," Sergeant First Class Hermanson explained. "If you hear explosions, that's when you move to the bunker."

The specialists all nodded, and Sergeant First Class Hermanson continued the walking tour. He pointed out the dining facility, latrines, motor pool, supply building, and other things. The one area he did not point out to them was the operations building. He still didn't have complete trust in Al Khafaji yet, and they would not be able to get into the operations building because they did not have a security clearance.

Once the tour was over, Sergeant First Class Hermanson took them to the dining facility for a meal. The food was not bad, but it was a far stretch from what they had been eating at Fort Campbell. Al

Khafaji thought the only good thing was the fact that they could get halal food . . . or at least it was labeled as such.

"Sergeant, what will we do when we are working with the locally hired linguists?" Wafiq asked while they were finishing their meal.

"You will not be working with them, Wafiq," Sergeant First Class Hermanson began to explain. "We would like you to observe them and let us know if you see or hear anything that does not look right."

"How would we know if it is not right?" Aisha questioned.

"Well, if something seems out of place or not normal," Sergeant First Class Hermanson replied, hoping she would understand.

"Oh, like if the children do not run after the ball, or if the shopkeeper closes his windows and door early," Aisha said, recalling the early portions of the interpretation training.

"Exactly," Sergeant First Class Hermanson responded, happy to know that the training had made its mark on her. That would be something he would share with Staff Sergeant Hall when he returned.

The five of them finished up and walked back to the little rooms. Sergeant First Class Hermanson told them to make sure their weapons were on safe and keep them close by just in case. He didn't want to scare them, but he also didn't want them running out without their rifles.

"In the morning, Chief Provanski will come and get you," Sergeant First Class Hermanson told them. "He is our assistant commander, and he will let you know where he wants you to be. I'm not sure how long we will be gone tomorrow. If I get back soon enough, we will all talk again after dinner tomorrow night."

"Yes, Sergeant," the specialists said as everyone headed into their own rooms.

The night went by without incident, and it seemed odd to Al Khafaji that their first day in Iraq was so quiet. Where were all the warriors? He couldn't understand why there had been no attacks on the infidels. Nothing at the airport and nothing at this outpost was near anything of importance in his mind. He had been able to see only one small village as the helicopter had made its descent on the flight to the base, and that must have been at least ten kilometers away. He would need to find a way to contact his group as soon as possible.

Chief Warrant Officer 2 Provanski saw the specialists at the dining facility at breakfast and came by to talk with them for a few minutes. Al Khafaji thought he was a very pleasant person, but he had a very thick accent that made it a little difficult to understand him at times.

"Meet me at the supply building at 0900 hours," Chief Provanski said. "You know where this is, correct?"

"Yes, sir," the specialists answered.

"Ha, good," Chief Provanski said with a deep laugh. "Maybe today we catch some spies."

"Don't just show us all the rest areas, Steve," Master Sergeant Mandess said to his friend as they drove down a poor excuse for a road. They had been driving for about fifteen minutes and had yet to see a person or animal.

"We'll make sure to show you all the points of interest," Master Sergeant Barker answered as the lead vehicle came to a stop.

"What's the problem, Steve?" Master Sergeant Mandess asked as Master Sergeant Barker looked out at the area in front of the lead vehicle.

"Looks like we may have another one," Master Sergeant Barker commented as he got out of the vehicle.

Master Sergeant Mandess and Master Sergeant Barker walked up to the lead vehicle. Off to the side of the road was one of their locally hired linguists. He had been beheaded. His torso had several bullet wounds, and his hands were tied behind his back. They had cut his tongue out and laid it next to his head.

"Do you recognize him?" Master Sergeant Mandess asked.

"I don't know his name, but he definitely had been working with us," Master Sergeant Barker murmured, looking closely to see if the body had been booby-trapped.

"Marcus," Master Sergeant Barker said to the driver of the first vehicle. "Call it in and have them send someone out to pick up the body so we can turn it over to the family."

"Will do," Marcus answered. He reached inside the vehicle and keyed the microphone, relaying the message to the outpost.

"We are getting closer to them," Master Sergeant Barker observed, pointing to a bend in the road about one hundred yards away. "That's where we got hit about two weeks ago. They had a vehicle take a few shots at us, and we went after them. They waited until the last vehicle made the turn and then opened up. I definitely think we are dealing with some folks who have a lot of training."

"Could be some of the folks from the Iraqi Army that we sent into early retirement," Master Sergeant Mandess noted. "Another well-thought-out plan."

"Yep, seems like our side has been full of that stuff during this war," Master Sergeant Barker sighed as he scanned the horizon for any signs of the enemy, but there was nothing left to see.

The truck from the outpost showed up within twenty minutes and picked up the body. Master Sergeant Barker pulled the perimeter guards back in, and they continued on their way. Master Sergeant Mandess could tell it was difficult for his friend to go back through the ambush site. He was glad that the decision had been made to send fresh teams to the outpost. The men who were at the outpost needed to get out of there.

The drive continued but turned in the opposite direction of where the ambush had taken place. Master Sergeant Mandess thought it was a conscious decision by Master Sergeant Barker to go that way, and he had no issues with it. The most important thing was the location had been identified, and it was something Master Sergeant Mandess would keep in mind when choosing routes.

"I want to take you through the little village near us," Master Sergeant Barker said while they continued down the road. As they drove on, the road seemed to get better until it got to the point where it looked like an actual road. Not paved but well used and well worn. It was clear there was a lot of traffic traveling in the same direction. "The village is a little under twenty kilometers from the outpost, and it has been pretty quiet until recently. Many of our local hires who have been killed are from this village."

They drove to the village and slowed down once they got within one hundred meters of the outskirts. Sergeant First Class Hermanson and the other occupants of the first vehicle checked the nearby buildings for anything suspicious, but everything looked good, so they slowly proceeded. The people in the village didn't pay much attention to the military vehicles anymore. They had become accustomed to seeing them on a regular basis.

The entire village consisted of no more than forty buildings, many of which had some type of store or business on the first floor. When Master Sergeant Mandess looked down the right side of the road, he didn't notice anything. Master Sergeant Barker came up with the same thing on the left side. However, when they approached the last building in the village, Master Sergeant Mandess looked up and noticed there were dozens of bullet holes at the top.

"We got that one before he even got a round off," Master Sergeant Barker said before Master Sergeant Mandess even had a chance to ask the question. Master Sergeant Mandess simply nodded his head as they continued to drive on.

They drove for the better part of the day, traveling about one hundred kilometers along an oblong route. It seemed like there were many more people populating the areas north and east of them, while the areas west and south of them were sparsely populated. Master Sergeant Mandess was most interested in what was going on in the two larger cities in the area. He thought that could pose the greatest threat, but it seemed like the attacks on Master Sergeant Barker's team were coming from the less-populated areas.

⁓

The four specialists were right on time as usual. Chief Provanski was already waiting for them by the side of the building. He walked out to meet them, and Aisha started to salute.

"No, we don't do that here!" he yelled, stopping her cold. Aisha lowered her arm. "That is how people get killed here. Why would you want to do that?"

"I am sorry, sir," Aisha said quietly.

"It is OK. You all just have to remember that," Chief Provanski said in a much calmer tone.

"Yes, sir," they replied, wondering if it was OK to say "sir."

"This is what I want you to do," Chief Provanski said in a quieter voice. "I have spoken with the supply persons, and two of you will work behind the counter with him. Sometimes the local hire people talk among themselves, and my Arabic is not good enough to understand everything. So I just want you to listen and say if something is wrong. The other two will walk around like you are looking for something that you need, and you will also be listening for anything wrong. If you hear anything, you come outside and tell me. OK, is everyone understanding?"

"Yes, sir," the specialists answered.

Chief Provanski sent Aisha and Sara in to work behind the counter and had Al Khafaji and Wafiq looking for something. They walked inside the building and started listening. They listened for two hours and heard very little of interest, although Al Khafaji did hear one person talking about a cell phone he had just bought. He remembered that he still needed to call his leader to confirm that he was in Iraq.

Wafiq saw Chief Provanski enter the building and motion toward him. "Get the others and come outside," Chief Provanski instructed.

Wafiq turned and went back inside. It was only a matter of minutes before all four specialists were outside again with Chief Provanski. "So tell me. What did you hear?"

Each of the specialists reported back that they had not heard anything. Chief Provanski thought for a minute and asked if they were sure. The specialists once again told him that there was nothing being said other than what supplies were needed.

"We will try again after lunch," Chief Provanski said. "Go on and get something to eat and be back by 1300 hours. No, wait. It is much better to be back at 1230 hours."

Chief Provanski turned and walked off toward the operations building while the four specialists retreated toward the dining facility. Suddenly, Al Khafaji stopped, and so did the others.

"I am going back to the supply building to ask a question," Al Khafaji said. "I will be at the dining facility in less than ten minutes."

"I will save you a seat at our table," Wafiq offered.

"Thank you," Al Khafaji replied as he turned to run back toward the supply building.

Al Khafaji entered and looked for the person with the new phone. He was about to give up when he saw the older man walking down an aisle. He quickly made his way over to him.

"I would like to use your phone to make an important call," Al Khafaji said to the man in Arabic. "I just arrived, and I have family here that I want to speak with."

"I do not think I can allow you to use my phone," the man nervously replied. He thought that Al Khafaji was trying to trick him into breaking the rules, and he did not want to be in any trouble. "The contracting official said that we must not share any items with the American soldiers."

"I am from Iraq," Al Khafaji said to the man in an attempt to try to reason with him. "My family is more important to me than American rules. If you do not let me use the phone, I will tell the Americans you were planning to steal things from them," Al Khafaji uttered, growing tired of debating with this fool.

"You cannot threaten me with lies," the man said with confidence.

"Only you and I know the truth," Al Khafaji said to the man quietly. "Who do you think the Americans will believe? You or a fellow soldier?"

"Can we go outside?" the man asked. "I do not want anyone to see me giving you the phone. It cannot be a long call."

"I will make it very short," Al Khafaji assured him as they walked outside.

Al Khafaji took the phone as they stood next to the building. He dialed the same code as before and waited for an answer on ring number two of the second call. When the woman picked up, he didn't wait to hear what she was going to say.

"It's Samir. I am here," Al Khafaji said.

"I will tell him. Get a new phone," the voice stated and then hung up.

Al Khafaji thanked the man and headed off to the dining facility. The three other specialists were already inside and seated at a table. Al Khafaji asked the Iraqi food worker for a halal meal and took it over to the table to be with the others.

After lunch, the four went back to the supply building, where they tried once again to catch someone doing something wrong. They spent more than three hours listening to the locals, but the results were just like what had happened in the morning. They had not overheard anything that seemed a bit suspicious. Chief Provanski was sure they'd missed something and said they would need to go back again in the morning. The specialists gathered their things and headed back to the dining facility for an early meal.

"Is this all we will be doing here?" Aisha asked the others. "I did not think we would be trying to find something bad while listening to how many bags of ice, hand towels, hairnets, and rolls of toilet paper were needed."

"I think it is good to try to listen," Wafiq commented. "If we hear only one thing, it could be very important."

"If you are content with staying here and spying on your own people, you can have it," Al Khafaji said before he could even think about what he was saying. "I would rather be out looking for the enemy with the soldiers."

"Don't be in such a hurry to use your rifle," Sara said in her usual calm and subdued manner. "I think we will have plenty of opportunities to do that before we are done here. What Chief Provanski has us doing must be very important to them."

"But we are soldiers," Al Khafaji replied, keeping his voice as calm as possible. "We should be acting like soldiers."

"Samir, the only reason we are here is because we speak the language and understand the culture," Sara countered. "If it were not for that, we would not be in the Army. We would all still be students or doing other things."

"That is true," Al Khafaji admitted, "but we are still soldiers."

"You be a soldier," Aisha said. "I just want to do this and go back home. I don't like being out here."

Al Khafaji wanted to call her a traitor and slap her for being so insolent, but now was not the time. Right now, he just needed to do as he was told and wait for his leader to tell him what he needed to do. He would check his messages on the computer after he finished his meal to see if anything had been sent to him.

When they got to the dining facility, they saw Sergeant First Class Hermanson sitting at a table with Master Sergeant Mandess and some other soldiers. Sergeant First Class Hermanson waited until they had their food and had sat down at a table before he came over to speak with them. Sara thought he looked tired, and he was, but his mind was focused on the discussion he had just had with the others. The way their area was aligned, he thought he would have to use all four of the specialists outside of the gate. He was hoping to be able to leave

one or two inside the outpost, but that just wasn't the way it was playing out. Plus, with the ramp-up in activity over the last month, he was
expecting attacks on the compound as well.

"How did you do with the work the assistant commander had for
you?" Sergeant First Class Hermanson asked.

"We did not catch any spies," Aisha blurted out.

"Spies?" Sergeant First Class Hermanson was a little confused; he
thought they were supposed to be helping with interpretation with
the locally hired people.

"Yes, Sergeant," Wafiq added. "We were in the supply building
trying to see if the local workers said or did anything suspicious. Chief
Provanski thought we might find a spy."

"OK, I understand," Sergeant First Class Hermanson said before
moving on to another topic. "We will be going out again tomorrow,
so the four of you will have another opportunity to find a spy."

"Sergeant," Al Khafaji said, "will we be able to go with you after that?"

"I will check with the boss and see what is planned," Sergeant
First Class Hermanson responded without promising anything. He
was just responsible for monitoring the work the specialists did. He
was not the one who decided what that work would be.

"Yes, Sergeant," Al Khafaji said.

That night, there was a rocket and mortar attack on the outpost. The first rocket missed the entire outpost and exploded a hundred yards beyond the wall. The alarm sounded, and soldiers began
moving toward fighting positions and bunkers. Sergeant First Class
Hermanson was running out the door when he saw the doors to the
specialists' quarters burst open with Sara and Al Khafaji the first ones
out the doors. Aisha and Wafiq were right behind them as they ran to
the nearest bunker.

A second missile hit just left of the far wall as Sergeant First Class
Hermanson was running toward a fighting position. A mortar round
landed near the dining facility, while another one landed near the

operations building. Both buildings were still intact, but the dining facility was pockmarked from shrapnel.

Staff Sergeant Pederson set up a sniper rifle in a fighting position near the front entrance. His spotter was another weapons specialist named Staff Sergeant Burleson.

"Target front left, 450 meters," Staff Sergeant Burleson shouted. Staff Sergeant Pederson scanned the area and located a person who appeared to be the individual feeding one of the mortars. He made sure the crosshairs on his scope lined up mid-chest and pulled the trigger. "Hit," Staff Sergeant Burleson called out. He scanned the area but could not identify any additional targets.

Two more mortar rounds exploded near the front entrance outside of the outpost. They were most likely fired in order to discourage any vehicles from trying to come out to pursue the invaders. Everything got quiet again, but the soldiers remained in the fighting positions for another thirty minutes. Once the attack seemed to be over and no additional targets were visible through the night-vision devices, manning on the perimeter was brought down to 50 percent and reduced to regular security levels thirty minutes after that. Team leaders inspected their areas within the outpost to determine whether there was any significant damage or unexploded ordnance left behind after the attack. When everything seemed to check out, the personnel in the bunkers were given the all clear, and the specialists filed out and headed back to their quarters. It was almost 0200 hours.

A voice came over the intercom asking everyone to prepare for landing. Sergeant Abdullah put his seat forward and made sure his seat belt was fastened. There was a small amount of turbulence as the plane came in for a landing, but the large passenger airplane landed without a problem.

"Welcome to Kuwait," the pilot said over the intercom system. "Thank you all for your service."

The soldiers on the plane clapped as they got up and secured their gear. When the door to the plane opened, it was like a blast furnace outside as the soldiers began to walk down the mobile stairs that had been positioned next to the plane. There were four buses and three two-and-a-half-ton trucks waiting on the tarmac.

The soldiers were instructed to get on the buses and take a seat. They were all heading to the same location. The military trucks would bring the duffel bags to the building they would be staying in. The first sergeant had told them that they would be staying in Kuwait for a couple of weeks before heading out to Iraq. In the meantime, they would be inspecting vehicles and making any needed repairs before the convoys left for Iraq.

"Wow, it's hotter than Hades," Sergeant Maczrakolski commented as they walked over to the buses.

"Oh, it is not that bad," Sergeant Abdullah said with a smile. "It is not even summer yet."

The buses filled up quickly and headed off to the equipment-holding area. There was a barracks area close by so the mechanics could spend as much time as they needed with the equipment. Sergeant Abdullah's unit got off the bus and walked to the maintenance building. The first thing they needed to do after grounding their gear was sign for their toolboxes. The tools were already laying out on a mat next to a large toolbox that was empty.

"OK," Sergeant First Class Broadmoor called out. "When I call out a tool, check to make sure you have it and then put it in your toolbox."

Sergeant First Class Broadmoor read the list of tools out loud. He looked up at the mechanics after he called each tool out to see if any of the mechanics were missing that tool. After forty-five minutes, they had gone through the entire list. Each mechanic wrote their name on a piece of tape and put it on their toolbox. Then, the toolboxes were secured with a lock and put into a fenced-in area with a lock on the door.

When the toolboxes were all secured, the soldiers were brought to the sleeping quarters. Since Sergeant Abdullah's unit was going to be in the area for only a few weeks or less, they were housed in a large room with cots. The armorer set up a line of rifle racks along the wall. The soldiers turned their rifles in so they could remain secured until the unit was set to depart the area. First Sergeant Holman made up a weapons guard roster that went from 2200 hours until 0600 hours. The shifts were four hours long. The armorer was responsible for the remainder of the time, and the administrative clerk filled in for meal breaks.

Since the guard roster was made out alphabetically, Sergeant Abdullah was first on the list. He walked over to the rifle rack about ten minutes early. The armorer gave him a pistol belt with a holster attached that held a nine-millimeter pistol.

"It's loaded," the armorer said. "Just leave it in the holster. The only time to take it out is if someone is trying to take these rifles."

"I understand," Sergeant Abdullah said.

"Specialist Addison will be your replacement," the armorer continued as he pointed to a cot a few rows over from where they were. The cot had a yellow reflective vest laying underneath it. "You can go over and wake him up five minutes before your shift ends. If he doesn't want to get up, just tip his cot over."

"No problem," Sergeant Abdullah replied.

The armorer went over to his cot to go to sleep. Sergeant Abdullah thought about reading a book but decided against it because it might make him tired. He took out a notebook and started writing down all the things he wanted to do when he returned to the United States. The first thing on his list was to visit his parents. He wanted to explain to them why he did not mention anything to them about going back to Iraq. This would be a difficult discussion, but he was sure that his parents would understand.

The time passed by quickly with no problems. When Sergeant Abdullah went to wake up Specialist Addison, he was already putting his boots on. Sergeant Abdullah took off the pistol belt with the handgun and handed it to him.

"Thanks, Sergeant," Specialist Addison said as he strapped on the pistol belt. He was the official new guy who had been diverted to the company for assignment due to personnel shortages.

"No," Sergeant Abdullah replied. "I thank you. I am going to sleep."

Sergeant Abdullah woke up before 0600 hours and got ready for the day. He saw civilian workers setting up tables outside of the sleeping area. He was going to walk out to see what they were doing, but when he got close to the door, he could smell the food. Breakfast was served.

Breakfast wasn't anything fancy. Scrambled eggs, potatoes, bacon, sausage, and something that looked like it might have been grits. Sergeant Abdullah picked up a paper plate and plastic fork and filled his plate. There was also hot coffee and boxes of juice.

Not bad, Sergeant Abdullah thought as he sat down to eat. He had been in much worse situations on his other deployments to Iraq. He knew it would probably be different once he got into Iraq again, but for now, this was a good start.

When he finished, Sergeant Abdullah walked over to the side of the building where the maintenance bays were located. He saw Sergeant First Class Broadmoor writing on a dry-erase board. There were vehicles already pulled into each of the ten maintenance bays and others waiting outside.

"Is there anything I can do to help?" Sergeant Abdullah askedSergeant First Class Broadmoor as he walked up near the board.

"Not right now, Carson," Sergeant First Class Broadmoor answered as he continued to write on the board. "Well, if you want to go and start moving the other folks in here, that would be great. We've got a lot of work to do today."

"Will do, Sergeant," Sergeant Abdullah said before turning to head back to the sleeping area.

When he got to where the breakfast tables were set up, it looked like many of the soldiers were already there. Sergeant Abdullah went from table to table, telling them that Sergeant First Class Broadmoor wanted them in the maintenance bay as soon as possible. When he got to the table that Sergeant Maczrakolski was sitting at, he only got halfway through his talk before Ski stopped him.

"Carson, if you want to tell everyone this, there is a better way," Sergeant Maczrakolski said. Then, he pushed his chair back, stood up, and yelled out to everyone in the dining area. "All right, folks, Big B needs us in the maintenance bay right now, so finish it up and let's get going. We're burning daylight."

Some of the soldiers started to move, but most of them just seemed to ignore Sergeant Maczrakolski. They didn't notice that Sergeant First Class Broadmoor had walked into the doorway.

"All right, you heard the man," Sergeant First Class Broadmoor boomed out across the area. "Now get your goat-smelling asses out to the maintenance bay, and I mean right fucking now!"

Every single chair in the dining area moved back as the soldiers picked up their trays and headed toward the door. Nobody asked a question, and nobody waited to finish their meal. There were dozens of soldiers heading out the door one after another as Sergeant First Class Broadmoor stood to the side and smiled.

"Now that's the way to do it, Carson," Sergeant Maczrakolski stated as he also headed toward the door.

When all the mechanics were standing in the maintenance bay, Sergeant First Class Broadmoor had them go one at a time into the fenced-in room and get their toolbox. He had them make sure the locks were still on before coming out of the fenced-in enclosure. When all the mechanics were standing in front of him with their toolboxes, he provided them with a couple words of advice.

"I want you to inspect every one of these vehicles by the book with no shortcuts," Sergeant First Class Broadmoor began. "If there is anything wrong, and I do mean anything, it will be fixed before it leaves this building. As far as all the filters go, don't even bother checking them. Just change every one of them. I guarantee you they will need it. If you have not had the pleasure of being in this neck of the woods before, this environment destroys filters. Now get to work because we have a shit-ton of vehicles to go through."

"Hooah!" a few of the soldiers yelled out.

"Really?" Sergeant First Class Broadmoor answered. "That's about a sorry-ass response right there. What's wrong with all of you? Now let's try that one more time. Let's all get to work!"

"HOOAH!" came the reply from every mechanic in the maintenance bay.

"That's more like it," Sergeant First Class Broadmoor said with a smile. "Now let's get to work."

The mechanics worked all day inspecting and repairing vehicles. They had gone through thirty vehicles, and all the bays were empty except for four vehicles that needed additional work to be fully operational. The mechanics only stopped long enough at lunch to have a sandwich and a small bag of chips that was provided by the contract meal workers.

"That's good enough for today," Sergeant First Class Broadmoor said when it got to be 1800 hours. "They'll still be here in the morning. Go grab some chow and be back in here by 0700 hours tomorrow."

The next four days were all the same. Every morning, the mechanics would wake up to a new line of vehicles that needed to be inspected. As the days went by, it seemed the vehicles were in worse and worse shape. By the end of the third day, all the bays were full with vehicles that needed more than an inspection and a quick fix. Each bay was now three vehicles deep.

The backlog of vehicles was so bad that Sergeant First Class Broadmoor now had at least three mechanics working on the same vehicle. Then, the mechanics started getting sick. Everyone thought it must have been a virus until Sergeant Abdullah heard the food workers talking one morning.

"This food doesn't seem right," one of the workers was saying to another.

"What difference does it make?" the other one said. "We don't have to eat it."

Sergeant Abdullah was next in line to get his food. He put his hand on the shoulder of the person in front of him.

"Do not eat that food," Sergeant Abdullah muttered to him. Luckily, Sergeant Abdullah was one of the first in line as usual. "The workers think it might be bad."

"How do you know?" the sergeant in front of him asked.

"I understand what they said. I speak Arabic," Sergeant Abdullah replied as he dumped the large pan of food onto the floor. The pan needed to be emptied out so the others could see the condition.

"What's going on here?" one of the food worker managers said to the workers in Arabic.

"They are serving bad food," Sergeant Abdullah replied. "I think you have been getting our soldiers sick."

"That is nonsense," the manager said to Sergeant Abdullah in English. "There is nothing wrong with this food."

"If you think it is good, then you can eat some," Sergeant Abdullah countered. He bent down and took a big scoop of the eggs with the serving spoon and tried to give it to the manager.

"What's the holdup?" Sergeant First Class Broadmoor said, striding up to the front of the line. "Carson, why am I not sitting down and enjoying my breakfast right now?"

"Sergeant, they are serving us food that is not good," Sergeant Abdullah said, still holding the large serving spoon of eggs in his hand.

"Are you sure?" Sergeant First Class Broadmoor asked while moving closer to the manager.

"Yes," Sergeant Abdullah replied. "I heard these two talking about it."

"Good enough for me," Sergeant First Class Broadmoor said as he moved toward the manager. "Take your folks and get out of here."

The manager looked up at Sergeant First Class Broadmoor and decided not to push the issue. He motioned to his workers to leave, and they started to pack up the food containers.

"Oh no," Sergeant First Class Broadmoor barked. "You'll be leaving that. I think there may be some folks who would like to take a look at what you have been doing."

The manager was not happy and tried to have his people remove the trays again, so Sergeant First Class Broadmoor escorted them out of the building with the help of a few other soldiers who were not very happy with what had happened. Sergeant First Class Broadmoor returned after a few minutes with the other soldiers.

"Now what do we do?" Staff Sergeant Feister asked. "What are we going to eat?"

"Take four other soldiers with you and go get five cases of MREs," Sergeant First Class Broadmoor replied. "That will have to do for now."

Sergeant First Class Broadmoor walked up to the serving line and looked down at the pan with the eggs in it. He saw the same thing Sergeant Abdullah had seen and knew there was something wrong with the food.

"Carson, you just keep amazing me every day," Sergeant First Class Broadmoor stated, raising his voice enough for everyone to hear. "Expert with the rifle, deployed with the snake eaters, speaks fluent Arabic, and a pretty darn good mechanic to boot. I'm happy as hell that you're on our side."

"HOOAH!" came the response from all the soldiers within earshot.

The unit had to eat MREs for the remainder of the day, but the next morning, there were hot meals once again. Sergeant Abdullah noticed that the servers and managers were different, and when he went through the line, the first server took a small portion of eggs and put it on a plate. She then ate them with a smile to show they were good.

It took another six days to finish all the vehicles. Once they were done, they were told that the convoys would begin in two days, and they would be in the third serial of vehicles to depart. That would put the maintenance vehicles near the middle of the convoys so they would be able to deal with any issues.

Many of the soldiers in Sergeant Abdullah's unit had not deployed to Iraq before and were concerned about leaving Kuwait. It was always difficult to deal with the unknown, but they also knew that this time would come eventually, and it was better to just move out and get it over with. The sooner they left Kuwait, the sooner they would be able to get into the fight.

12

"Good morning, soldiers," Chief Provanski greeted, stopping at the table the specialists were sitting at for breakfast. "Did you enjoy the fireworks last night?"

"It was very exciting," Wafiq said.

"Yes. Every time they shoot at us, I want to go out and kill them all with my bare hands," Chief Provanski commented with an odd smile on his face. "It makes me very pumped up with energy. So were any of you injured?"

"No, sir," Aisha answered.

"Oh, well, that is good," Chief Provanski said. "No paperwork to fill out. Maybe next time we get you a Purple Heart. OK, so today we are going back to work. I have a meeting first, and then we will begin. You can do other things first and then meet me by the supply building at 1000 hours."

Al Khafaji used the extra time to check his messages. He didn't find anything of note in his email or junk folders. He tried to find information on the general situation in Iraq, but there wasn't much available. There seemed to be much more activity in Afghanistan. He shut the computer down and headed over to the supply building.

The four specialists waited for Chief Provanski outside for almost ten minutes before they saw him walking quickly over to the supply building.

"I cannot look for spies right now," Chief Provanski said, a little out of breath. "You all can go do something else useful for today. I will speak with Sergeant First Class Hermanson about tomorrow."

The four specialists went back to their quarters to wait for lunch. Al Khafaji was upset that he'd wasted the morning when he might have been able to go out on patrol with Sergeant First Class Hermanson. He needed to find a way to see what was happening outside of the outpost so he could pass information on to his cousin. Sitting around his quarters waiting for something to happen was not good enough for him. He was just going back to the computer room to check his messages when he thought he heard Sergeant First Class Hermanson's voice outside.

Al Khafaji picked up his rifle and gear and walked outside to see Sergeant First Class Hermanson talking with Staff Sergeant Pederson. He stood still for a few seconds until Sergeant First Class Hermanson waved him over.

"Samir, what are you doing here?" Sergeant First Class Hermanson asked. "I thought you were all looking for spies again with Chief Provanski."

"We were, Sergeant," Al Khafaji began, walking closer. "But Chief Provanski had to go do other things and told us to find something to keep busy. Would it be possible to go with you, Sergeant?"

"Sure, why not?" Sergeant First Class Hermanson said, glancing at Staff Sergeant Pederson.

"Fine with me, Herm," Staff Sergeant Pederson said. "Wouldn't hurt to have a linguist with us just in case."

"OK, Samir, you can meet us over at the vehicles at 1300 hours," Sergeant First Class Hermanson said as he looked at his watch. "Make sure you have at least four twenty-round magazines and bring your rucksack with at least one MRE and a couple canteens of water."

"Yes, Sergeant. Thank you," Al Khafaji replied before hurrying back to his quarters to make sure everything was ready prior to going to lunch. He would stop by his quarters on the way to the vehicle. He did not want to say anything to the others because they might also want to go, and Sergeant First Class Hermanson might change his mind.

"I am going to leave for lunch. Are you coming?" Al Khafaji asked Wafiq after organizing his gear. "I have been told that the food is better if you get there early."

"OK," Wafiq replied without much enthusiasm. He was hoping to look for spies again. "It isn't as if we have anything else to do. Maybe there will be some spies at lunch with us."

"You never know with spies," Al Khafaji said, smiling. "They could be anywhere."

"Yes, they can be anywhere except the supply building," Wafiq added, grinning back at him.

Wafiq and Al Khafaji stopped and asked Aisha and Sara to join them. The four specialists walked to the dining facility and joined the relatively short line. They got their food and ate. When Al Khafaji looked at his watch, it was only 1200 hours. He tried to keep the others occupied by talking instead of eating, but nobody seemed to be interested.

He didn't think his original plan of sneaking out without the others noticing was going to work. Al Khafaji saw Staff Sergeant Pederson sitting with some other soldiers and walked over to his table.

"Excuse me, Sergeant," Al Khafaji said to Staff Sergeant Pederson. "I just wanted to check to see if there was anything else I needed to bring with me today."

"No, I don't think so," Staff Sergeant Pederson responded, not really understanding why there was a need to ask. "I think Sergeant First Class Hermanson covered it pretty well."

"Yes, Sergeant," Al Khafaji said and walked back to the table with the other specialists.

"Sergeant First Class Hermanson wants me to go with them this afternoon," Al Khafaji revealed to the other specialists. "But he wants you to stay here in case there are any spies. He will take all of us with him soon."

"Well, at least one of us gets to actually do something," Wafiq said. "You will have to tell us how it goes when you return."

"Yes, we can all talk about it when I get back," Al Khafaji answered, rising from the table to leave.

"I will be looking for spies in my sleep," Aisha said.

Al Khafaji went back and picked up his gear. It wasn't 1300 hours yet, but he decided to walk over to the vehicles. Maybe there was something he could do to help.

"Samir, you are early," Sergeant First Class Hermanson said when he saw Al Khafaji walking up. "That's good. The sooner we leave, the sooner we will be back. Are you ready?"

"Yes, Sergeant," Al Khafaji replied.

"OK, take a seat in the back and get comfortable," Sergeant First Class Hermanson instructed as he got into the vehicle.

Al Khafaji got in the back with three other soldiers. Sergeant First Class Hermanson sat in the passenger seat up front while one of the soldiers from the other team drove the vehicle. Staff Sergeant Pederson rode in the back with Al Khafaji, Sergeant First Class Frederick, and Staff Sergeant Perez. Another vehicle followed with six additional soldiers.

They pulled through the gate and headed down the same route they had taken on the first day. The only difference would be that they would turn around after going through the small village and head back to the outpost. The idea was to get everyone used to the areas the team was responsible for while also maintaining a presence in the outpost.

Al Khafaji could not tell which direction they were heading, so there would not be much he could relay to his cousin about this trip, but he still thought it was good for him to be out and seeing what the soldiers saw. They stopped several times along the route but never dismounted the vehicle until they came to a complete stop and Sergeant First Class Hermanson signaled for everyone to get out. When Al Khafaji exited the vehicle, he noticed they were outside of a small village with only one road. He did not recognize the village, and there were no signs to indicate which village it was. He looked around and saw people walking into the shops, but there were no vehicles in the village or driving through it. There seemed to be a steady line of people walking in and out of the village on the road they were on.

"Samir," Sergeant First Class Hermanson called. "Come with me."

Al Khafaji hurried over to Sergeant First Class Hermanson and walked on his left side but two steps behind as he had been trained. By doing so, he was not in the way if Sergeant First Class Hermanson had to fire his rifle, but he was also close enough to say something if he noticed anything. They walked into the village while the soldiers in the other vehicle stayed outside for protection. The machine gun on top of the other vehicle moved slowly from side to side looking for any sign of the enemy.

Sergeant First Class Hermanson and Al Khafaji led the three others down through the village. Sergeant First Class Hermanson stopped every so often to say hello to one of the inhabitants of the village. Most of them merely nodded their heads without speaking. Al Khafaji recognized it as a sign the villagers were concerned about being seen speaking with the Americans. He thought there most likely was a group of true believers in the village that would take revenge for helping the infidels.

Al Khafaji noticed a group of younger men gathered near the side of a building twenty yards ahead of them. He checked the buildings on the other side of the street, and when he looked back, the young men were gone. An elderly man was now standing in their place.

"Sergeant," Al Khafaji said to Sergeant First Class Hermanson. "Maybe we should try talking with the elder."

"It's worth a try," Sergeant First Class Hermanson agreed as they moved to the other side of the street.

The old man did not move as the soldiers approached him. Al Khafaji was not surprised. The elders had been through much in their lives and were highly respected. He probably would not talk much with them, but Al Khafaji was sure it would not be out of fear.

"Peace be with you," Sergeant First Class Hermanson greeted, extending his hand. The elder reached out and shook hands but only nodded his head. "Samir, see if he will speak with you."

"Peace be with you," Al Khafaji repeated and slowly nodded his head as he extended his own hand.

"And peace be unto you," the elderly man replied as he grasped Al Khafaji's hand and pulled him closer. "You look familiar. Are you Iraqi?"

Al Khafaji again nodded his head. He turned to Sergeant First Class Hermanson, still gripping the man's hand.

"Sergeant, the elder has a problem with his voice," Al Khafaji said. "Is it OK if he talks close to my ear so it does not strain his voice?'

"Give me your rifle and be careful," Sergeant First Class Hermanson. Al Khafaji quickly complied.

"Yes, I was born and raised in Iraq," Al Khafaji said to the elder. "I have family in Iraq. My cousin is Abdurrahim Baghdadi."

"How can that be?" the man asked in disbelief.

"I am a true believer. Do not be surprised," Al Khafaji replied quietly. "If you know of my cousin, please tell him I am safe."

"Yes, I will," the elder said as they once again shook hands.

Al Khafaji turned and stood near Sergeant First Class Hermanson again. The small group continued to walk down the street. When they got to the end of the village, they noticed that the foot traffic was heavier from that direction as people walked along the side of the road.

"So, what did he have to say?" Sergeant First Class Hermanson asked Al Khafaji. He'd understood some of it but had difficulty hearing what the old man was saying.

"The elder thought that I looked familiar to him," Al Khafaji said, "but I explained to him that I had never been here before, and it might have been one of my cousins."

"Good job, Samir," Sergeant First Class Hermanson said, but he had a feeling Al Khafaji was not telling him everything. He would make sure to talk with Master Sergeant Mandess about what happened.

The group waited for a few minutes just outside of the village. There didn't seem to be anything odd about what was happening, even though it seemed like a lot of people to be traveling back and forth from such a small village. There were two shops that many people were going to. One was like an Iraqi version of a small Dollar General that sold a wide variety of things, and the other seemed to be some type of electronics shop. The electronics shop was close to the place where the elder had been standing. Sergeant First Class Hermanson contacted the vehicle at the other end of the village to let them know they were heading back.

The group walked down the road, led by Sergeant First Class Hermanson with Staff Sergeant Pederson covering the six. When they passed by the electronics shop, a small vehicle pulled out from the side of the building. Al Khafaji recognized two of the young men from before. The vehicle turned left and went in the opposite direction of the group. The vehicle posed no threat, so nobody was overly concerned; plus, had anything happened, the machine gun on the other patrol vehicle would have taken out the small vehicle with little effort.

"Everybody, mount up. We're heading home," Sergeant First Class Hermanson said as they reached the vehicles.

On the way back, they stopped at the ambush site again. Staff Sergeant Pederson wanted to see if he could estimate the enemy positions just in case there was another attack in the same location. He walked the area for about ten minutes before getting back into the vehicle. He spent the remainder of the drive back to the outpost looking over the sketches he had made of the area.

When the vehicles finally pulled through the outpost gate, it was almost 1700 hours. Sergeant First Class Hermanson stood by the vehicles until everyone had gotten out. He checked the notes he had made on the route and asked everyone to gather around.

"I think we have some trouble brewing in the little village," Sergeant First Class Hermanson said. Al Khafaji was a little shocked.

He didn't think that Sergeant First Class Hermanson had noticed anything wrong.

"I agree, Herm," Staff Sergeant Pederson said. "Stuff ain't what
it seems to be. The normal folks are afraid of something, and that old
dude probably has something to do with it."

"I'm going to talk with Top about that electronics shop as well,"
Sergeant First Class Hermanson added. "Those three guys hanging
out when we got there disappeared awfully fast, and when two of
them pulled out in the little vehicle, the back end was carrying a lot
of weight. Someone has been setting the IEDs in the road, and my
guess is that electronics shop has something to do with it. Samir, what
do you think?"

"Sergeant, I think that I missed many things today," Al Khafaji
said, sounding a little embarrassed. "The elder just seemed like a normal elder to me. I thought he was just concerned for his people."

"You'll get plenty of chances to learn," Sergeant First Class Hermanson replied. "I'm just glad you were able to get him to talk with
you."

"Yes, Sergeant," Al Khafaji said. "Is there anything else I can do?"

"No, but maybe you can go with us again tomorrow," Sergeant
First Class Hermanson suggested. "I will have one more of you ride
in the other vehicle tomorrow. I will stop by later and say who I have
picked. Why don't you go find the others and go to dinner."

"Yes, Sergeant. I am looking forward to going with you again
tomorrow," Al Khafaji said, hoping they would go to the village again.

Al Khafaji found the other specialists in their quarters, and they
went to dinner. He spoke with them on the way about the trip to
the village. He only talked about how the ride was and where they
stopped. He didn't add any details about what they did in the village
or the fact that they'd stopped at the location of the ambush. He also
did not say anything about Sergeant First Class Hermanson wanting
to take another one of them tomorrow, but he did tell them that he
would be going again.

"Top, any way we can get someone to take a look down the road heading out of the village to the north?" Sergeant First Class Hermanson said to Master Sergeant Mandess when he walked into the operations area.

"Why? Did something happen?" Master Sergeant Mandess asked as he examined the map.

"Well, we had a weighted-down car heading in that direction when we were in the village today," Sergeant First Class Hermanson replied. "Just thinking maybe they might be heading out to set up an IED."

"We can look into getting a drone to do a flyover," Master Sergeant Mandess said. "They are probably long gone by now, but there might be some signs of digging on the road. How did Al Khafaji do?"

"Not bad for a first time out, but I'm taking him out again tomorrow," Sergeant First Class Hermanson said. "I think I might take Aisha out as well. I don't think I will be able to take her on any breaching missions, but tomorrow's run should at least give her a chance to get out and do something before we put her on contract security."

"Your call, Herm," Master Sergeant Mandess replied. "I'll let you know if I can get a drone."

"Thanks, Top," Sergeant First Class Hermanson said as he left to find the specialists. He checked their quarters, but they were not there, so he figured they were most likely eating dinner.

Sergeant First Class Hermanson walked to the dining facility and saw the specialists sitting at a table. They were finishing their meal, so he guessed that Al Khafaji had already talked with them about what had happened.

"I spoke with Master Sergeant Mandess, and it looks like I am going to be taking Samir and Aisha with me tomorrow," Sergeant First Class Hermanson said as he sat down at the table. "I will make sure to get all of you out soon to be familiar with our area."

"Yes, Sergeant," Aisha said. "Are there any certain things I should bring with me tomorrow?"

"Samir, can you help Aisha get ready?" Sergeant First Class Hermanson asked. He was a little surprised that Al Khafaji had not discussed that with them, but as he thought through it, he hadn't been very specific on what to share with his fellow soldiers.

"Yes, Sergeant," Al Khafaji said. "We can all sit down after the meal and go over what is needed. That way, everyone will be ready when it is time to go with you."

"Sounds good," Sergeant First Class Hermanson said as he got up from the table. "Be at the vehicles by 0700 hours. Need to get chow early if you want any breakfast. We will probably not be back until late in the day, but you should still be able to eat dinner here tomorrow night."

"Yes, Sergeant," Al Khafaji and Aisha answered.

After Sergeant First Class Hermanson left the table, Al Khafaji began to explain what was needed to go with Sergeant First Class Hermanson. He said to bring half as much water as he was told and enough MREs for two to three days. Al Khafaji said that was because they may get attacked or have to travel in different directions, which might take several days.

"Wow, that sounds like fun," Aisha sarcastically replied. "I can hardly wait."

It took the better part of a day to travel the three hundred kilometers to the forward operating base they would be located at for the next eleven months. The slow-moving convoy of wheeled vehicles made several refueling stops along the way. By the time the last vehicle pulled into the base, the fuel tankers were almost empty.

Everything seemed familiar to Sergeant Abdullah, but things had changed significantly since the last time he had been in Iraq. The biggest change was the resurgence of the small militant Islamic groups. He had been reading about increased IED attacks and contractor deaths in Iraq. One thing that had not changed was the large number of abandoned or destroyed vehicles alongside the road. He wondered if they would ever be moved.

By the time the vehicles pulled up to the base, everyone was more than ready to be done for the day. The security people at the gate were waving the vehicles through. There were only a handful of vehicles that had any issues. Three of them were able to be fixed en route, while two others were being towed to the base. A security detachment was sent two hundred yards up from the gate to engage any vehicles that tried to infiltrate the convoy, but there were none. It was a long, dusty drive, but there were no incidents along the way.

Sergeant Abdullah's unit was directed to park their vehicles near the left rear quarter of the base. When they got there, they saw a small building next to what looked like a drive-through pole barn capable of fitting five or six vehicles. The bays were currently empty, but there were vehicles parked nearby in various states of disrepair. Sergeant Abdullah thought they looked like donor vehicles for parts. Some of them were damaged way beyond repair.

"Start parking those vehicles out in back of the damaged vehicles," First Sergeant Holman called out as he got out of the vehicle he was in.

The other vehicles pulled around the far end of the covered maintenance bays and started to back into place. It took only about fifteen minutes before all of the unit's vehicles were in place. The soldiers walked up to the covered bays and waited to see what needed to be done next.

"Pick up your gear and start filling up the sleeping quarters," Sergeant First Class Broadmoor commanded from the door of the small building. "When you are done, come back here and tell me who is in which of the hooches. Get a move on. Dinner is going to end in forty-five minutes."

"Carson, come on over," Sergeant Maczrakolski called out from the door of one of the two-person sleeping quarters. "I got us a good one."

Sergeant Abdullah picked up his gear and headed over to Sergeant Maczrakolski. The hooch looked a little bigger than the others, and it had a desk. Sergeant Abdullah threw his gear on the bed closest to the door.

"Home sweet home," Sergeant Maczrakolski sighed as he lay down on the bed.

Sergeant Abdullah didn't want to ruin his friend's time, but he had been in much better quarters in his previous deployments. For now, this would do, and he would be fine. Sergeant Abdullah put the duffel bag at the end of the bed with the top end facing toward him. Sergeant Maczrakolski watched as he took out a roll of tape and put it around the flaps that closed the bag. When he was done, he threw the roll over to Sergeant Maczrakolski.

"Put some on the top of your bag," Sergeant Abdullah said, smiling as he pointed to the flaps. "You don't want anything going into your bag that you didn't put there. The tape makes it easy to get in and out, and it will stay sticky for days."

Sergeant Maczrakolski didn't ask why. He just took the tape and tried to put it on the same way Sergeant Abdullah had done to his own bag. It didn't look as good as Sergeant Abdullah's, but Sergeant Maczrakolski figured it was good enough to get the job done. He tossed the tape back over to Sergeant Abdullah.

"Let's go tell Big B where we are staying so we can head to eat," Sergeant Maczrakolski said.

"OK, I could use a good meal," Sergeant Abdullah replied as he picked up his rifle.

The pair walked over to the little building and told Sergeant First Class Broadmoor which hooch they were in. There was a small map on the wall that showed where the dining facility was located.

It wasn't too far away, so they figured they wouldn't have an issue getting a meal.

The problem was the entire convoy had the same idea, and the line was very long to get in. A dining worker came out and told everyone they had plenty of food, but Sergeant Abdullah and Sergeant Maczrakolski weren't really all that excited about standing in line for thirty minutes. They both had plenty of water left from the trip and a few MREs, so they decided to just go back to the room.

As they were heading back, they saw explosions off in the distance. Sergeant Abdullah watched as several more bombs exploded. It looked like it was farther up the road they had traveled on and closer to Baghdad.

I am now officially back in Iraq, Sergeant Abdullah thought to himself. The explosions came to an end and they continued on to their quarters.

Al Khafaji and Aisha were at the dining facility by 0600 hours. The thought of eating MREs for breakfast and lunch was not something that appealed to either one of them. Aisha could not quite understand how someone could make food, put it inside a plastic wrapper, and say it was still good days, weeks, months, or even years later.

The two specialists finished their meals and stopped by their quarters before heading to the vehicles. Wafiq and Sara were already awake and wished them well. They were hoping they would not have to go back to the supply building. They were planning to go to breakfast but thought they might run into Chief Provanski.

"Come on, Wafiq," Sara said as she stood outside the door. "Let's go to breakfast. If Chief Provanski wants us to help him, we can't hide all day long."

"Yes," Wafiq grumbled. "You are right, and I am hungry."

Aisha and Al Khafaji walked over to the vehicles and waited for the others. It was 0645 hours, but they were the only ones there. Al Khafaji wondered if something had changed. A group of soldiers walked their way about five minutes later, but Al Khafaji did not see Sergeant First Class Hermanson.

"Are you the two linguists who are working with Sergeant First Class Hermanson?" one of the soldiers asked.

"Yes, Sergeant," they replied.

"Sergeant First Class Hermanson said that he may not be able to go on the drive today," a sergeant first class explained. "But he wanted the two of you to go out with us. My name is Sergeant First Class Wichman, this is Staff Sergeant Vincent, and that big guy is Staff Sergeant Ivory. Specialist Al Khafaji will be riding with us, and Specialist Hassan, you will be going with the second vehicle."

The two specialists walked to their respective vehicles and prepared to depart. The plan was to traverse the entire oblong route that the team had taken a few days ago. The goal was to establish a presence in the area but not to always be on the same schedule. They wanted to avoid being stuck with a predictable route or timeline. Today, they would travel in the opposite direction, which would put them in the little village late in the day. Sergeant First Class Hermanson had told them to pay particular attention to the reactions of the people and check to see if the old man was standing near the electronics shop again.

The team for the second vehicle showed up shortly before 0700 hours. The two teams got together for a quick huddle and went over the route and objectives for the day. It wasn't long before they were out on the road.

They didn't see many other vehicles until they reached the improved road heading toward the first of the two larger cities. There seemed to be quite a bit of traffic heading north. There wasn't much concern about an attack on the two vehicles, but the second team was constantly increasing their speed to close the gap between them and the first vehicle—it was not a good idea to let a civilian vehicle get between the two military ones.

When the local people were frightened or in a hurry, they didn't really care which side of the road they drove on. This caused a lot of problems, and there were several accidents as they continued to move farther north. Most of the accidents didn't seem to be very bad, but one most likely resulted in several fatalities with both vehicles in flames and a body lying in the road.

A few minutes later, they saw three military vehicles on the side of the road. There were soldiers standing around, and they seemed to be waiting for something. Sergeant First Class Wichman told the driver of the first vehicle to pull over in front of the others. He contacted the second vehicle to let them know he was going to get out and see if they needed any help.

"Is there anything we can do to assist?" Sergeant First Class Wichman called out as he walked toward the vehicles.

The soldier closest to him turned toward him, and Sergeant First Class Wichman noticed that he was a second lieutenant. The lieutenant looked at him and took a step closer.

"Sergeant, aren't you forgetting something?" the young lieutenant asked. He looked very young, and Sergeant First Class Wichman guessed that he was probably no older than twenty-three or twenty-four.

"Sorry, sir, but my hearing is not as good as it used to be," Sergeant First Class Wichman said without showing a bit of emotion. "Would it be possible to move over this way a little so I can maybe hear you over the traffic noise?"

The young lieutenant walked toward Sergeant First Class Wichman, who took about ten steps further away from the road.

"Sergeant, I am still waiting for a hand salute," the lieutenant said as he stood a couple feet away from Sergeant First Class Wichman.

"Sir, I would be happy to salute you if we were back in the States," Sergeant First Class Wichman began. "Heck, I would give you one of the finest salutes you've probably ever seen because I have a ton of respect and faith in junior officers. We are not in the States, and this is a war zone. If you don't want to leave this place in a body bag, you should quit expecting folks to salute you."

The lieutenant stood still without saying a word. He was starting to feel a little uncomfortable with the way the sergeant was speaking to him.

"You see, here, the enemy doesn't really get close enough to tell which ranks folks are," Sergeant First Class Wichman continued. "They just look out and see a bunch of soldiers. If you demand for everyone to salute you, then they have a target, and that target is you. I know this is your first time here, and there is a steep learning curve, but you need to be able to adjust to be able to take care of yourself and your soldiers."

"How do you know this is my first time here?" the lieutenant asked.

"Well, sir," Sergeant First Class Wichman said. "First, you are not wearing a combat patch. Second, you are a second lieutenant. If you had been here before, you would be at least a first lieutenant by now. And lastly, you seem to be a very young man."

"OK, Sergeant," the lieutenant said. "I get it, and thanks for not telling me this in front of my soldiers."

"I would never do that, sir," Sergeant First Class Wichman said. "Can I give you one more piece of advice?"

"Absolutely," the young lieutenant responded.

"If you are going to be here for a while, you may want to have your folks set up a hasty perimeter," Sergeant First Class Wichman recommended as he pointed to the vehicles. "And never allow your soldiers to get out of those vehicles without their rifles. If you can't fix whatever is broken quickly or tow it yourself, call a wrecker. You don't want to be sitting out here any longer than you need to be."

"Roger that, Sergeant," the lieutenant replied. "Thank you."

Sergeant First Class Wichman walked back over to his vehicle and got in. He took a look back at the three vehicles and smiled as he saw the soldiers scurrying around to find their rifles. *Good job, Lieutenant.*

The two vehicles pulled back onto the road and continued on their route. Between the traffic and the unscheduled stop, they were well behind the timeline Sergeant First Class Wichman had in his head. They had originally planned to stop in the city and conduct a short foot patrol. Sergeant First Class Wichman looked at his watch and decided they would just drive through and save the foot patrol for another day.

"Hey, Jim," Sergeant First Class Wichman said to the driver. "When you get up to the city, just drive through. We aren't going to be stopping today."

"Roger that," the driver answered without hesitation.

Sergeant First Class Wichman got on the radio and relayed the same message to the other vehicle. He looked at the map and estimated that they would be nearing the city in about twenty minutes.

"I want you all to be on your toes when we get to this city," Sergeant First Class Wichman said as he looked at the soldiers in the back of the vehicle. "I'm not expecting any issues but better to be alert than eating an MRE. Once we get through the city, chow down if you are hungry."

Al Khafaji and the others in the back of the vehicle nodded their heads or gave Sergeant First Class Wichman a thumbs-up. They had already been driving for a while, and now that the stop in the city had been canceled, there was no telling when the next stop would be. The others in the back of the vehicle joked about having to wear adult diapers when they went out on a mission with Sergeant First Class Wichman. They said that he never liked to stop.

They finally made it to the city, and the traffic seemed to thin out a little. Al Khafaji tried to look out as they drove along, but the seats in the vehicle were all facing in, which made it difficult. There were firing ports in case the vehicle came under attack, but Al Khafaji had no idea how they would work, especially if the vehicle was moving.

Everything seemed quiet, and there were no issues as the two vehicles drove through the streets of the city. Sergeant First Class

Wichman looked for any issues along the way but didn't see anything that seemed alarming or out of place. At one point, he was a little concerned about a van that seemed to be following them. He had the vehicles slow down a little to see what the van would do, and it just passed them and kept moving.

Shortly after the van had passed, a motorcycle with a driver and a passenger came alongside the second vehicle. The passenger looked over to the vehicle and then said something to the driver. The motorcycle sped up and was starting to pass the lead vehicle when the passenger began firing with an AK-47. The driver of the lead vehicle tapped the brakes, and the motorcycle cut in front of them and went down a side street. Sergeant First Class Wichman looked down the street and thought he saw the van.

"Nope, not going to suck us into that one," Sergeant First Class Wichman said. "Give them a couple bursts from the turret."

The turret moved in the direction of the side street and fired off a couple bursts. Sergeant First Class Wichman thought he saw the motorcycle go down but didn't want to stop the vehicle. They continued to move through the town until they were about a mile away from the closest buildings. Sergeant First Class Wichman told the driver to move to the side of the road and stop. The second vehicle halted behind them, and Sergeant First Class Wichman got out and walked back to it.

"Hey, Doc, what's going on?" the commander of the second vehicle, Sergeant First Class Evans, asked.

"Just trying to avoid running into a setup," Sergeant First Class Wichman responded. "I noticed that white van parked down the street when the motorcycle turned. I figured they had a little surprise for us if we would have followed. Did we hit the motorcycle?"

"The guy in the back with the AK went down pretty hard, and I think the motorcycle got dumped as well," Sergeant First Class Evans said. "Other than that, I couldn't really tell."

"OK, well, let your folks know that now would be a good time to try to eat something," Sergeant First Class Wichman said. "The next stretch of road on the way up to the next city should be quiet."

"Roger," Sergeant First Class Evans said. "Oh, and thanks for giving us the linguist. She about jumped through the firing port when she heard your gun go off. I think she is a little skittish."

"I would have given you the other one, but Herm told me to keep an eye on him," Sergeant First Class Wichman explained.

The two of them got back into their vehicles and continued traveling north on the road. Al Khafaji opened an MRE and was happy to see it was some type of chicken. One of the other soldiers asked him if he wanted to trade, so he figured it must have been one of the good meals. The chicken was very spicy, but he had plenty of water to wash it down. It made him miss the dining facility.

The drive to the next city took almost forty-five minutes. Most of the soldiers in the vehicles were finished with what they wanted to eat in the MREs long before they arrived. As they entered the southern end of the city, Sergeant First Class Wichman noticed a gathering of young men on the side of the road. When the lead vehicle passed the group, the men threw rocks and bottles at them. It was mostly just a nuisance, but there had been times when it started with rocks and bottles, and it ended up with rocket-propelled grenades and automatic weapons fire. The senior person in each vehicle kept an eye on the crowd to try to determine when or if the action might escalate.

Thankfully, nothing else happened, and both vehicles moved on through the city without issue. The next stretch of the route was the less-improved road that led to the little village. Sergeant First Class Hermanson had told them that he was very suspicious of the vehicle that drove out of the village during their last trip. He wanted everyone to be very cautious of that road and report anything that looked like a possible IED. The drone they had tasked didn't find anything that seemed out of the ordinary, but those two guys had been taking something somewhere.

The wind started to pick up, so Sergeant First Class Wichman directed the driver to reduce his speed as they turned down the less-improved road. It was a little difficult to see far in front of the vehicle, so they reduced their speed even further. The drive took much longer than it should have, but time would have been the least of their worries if they had driven over a mine. There were only a couple of areas where the road seemed to look different, but each time as they got closer, they realized there was nothing there.

They were only about a mile from the small village when the wind started to decrease and Sergeant First Class Wichman told the driver to stop. The foot traffic into and out of the village was still fairly constant. Sergeant First Class Wichman noticed that the people were still walking in the road. He told the driver to continue at regular speed. Whatever had been in the little car wasn't buried on this road, at least not on this trip.

Sergeant First Class Wichman told everyone to keep watching for anything suspicious, but he knew that there was nothing there. He would make sure to tell Sergeant First Class Hermanson when he got back. For now, he was focused on the amount of foot traffic that was heading out of the village. He thought it was probably more because the village was so small than anything else. It was almost like living in a small town in the States that was close to a big city. He remembered growing up in a small town south of Chicago that didn't even have a grocery store and having to go to another town with his parents just to go grocery shopping.

"Pull up short of the village," Sergeant First Class Wichman told the driver and then contacted Sergeant First Class Evans on the radio. "Time for a walkabout. We'll hold tight."

"Roger, on the way," Sergeant First Class Evans responded as everyone but the driver exited the vehicle. "Specialist Hassan, stay with me."

"Yes, Sergeant," Aisha said as she walked behind Sergeant First Class Evans. She was more nervous than scared, and she thought that was funny. A year ago, people would have laughed at her if she'd told them she was going back to Iraq to protect the people from militants.

Sergeant First Class Evans and his team strode down the street as normally as possible. They were here today to just show a presence. In the future, they would wear different clothes and park the vehicles away from the village and walk in like everyone else was doing, trying to blend in.

Sergeant First Class Evans stopped near the store to say hello to the elder. He would only nod to Sergeant First Class Evans as he spoke to him in Arabic.

"Maybe he will speak with you," Sergeant First Class Evans suggested to Aisha.

"Peace be with you," Aisha said to the elder.

"And peace be unto you," the elder replied. "Are you also Iraqi?"

"Yes, I am," Aisha replied, not knowing what to say next.

"Where is the young man who was here before?" the elder asked. "I would like to speak with him again."

"Sergeant, the gentleman would like to speak with Specialist Al Khafaji again," Aisha said to Sergeant First Class Evans.

"Doc, are you up?" Sergeant First Class Evans said into his headset microphone.

"Go ahead," Sergeant First Class Wichman replied.

"The old man here wants to speak with your terp," Sergeant First Class Evans said. "Seems like he was with Herm the last time, and they must have hit it off."

"OK," Sergeant First Class Wichman replied. "I'll send him over."

"Specialist Al Khafaji, grab your gear and go up to Sergeant First Class Evans," Sergeant First Class Wichman instructed as he turned to Al Khafaji. "The old man you spoke with before wants to speak with you again."

"Yes, Sergeant," Al Khafaji responded, grabbing his gear and stepping out of the vehicle. He walked quickly up the street toward Sergeant First Class Evans.

"Specialist, this gentleman would like to speak with you," Sergeant First Class Evans said.

"It is good to speak with you again," the elder said to Al Khafaji. He leaned forward to shake Al Khafaji's hand with both of his. Al Khafaji could feel something hard against his palm. "Put this in your large pocket. Your friends would like to speak with you."

Al Khafaji surreptitiously dropped the phone into the large cargo pocket on his right side.

"And were you able to speak with my cousin?" Al Khafaji whispered, as they were still close to each other.

"Yes, he is very happy that you are here and OK," the elder replied. "He will contact you soon."

"Have there been any problems in the village?" Al Khafaji asked more loudly.

"No, everything here is as normal as possible," the elder said, looking straight at Sergeant First Class Evans. "The only people we are in fear of attacking us are the Americans."

"The gentleman said the only ones they are afraid of are the Americans," Aisha said to Sergeant First Class Evans.

"Thank you," Sergeant First Class Evans replied in Arabic.

Sergeant First Class Evans and the remainder of the team finished the walk through the village and went back to the vehicles. The only thing they noticed that seemed odd was the electronics shop that Sergeant First Class Hermanson had mentioned seemed to be closed. Sergeant First Class Evans checked to see if the little car was parked next to the electronics shop but didn't see anything.

"Nothing out of the ordinary that I saw," Sergeant First Class Evans reported to Sergeant First Class Wichman as he got back to the vehicles.

"OK, let's get back to the base," Sergeant First Class Wichman said to the driver as everyone got back in their vehicles.

The two vehicles were able to make good time along the remainder of the route and were at the front gate before 1800 hours. When they pulled into the parking area, Sergeant First Class Hermanson was waiting for them.

"Hey, Doc, any issues?" Sergeant First Class Hermanson asked.

"Nothing to write home about," Sergeant First Class Wichman said. "We had a little dust-up with a pair on a motorcycle who wanted us to follow them down a road. The electronics shop was closed. We didn't see any sign of the small car, and the old man insisted on speaking with Specialist Al Khafaji instead of Specialist Hassan."

"Did you see any sign of IEDs?" Sergeant First Class Hermanson inquired.

"Nope, not a thing," Sergeant First Class Wichman said. "The road was absolutely clean."

"OK, tomorrow is another day," Sergeant First Class Hermanson said, but he was trying to figure out in his mind why the elderly man was insistent on speaking with Al Khafaji. Was he trying to get information from him, or did he just know him from an earlier time before the war?

For the next several weeks, Sergeant Abdullah's unit fell into a routine that was a lot like what they had been doing in Fort Bragg. The vehicles that actually ran over an IED were taken to a higher-level maintenance unit. Most of the vehicles they worked on were results of usual wear and tear, but on occasion, a vehicle would come in that had been near an IED or had been shot at by small arms fire. When Sergeant Abdullah saw these vehicles, he wished he was back in the fight and not repairing vehicles and replacing filters. He knew that he was not officially ever a member of the Special Forces, but having worked with them, he held a great deal of respect for what they did. It was difficult to have such a different role now, but he reminded himself this was his choice. He was still supporting the war effort, just not in the same role.

13

"Mac, the boss wants to see you in his office," Captain Taylor said to Chief Warrant Officer 2 MacKenzie.

"Any idea what's up?" Chief MacKenzie asked, hoping it wasn't anything bad.

"Nope. You know how the boss is when he gets in a mood," Captain Taylor responded.

Unfortunately, Chief MacKenzie knew exactly how he got when something was bothering him. He had known Major Palmer for years and thought of him as a great person and an even better leader, but when something was bothering him, it was a good thing to just stay out of the way until he either figured it out or asked for your help. Chief MacKenzie figured if the boss had asked for him, it might not be as bad as he thought.

He walked down to Major Palmer's office and saw Segreant Major Wagner standing in the doorway.

"What took you so long, Chief?" Segreant Major Wagner said. "Did you do some sightseeing along the way?"

"Come on in, Mac," Major Palmer said. "I need your take on . . . Chief, I can't believe what I am seeing. You are out of uniform, Mr. MacKenzie."

Chief MacKenzie was completely lost about what was going on. He took a quick look to double-check, but he was completely dumbfounded by the comment. Then, he saw Captain Taylor coming down the hallway.

"Boss, are you shitting me?" Chief MacKenzie asked.

"I wouldn't shit you, Mac. You're my favorite turd," Major Palmer said as he started to smile. "Congratulations, Chief. You are now officially a chief warrant officer 3. Your orders finally came through."

"So, you are shitting me," now Chief Warrant Officer 3 MacKenzie finally said with a sigh of relief. "You couldn't just give me the orders and say congratulations."

"Well, hell, what fun would that be?" Sergeant Major Wagner said. "Congratulations, Chief."

The boss made Chief Warrant Officer 3 MacKenzie go through a formal promotion ceremony in front of all the folks on the support team. He didn't really want all the fancy stuff—heck, all he wanted to do was pin on the new rank and look for the bump in his next leave and earnings statement.

Chief MacKenzie had a ton of things to do, so he went back to his office after the dog and pony show. One of things he needed to try to figure out was how to fix the problems with the local hires. His units needed more linguists fluent in Arabic to support them. The escalating casualty rate for locally hired contractors was really putting a damper on the market. There was also a fairly high uptick in IED events and unrest in the two cities his teams were keeping an eye on. Supposedly, according to the intelligence reports, there was a new militant cell operational that was being run by former members of the Iraqi Army. He knew there was a strong tie between both of his major problems and felt that if he were able to find the head of the organization and take him out, the cell would fall apart from a lack of leadership.

Captain Taylor stopped by around dinnertime to see if he wanted to try to get something to eat, but Chief MacKenzie was knee-deep into working on his two issues and took a rain check instead. He was trying to see if there were any contract linguists available. He left three messages with folks inside the Green Zone but hadn't received a single call back. Captain Taylor said he would bring him back something if he was going to be around a while.

"Thanks, that would be great," Chief MacKenzie replied without looking up from his computer. "Anything would be fine."

"I think you have been working with the boss too long," Captain Taylor observed, trying one last time to get him out of the office.

"Yep, I guess he does rub off on you after a couple deployments," Chief MacKenzie commented, finally looking up from his computer screen. "I really want to get this knocked out first. How about we grab something tomorrow and celebrate the promotion?"

"Sure thing," Captain Taylor said. "But somehow I'm thinking you'll still be trying to fix whatever it is you are working on."

Chief MacKenzie wanted to make a call to the outpost and speak with Master Sergeant Mandess. He wanted to see how the MAVNI linguists were working out. Maybe he could find a few more around to ship over to his A Teams. That would help solve at least one of his problems, but he would probably only be able to get extra personnel on loan for specific missions, and that wouldn't be the best option. Then again, if he got contract linguists, he might not be able to take them on a combat mission, and they also would not be armed.

"Operations, Master Sergeant Mandess speaking," Master Sergeant Mandess said in his normal phone-answering routine.

"Top, you got a minute or two?" Chief MacKenzie said.

"Sure thing, Chief. What can I do for you?" Master Sergeant Mandess answered.

"Well, I wanted to ask you how your four specialists were doing?" Chief MacKenzie said. "Hopefully you haven't lost any of them yet."

"Nope, we keep a little beeper on them, so we know where they are all the time," Master Sergeant Mandess jokingly replied. "But seriously, I think they are doing just fine so far. We are working them into the routes before we shift gears and start moving out to try to mix in with the locals."

"Good stuff," Chief MacKenzie said with relief. Things would have been much worse if those linguists could not function. Most of the soldiers on the team had a solid knowledge of the Arabic language and understood much of the Iraqi culture, but their focus needed to be on other things. Having a native speaker of Arabic was a huge combat multiplier for the teams.

"I'm thinking about coming out your way in the next week or so," Chief MacKenzie said, just to make sure there weren't any issues. "No dog and pony show. I just want to see how things are going and get a better feel for the MAVNI folks."

"Mac, you know you're always welcome down here," Master Sergeant Mandess said. "You will always be a great teammate to me. Getting to be a warrant officer was a great accomplishment, and I am always proud to say I know you. The best part is you will always be Mac, and I know that guy like the back of my hand."

"Thanks, Top, much appreciated," Chief MacKenzie said in a humble manner that also was exactly what Master Sergeant Mandess expected. "I'll let you know when I can make it."

"No worries. Take care," Master Sergeant Mandess said before the line disconnected. *Another thing that hasn't changed: he's always in a hurry.*

Al Khafaji wanted to use the phone to contact his cousin, but he needed to wait until the others went to the dining facility. He wondered why Wafiq was waiting so long to eat. He usually liked to go early. There was a knock on the door, and then they heard Aisha.

"Are you guys going to eat?" Aisha asked from outside the door.

"Sure, we'll be right out," Wafiq answered, and then he noticed that Al Khafaji was not moving. "Aren't you coming?"

"No, I want to finish up some letters," Al Khafaji said. "I will go a little later."

"We can just wait for you," Wafiq offered.

"That's OK," Al Khafaji replied. "I don't know how long I will be, and I don't want you to miss out on anything. It's always good to be near the front of the line."

"Yes, you are right, Samir," Wafiq said, grabbing his gear and rifle. "I will save a seat at our table for you."

Al Khafaji waited a couple of minutes to make sure the other three had left. Then, he took out the phone. It had several numbers in the contact list. He went down the list, but there was nothing that would indicate which one was his cousin's.

He started calling each number with no luck. They each seemed to be disconnected and no longer in service. When he got to the ninth number, his cousin answered.

"It is good to hear your voice," Al Khafaji said.

"I will not call you from this phone," his cousin explained. "If I call, we will use the same process. I will call for five rings, then call back with two rings. You should call this number after that."

"I understand," Al Khafaji said, and the phone call ended. Al Khafaji picked up his rifle and went to the dining facility. He felt good that he was able to speak with his cousin.

Sergeant Abdullah was finally feeling comfortable in his role as a mechanic. He usually had at least one or two vehicles under his name to work on every day on Sergeant First Class Broadmoor's work board. He also felt very safe inside the base. It was very well defended. There were security points that provided an early warning system for possible attacks, and so far, they seemed to be working very well. There had been only one rocket attack in the three weeks they had been there, and that rocket had fallen well short of the defensive perimeter.

The maneuver elements of the brigade were constantly moving to potential contact with the enemy and had taken several casualties, including two soldiers who were killed by an IED and one who was shot. There were about a dozen with lesser injuries who were still able to fight.

There was some good news at the beginning of the third week. Staff Sergeant Feister received a package from his wife. When he opened it, there was a note that said, "The rabbit died! :) I love you." Inside the box wrapped in paper were a dozen cigars. Staff Sergeant Feister didn't know what it meant at first and told someone that they didn't even have a rabbit. After he thought about it for a minute or so, he developed a huge smile from ear to ear.

"I'm going to be a dad!" Staff Sergeant Feister yelled out and started going around passing out the cigars and shaking hands.

There were other folks that got not-so-good news. Mostly issues with their marriages, but there was also an occasional missed payment of a bill or an accident with a vehicle they let someone else use while they were gone. Mail call was like playing the slot machines in Vegas. You never knew what was going to happen. Sergeant Abdullah received letters from his parents, and on special occasions, they would send a small package. They had done this on all of his deployments and had learned that sending large boxes was not a good idea. If their son was lucky enough to receive a large box still intact, he had no place to store what was inside.

Sergeant Abdullah wrote back to his parents when he could, but it was not very often. The work he had so desperately wanted to do while he was back in Fort Bragg was now more than he could keep up with. He actually enjoyed when there was a need for a wrecker and a mechanic and found himself volunteering to go outside of the base. Most of the other mechanics didn't want to take any chances outside the gate unless they had to, so it was usually just himself and Sergeant Maczrakolski heading out to wherever they were needed.

The maneuver brigade that Sergeant Abdullah's unit deployed with was beginning to put a lot of pressure on the local militant groups. They were setting up checkpoints, conducting more vehicle patrols, and working with local forces to raid bomb factories and weapons storage sites. As the pressure mounted, the militant groups fought back by using more powerful IEDs and conducting ambushes on local forces. The increased attacks on locally hired contractors was another sign of the growing unrest in the local groups.

One day, as Sergeant Abdullah worked on replacing the filters on a vehicle, a call came in asking for support with a vehicle that had broken down on one of the patrols about thirty minutes further north on the road toward Baghdad. The unit did not request the wrecker but sent a partial list of parts to bring. From the sound of it, Sergeant Abdullah thought they may have run over a small-sized IED. Sergeant Abdullah and Sergeant Maczrakolski grabbed the keys to the maintenance contact truck and loaded up what parts they could find.

The brigade operations officer sent an infantry squad with the two mechanics to provide security. The two vehicles made good time getting to the location. Sergeant Abdullah was partially right with his guess. One vehicle was damaged but could easily be fixed while the vehicle that had actually run over the IED was much worse.

Sergeant Abdullah noticed a large amount of blood on the severely damaged vehicle. The driver and vehicle commander must have already been evacuated to the field hospital by helicopter. The other occupants of the vehicle seemed to have only minor injuries and were sitting off to the side getting treatment from a medic.

Sergeant Maczrakolski started getting the parts from the contact vehicle while Sergeant Abdullah did a quick inspection of the damaged but repairable vehicle. He noticed several possible issues in addition to what they had been told. He made a quick list and gave it to Sergeant Maczrakolski who, in turn, went back to the vehicle and started looking. He found a couple of the additional parts and brought them back to the damaged vehicle.

The two mechanics worked quickly to remove the old parts and put on new ones. There wasn't enough time to do in-depth repairs. All they wanted to do was make the vehicle operational so the unit could get it back to the base. It wouldn't look pretty, and it would need additional work before going back on mission again, but it at least would be able to make it back to the base.

Sergeant Abdullah was almost done with the repairs when they received a call on the radio.

"Bravo three one, this is Bravo three six, over," the voice said. Sergeant Maczrakolski picked up the handset and replied, "This is Bravo three one, over."

"Bravo three one, we got a call for support about thirty minutes north of your location," the voice said. "Can you handle this, or do we need to send another team out, over?"

"Almost done here," Sergeant Maczrakolski replied. "What about the eleven Bravo support, over?"

"It's all good and been cleared with their higher," the voice responded. "So is it a go, over?"

Sergeant Abdullah nodded his head and told Sergeant Maczrakolski he would be done in about five minutes.

"Roger that," Sergeant Maczrakolski answered. "ETA thirty-five mikes, over."

"Roger, Bravo three six out," the voice said as the transmission ended.

Sergeant Abdullah finished up, and the two vehicles started to move north to the next location. The infantry unit had sent the new grid coordinates to their squad. According to the coordinates, the vehicle would be about ten minutes off the main road. The infantry squad leader said something about some folks from the Green Zone going out to spend time with a unit, and their vehicle stopped running. They all joked that the visitors probably ran out of fuel.

The infantry vehicle slowed down as it came to the dirt road and turned to the left with the maintenance vehicle less than twenty yards behind. The infantry vehicle continued down the road at a slow speed; Sergeant Abdullah could not understand why they did not speed up after making the turn. They drove about three miles before they saw another vehicle sitting near the side of the road. The infantry vehicle stopped about fifty yards away, and the soldiers dismounted and moved quickly up to the other vehicle. As they approached, the driver turned his head, smiled, and waved at them.

"Whatever you do, don't fucking shoot," a voice called out from the inside of the vehicle. "The last thing I want to do is try to explain to my wife how I got shot by a bunch of Americans."

Sergeant Abdullah could see what was happening but could not hear what was being said. He did not like waiting on a side road. He thought it would be too easy to get boxed in. There were too many things that could happen, and one squad of infantry might not be enough to deal with the threat.

The soldiers lowered their rifles and stepped back as the driver and passenger in the front seat got out of the vehicle. The three soldiers in the back stayed put momentarily and then opened the rear door and exited as well. The infantry squad leader motioned for Sergeant Abdullah and Sergeant Maczrakolski to come over. As Sergeant Abdullah got closer, he thought he recognized one of the men.

"Sergeant Mac," Sergeant Abdullah said, almost as a question.

Chief MacKenzie turned his head and saw Sergeant Abdullah carrying one of the toolboxes.

"Carson!" Chief MacKenzie yelled, turning to face him.

"My apologies, sir," Sergeant Abdullah said as he noticed the CW3 rank on Chief MacKenzie's uniform.

"Oh, hell, Carson," Chief MacKenzie said, stepping toward Sergeant Abdullah. "I think I can let that slide this time."

"Wait, did you say Carson?" Captain Taylor asked. "Is this the same Carson you are always talking about, Mac?"

"Yes, sir," Chief MacKenzie proudly said as he stood next to Sergeant Abdullah. "The guy who made it possible for me to be standing here right now."

"Sir, you are too kind," Sergeant Abdullah replied, feeling a little embarrassed. "I did nothing that anyone else would not have done."

"Carson, you shielded me with your body and took rounds that would have killed me," Chief MacKenzie countered.

"My man Carson," Sergeant Maczrakolski said quietly to himself.

"Whatever happened, we appreciate the fact that Mac is still with us," Captain Taylor said. "Thanks, Carson."

"Sir, I think we should try to fix your vehicle so you can finish your mission," Sergeant Abdullah said in an effort to make sure nobody stayed on the side road for very long.

"So how did you get here?" Chief MacKenzie asked Sergeant Abdullah as they walked to the front of the vehicle.

"I am a mechanic now, sir," Sergeant Abdullah responded. "I had to change my MOS when the Army closed the 09L program."

"When I heard the 09L program closed, I just thought you would get out and get a job as a civilian," Chief MacKenzie said. "That's where the big money is."

"That is the same thing my first sergeant told me when we found out about the program being closed," Sergeant Abdullah explained, although he was a little surprised that Chief MacKenzie did not understand why he'd decided to stay. "Sir, you should know better than anyone else that I would choose to stay in the Army. I am a soldier."

"Sergeant Abdullah, you are still one of the finest soldiers I have ever worked with," Chief MacKenzie said. "Thank you for wanting to stay in the Army."

Chief MacKenzie walked back to the rear of the vehicle and let Sergeant Abdullah do his work with Sergeant Maczrakolski. They found several things that may have been causing a problem, and they also found a slight cut in the fuel line. It did not appear that correct operator maintenance was being done either, but the vehicle was most likely part of a fleet of vehicles available to personnel in the Green Zone.

The two mechanics working together had the vehicle in running condition in less than an hour. When they were done, Sergeant Abdullah walked over to say goodbye to his old friend.

"Sir, I am very proud to see you as an officer," Sergeant Abdullah said. "You were a very good leader, and I am sure you are a very good warrant officer. Chief Mac. That sounds very good, and I am very happy for you."

"Thank you, Sergeant Carson," Chief MacKenzie replied. "I know you will continue to be a great soldier for as long as you want to stay in the Army."

"Dang, Carson, I can't believe you," Sergeant Maczrakolski said once Sergeant Abdullah got into the vehicle and started the engine.

"What do you mean, Ski?" Sergeant Abdullah asked as he worked to turn the vehicle around.

"You really are a bona fide hero," Sergeant Maczrakolski excitedly proclaimed. "I can't wait to tell the folks about this. Heck, even the snake eaters think you are badass."

"Ski, please do not say anything," Sergeant Abdullah said. "I just want to be a good soldier and a good mechanic. All that is in the past, and I would rather just leave it there."

"Come on, Carson, how can you not let me tell your story to everyone?" Sergeant Maczrakolski asked.

"I only ask you as a friend to not do this," Sergeant Abdullah explained. "I think that is enough."

"OK, I can live with that. I won't say anything," Sergeant Maczrakolski conceded, sounding a little disappointed.

The vehicles all pulled away from the location, with the one repaired vehicle heading toward the outpost and the other two heading back to the base. As they drove along the road, Sergeant Abdullah was amazed to be able to see Chief MacKenzie again. He thought it was odd how things worked out sometimes. He had to remind himself that nothing happens by chance and there is a reason for everything. He didn't really understand what the meaning of this chance meeting with Chief MacKenzie was, but he was sure that in time it would be clear. For now, he just had to focus on getting back to the base.

14

By the time the group of headquarters personnel pulled up to the front gate of the outpost, it was hours beyond their expected arrival time. They had already contacted Master Sergeant Mandess to inform him of the vehicle problems, but there was still a level of concern for their well-being. Captain Starn and Chief Provanski met them at the gate and gave them a quick overview of what was happening as they walked to the operations building.

"We haven't really had much in the way of problems yet," Captain Starn said as he began to update the headquarters personnel on recent activity in the area. "We are thinking that there are issues in the village but haven't been able to pin anything down quite yet. Luckily, one of the terps seems to have developed a level of trust with one of the village elders."

"So, the MAVNI soldiers are working out for you?" Captain Taylor asked, trying to clarify the performance levels of the four specialists.

"Well, just like anything else, there are some that are better than others, but they are all pulling their weight so far," Captain Starn replied. "Master Sergeant Mandess and Sergeant First Class Hermanson can give you a more detailed evaluation of their capabilities once we get to the operations building."

The group continued to walk across the outpost grounds until they reached the operations building. Master Sergeant Mandess and Sergeant First Class Hermanson were waiting at the entrance when they walked up.

"How are you doing, Captain T?" Master Sergeant Mandess asked. "I see you brought the entire crew with you."

"Doing good, Top, all things considered," Captain Taylor replied. "Wish we could have gotten here earlier, but I guess the Green Zone motor pool is kind of falling behind on maintaining their vehicles."

"Well, it's all good," Master Sergeant Mandess said. "Let's get inside, and we'll give you the nickel tour of what we've got going."

Everyone headed into the building and followed Master Sergeant Mandess to a room that had a large folding table and chairs. They had folded over three-by-five cards for nameplates. Chief MacKenzie's nameplate read *CW2* lined through and followed by *CW3 MacKenzie*. Master Sergeant Mandess had placed a piece of pound cake in front of the nameplate.

"Congratulations, Mac," Captain Starn said as everyone gave Chief MacKenzie a round of applause.

"Thanks, sir," Chief MacKenzie grinned. "But you shouldn't have gone to so much trouble."

"Come on now, sir," Sergeant First Class Hermanson said. "You deserve every ounce of that amazing dessert."

"Great. Now tell us about the specialists," Captain Taylor said in an attempt to get things back on track.

"Well, out of the four of them, two are definitely ready to move out on a mission," Master Sergeant Mandess began, "while the other two need more time. Specialist Hassan is probably the least prepared to take on an actual mission. Not because of her language skills; she has not lived in Iraq for more than half of her life. Her parents sent her to Egypt for school, and from there, she went on to Princeton where she was attending college when she decided to enlist."

"She did go out on a patrol the other day," Sergeant First Class Hermanson added.

"The next one we have that has a way to go would be Specialist Ghulam," Master Sergeant Mandess said as he continued the evaluations. "He is a hard worker, and there isn't any problem with the effort he puts into things. If you told him to guard a door and not let anyone in, he would keep everyone out or die trying. His Arabic is good, and his cultural knowledge is above average, but he is a terrible shot and couldn't hit the side of a barn from ten meters away.

"Next up we have Specialist Al Khafaji," Master Sergeant Mandess continued after a short pause. "His language skills and cultural expertise are very good. The village he is from found a way to sponsor him for a student visa, and he was going to school at USC when he enlisted. He did well on the range and has established a connection with an elder in the village. It's really difficult to read him. He seems to do all the right things but doesn't show any emotions.

"Lastly, we have Specialist Rashidi." Master Sergeant Mandess smiled as he began to talk about her skills. "She is an expert with the rifle and has already worked with the Army as a locally hired linguist. She is very cool under pressure and excelled during the breaching exercises back in the States. I wouldn't hesitate to take her on any mission we run. The only reason she has not gone out with us yet is because she is already good to go."

"Isn't she the Kurdish one?" Captain Taylor asked.

"Yes," Sergeant First Class Hermanson said, "but we tried to keep that very low key with the others. I don't think that Specialist Ghulam or Specialist Hassan would have an issue, but Specialist Al Khafaji could be a different story. So far, we have not heard him saying anything about it, but he carries the male macho attitude along with him. He was a little put off when Specialist Rashidi outperformed him in marksmanship and in the breaching exercises."

"Don't tell me that she is the one who was going to kill Staff Sergeant Pederson with the pen," Chief MacKenzie smiled.

"Yep, the one and only," Sergeant First Class Hermanson said.

"The only problem we have now is the shortage of locally hired linguists," Master Sergeant Mandess said. He was hoping to hear some good news.

"I know, Top, and I'm going to fix it. I just haven't figured it out yet," Chief MacKenzie answered. "But guess who I saw on the way down the road?"

"I wouldn't even know where to begin to guess on that one," Master Sergeant Mandess said.

"Carson," Chief MacKenzie replied. "He was the one who came and fixed our vehicle."

"What the heck was he doing fixing your vehicle?" Master Sergeant Mandess asked and continued without waiting for an answer. "It's a damn shame we couldn't have kept him. I would have expected him to get out and work as a contractor."

"I said the same thing to him," Chief MacKenzie replied. "He looked me in the face and said, 'I could not do that because I am a soldier.'"

"Yep, that's Carson for you," Master Sergeant Mandess chuckled. "Too bad we can't get him working with us again. We could send him and Rashidi out together and just sit back here and tally up the body count."

"Great idea, Top," Chief MacKenzie said as he wrote something in his notebook. "Let me see what I can do."

The group continued to talk about other aspects of the mission like supplies, communications equipment, engineer support and explosives, and medical issues. After about forty-five minutes, the last question had been answered, and the headquarters support team was headed back to the Green Zone. With any luck, it wouldn't take more than ninety minutes before they were back in Baghdad. Chief MacKenzie sat and wrote notes in his notebook the entire way. By the end of the trip, he had a smile on his face as he looked at what he had written.

The next day, Chief MacKenzie submitted a by-name request to Captain Taylor for his approval. Captain Taylor took a look at it and handed it back to Chief MacKenzie. He looked at the request for a few seconds without saying anything. He thought this would be the easy part.

"Mac, you know I want to get Carson here as much as you do," Captain Taylor began, trying to explain his decision. "But we already have a couple other things out there that we need to let work through the system first."

"Come on, Boss," Chief MacKenzie persisted. "You know anybody they come up with won't be as good as Carson, and Herm looks like he is in a bind with the four he has now."

"All true, Mac," Captain Taylor said, "but I don't think we can make this work until we at least see what shakes out. If we don't get any feedback on our request by the end of the week, I'll push it forward."

"Fair enough, but don't you want to hold onto this just in case?" Chief MacKenzie said as he handed the request back to Captain Taylor.

"Fine. Just set it down on the desk," Captain Taylor sighed, but Chief MacKenzie still held the request in his hand. "Now what, Chief?"

"Well, maybe you should just go ahead and sign it so you don't forget," Chief MacKenzie insisted as he handed the request to Captain Taylor once again.

"Chief, don't push it," Captain Taylor warned, taking the request. Chief MacKenzie was still looking at him.

"Who, me?" he said, smiling.

"Fine," Captain Taylor huffed as he signed the request. "But it stays here on my desk until the end of the week."

"Yes, sir, anything you say," Chief MacKenzie grinned as he turned to leave the office. "You're the boss."

Sergeant Abdullah was working on a vehicle when he received word that the field artillery unit had a vehicle that was nonoperational. They had also asked for another vehicle to tow a piece of equipment, so Sergeant Abdullah would need to have three other people go out on the call with him. He went to Sergeant First Class Broadmoor and asked who else was available to accompany him. Sergeant First Class Broadmoor looked at the information from the support request.

"Well, this one is easy," Sergeant First Class Broadmoor said as he gazed out at the maintenance bays. "Hey, Uncle, your queen is broken down again."

"I don't know why they even decided to bring that piece of shit with them," Staff Sergeant Feister griped as he walked over to the maintenance building. "So, who is going with me?"

"Sergeant Maczrakolski and I will go with you," Sergeant Abdullah said.

"Fine, but I'm going to be driving the wrecker," Staff Sergeant Feister said, grabbing the keys.

"Uncle, take Sergeant Maxwell with you, but don't let him drive," Sergeant First Class Broadmoor instructed.

"Sure, no problem. Hey, Max, let's go. We got a vehicle to drag in," Staff Sergeant Feister called out.

The two vehicles pulled out of the outpost and headed to the reported area where the nonoperational vehicle was located. This time, the damaged vehicle was closer to the city where the large explosions had occurred weeks before. The city had a large contingent of militants, and the plan was to slowly encircle the city and cut off the group from outside support. According to the field artillery unit, the vehicle had gone about eight hundred meters off the improved road before it stalled out, and they were unable to get it restarted.

When the two maintenance vehicles turned off the improved road, they could see the vehicle that needed their support off in the distance. The other vehicles from the artillery battalion were set up further down the road and were conducting a fire mission. The first thing that Sergeant Abdullah noticed was how close this vehicle was to the location where the other vehicle had broken down just a short while ago.

"Uncle, before you hook this up and take it back, give me a minute to take a look," Sergeant Abdullah said as he got out of the maintenance truck.

"Sure, but don't take too long," Staff Sergeant Feister replied as he looked around to see whether there was anyone nearby.

Sergeant Abdullah got out and took a quick glance at the engine bay and undercarriage. He noticed a fluid leak, and when he looked closer, he noticed there was a small cut in the fuel line. He was concerned that this was not just a coincidence. He asked Sergeant Maczrakolski to try to start the vehicle. When Sergeant Maczrakolski tried, the engine did nothing.

"OK, Uncle, this doesn't look like something we can fix out here," Sergeant Abdullah stated, standing by the vehicle to help Staff Sergeant Feister hook it up to the wrecker.

Staff Sergeant Feister got out of the wrecker and started to walk back to the vehicle that he had spent so much time working on. As he continued to get closer, Sergeant Abdullah noticed that he had left his rifle. Sergeant Abdullah was about to say something when he noticed a vehicle, and then another, in the distance driving in their direction. Suddenly, he could tell that one was a covered vehicle while the other had people in the back firing at something further down the unimproved road. As the vehicles got less than two hundred yards from their location, the people in the open-bed truck started firing in their direction.

"Take cover and return fire," Sergeant Abdullah yelled as he crouched behind his vehicle, firing at the oncoming truck. Just then, someone began firing at the open-bed truck from somewhere near the artillery battalion location, and the truck flipped over with several passengers flying through the air.

"Keep firing at the other truck and don't stop!" Sergeant Abdullah cried.

The truck was about one hundred yards away and still closing on their position. As the others continued to fire their rifles, Sergeant Abdullah dropped a round into his grenade launcher and fired. The round hit short of the truck, which was still coming in their direction. Sergeant Abdullah loaded another round and fired again. This time, he did not miss, and as the round impacted near the back of the cab, there was a small explosion followed almost immediately by a huge explosion that shook the ground.

"Holy shit, what the hell was that?" Sergeant Maczrakolski asked as he got up from the ground. "That didn't sound like any 203 round I have ever heard."

"I think that truck was probably full of explosives," Sergeant Abdullah explained. "That's why there wasn't anyone firing at us from that truck and also why the other truck was trying to get us to focus on them instead."

"Fuck!" Sergeant Maxwell screamed as he opened the passenger side door to the wrecker and fell out onto the ground.

Sergeant Abdullah ran over to see what was wrong. Sergeant Maxwell had a large cut below his left eye that went all the way down his face and ended just below his left ear. He also had a bullet wound in his left upper arm, but Sergeant Abdullah could not find an exit wound. While Sergeant Abdullah was trying to stop the bleeding in Sergeant Maxwell's arm, Sergeant Maczrakolski went to check on Staff Sergeant Feister.

"Uncle! Oh, hell, no! Uncle!" Sergeant Maczrakolski yelled from the other side of the wrecker. "You dirty bastards!"

"Max, keep pressure on this bandage," Sergeant Abdullah instructed as he grabbed his rifle and ran around to the other side of the wrecker.

When he got to the other side, he saw Sergeant Maczrakolski standing over Staff Sergeant Feister just behind the left rear of the disabled vehicle. Sergeant Abdullah got closer and could tell that Staff Sergeant Feister had sustained a mortal wound. He couldn't tell if it was a result of shrapnel or rifle fire, but he was definitely no longer alive. Sergeant Abdullah reached down to check for a pulse just in case, but there wasn't any.

"Ski, there isn't anything else we can do for Uncle," Sergeant Abdullah said, trying to console his friend. "Could you go back to the truck and call for medical support? We need to get Sergeant Maxwell to a hospital."

Sergeant Maczrakolski turned toward what was left of the explosives truck and started to fire his machine gun. "Motherfuckers, rot in hell!"

Sergeant Maczrakolski finally took his finger off the trigger and lowered the smoking barrel. He looked at Sergeant Abdullah and had tears streaming down his cheeks.

"It's OK, Ski," Sergeant Abdullah murmured, putting his arm around his friend's shoulder. "Come with me so we can call the medics."

The pair walked over to the maintenance truck to make the call for medical support. A vehicle from the artillery battalion pulled up in front of the disabled vehicle, and soldiers began to get out and set up a hasty perimeter around the maintenance vehicles. A first lieutenant walked over to Sergeant Abdullah and Sergeant Maczrakolski.

"Is everyone OK?" the lieutenant asked.

"No, sir, we have one KIA and a WIA," Sergeant Abdullah replied.

"Charlie three zero, this is Charlie three one, over," the lieutenant said into his headset.

"Charlie three zero, over," the voice answered.

"Charlie three zero, need a med evac at my location. One WIA, one KIA, over," the lieutenant said.

"Charlie three one, roger, out," the voice replied as the transmission ended.

Sergeant Abdullah continued to try to help Sergeant Maxwell until the helicopter arrived about twenty minutes later. The artillery battalion soldiers helped carry Staff Sergeant Feister's body to the helicopter, and Sergeant Maczrakolski helped Sergeant Maxwell. Once Sergeant Maxwell was on the helicopter, Sergeant Maczrakolski returned to the maintenance vehicle.

Sergeant Abdullah had already hooked the disabled vehicle up to the wrecker. He'd also tried to wipe off some of the blood from Sergeant Maxwell before heading back to the base. When Sergeant Abdullah saw Sergeant Maczrakolski walking back his way, he got out of the wrecker and approached the maintenance vehicle.

"Ski, can you drive the maintenance vehicle back?" Sergeant Abdullah asked. "I'll take care of the wrecker."

"Sure, Carson," Sergeant Maczrakolski muttered and then paused. "You don't have to worry about me. I'll be fine."

They drove back to the base, and when they got there, Captain Pickett, First Sergeant Holman, and Sergeant First Class Broadmoor were all waiting for them inside the gate, along with two other mechanics. The captain motioned them to stop and get out of the vehicles. The other two mechanics took the wrecker and maintenance vehicle back to the parking area.

"I'm glad to have both of you back," Captain Pickett said as he tried to find the words to express his feelings over losing a soldier.

"We don't want to try to go over what happened now, but we are going to have to talk with you about it tomorrow," First Sergeant Holman said. He also was trying to hide his grief over the loss of Staff Sergeant Feister.

"I'm sure you both did everything you could out there," Sergeant First Class Broadmoor said to them. "I'm proud of both of you. Sometimes it's hard to move on, but that's what you need to focus on. If either of you want or need to talk about it, just come see me."

Once again, Sergeant Abdullah was amazed at the leadership qualities of Sergeant First Class Broadmoor. He knew that Sergeant Maczrakolski would have a difficult time with what had happened, and he would help him as much as he could, but there are battles a person faces that only he can win.

$$\backsim$$

Al Khafaji was preparing to go to breakfast when his phone rang five times, stopped, and then rang another two times before stopping once more. Wafiq had left to go to the latrine, so Al Khafaji quickly called his cousin's number.

"The infidels hit one of our bomb-making locations very hard," his cousin said. "We will be making plans to make them pay for their actions. The elder in the village will tell you more tomorrow."

Al Khafaji wanted to ask a question, but the line was dead. Wafiq came in shortly after Al Khafaji had put the phone away. Using the phone was becoming risky, and Al Khafaji didn't want to get caught. He hoped that whatever was being planned would include bringing him back into the group to help fight for his country.

Al Khafaji and Wafiq waited for Aisha and Sara and then went to breakfast. Sergeant First Class Hermanson had not mentioned anything about what they would be doing today. All he'd said was to be at the operations building by 0730 hours. The four specialists finished breakfast and had plenty of time to pick up their gear and walk to the operations building.

"Today, we will be going out again, and we will be taking Samir and Sara with us," Sergeant First Class Hermanson said. Al Khafaji raised his hand in the air to ask a question. "Yes, Samir."

"Sergeant, I know that Wafiq had hoped he would be selected today," Al Khafaji began. "I would be happy to have him take my place."

"I understand the elder in the village enjoys speaking with you," Sergeant First Class Hermanson said.

"Sergeant, I think the elder just would prefer speaking with a man," Al Khafaji explained.

"You may be right," Sergeant First Class Hermanson said as he thought about what Al Khafaji suggested. "Wafiq, are you able to go with us today and talk with the elder?"

"Yes, Sergeant," Wafiq said with a smile. "I would be happy to go today."

"OK, well, let's get going," Sergeant First Class Hermanson said before picking up his rucksack and heading down to the vehicles. Wafiq and Sara picked up their gear and followed closely behind him. Al Khafaji and Aisha had just started back toward the rooms when Master Sergeant Mandess saw them.

"OK, you two are going to be sitting in on new contractor interviews today," Master Sergeant Mandess said. "Specialist Al Khafaji, I thought you were supposed to be going with Sergeant First Class Hermanson."

"Yes, Sergeant, but Specialist Ghulam has not been out yet, so I changed with him," Al Khafaji explained.

"OK, as long as Sergeant First Class Hermanson was good with it," Master Sergeant Mandess said. "But after sitting through interviews all day, you might wish you had done something different by the end of the day."

Master Sergeant Mandess took them inside the building. A room to the right of the doorway had been reconfigured to accommodate the interviews. It originally was a small break area for personnel on duty.

"You two can use the facilities right across the hall if you need them," Master Sergeant Mandess said. "This is a one-size-fits-all latrine, young lady. It would be best if you knock before going in and lock the door once you are inside."

"Yes, Sergeant," Aisha said.

"Mac, we got a response back on one of the support requests," Captain Taylor yelled out from his desk to Chief MacKenzie. "Come on over so we can talk about it."

"On the way," Chief MacKenzie answered. He got up and walked over to Captain Taylor's desk and sat down. "What do we got, Boss?"

"Well, it looks like the request we sent out for uniformed Arabic speakers came back with three matches," Captain Taylor commented as he read through the official response. "Bad part is that only one of them is available. The other two are being considered as mission essential."

"OK, so Carson is the only guy available?" Chief MacKenzie said.

"Nope, that's the odd part," Captain Taylor said as he continued to read the names. "Carson isn't even on here. So, it's kind of clear his unit is trying to hide him from the list."

Captain Taylor sat back in his chair, thinking for a few minutes. He didn't show it, but he was not happy with the results of the support request. He wondered how many other qualified people had been left out.

"Chief, I don't like the way this played out," Captain Taylor finally said as he picked up the by-name request paperwork. "Let's go take a walk over to see Major Palmer. I don't think he'll have an issue with sending this up the chain now."

"OK, Boss, but it's not even Friday yet." Chief MacKenzie smiled, rising from the chair.

"Don't start, Chief," Captain Taylor said as they started down the hall.

"Yes, sir, starting stopped," Chief MacKenzie quipped back.

Sergeant Abdullah and Sergeant Maczrakolski had a meeting with the chain of command the next morning. Sergeant Maxwell had very serious injuries that required him to be transported to Germany for treatment. The doctors believed he would recover, but it would be touch and go whether he could keep his left arm or not. Sergeant Abdullah felt bad that he couldn't do more for Sergeant Maxwell, but First

Sergeant Holman and Captain Pickett said that he might have died if Sergeant Abdullah hadn't done what he did to stop the bleeding. Sergeant Abdullah appreciated the kind words, but it didn't change anything in his mind. He had done what he could to stop the militants, but his friend was still dead. He felt like he needed to be doing more.

Captain Pickett and First Sergeant Holman planned to have a memorial ceremony for Staff Sergeant Feister that afternoon. They said they would not ask Sergeant Abdullah or Sergeant Maczrakolski to make any comments, but if they wanted to, they would make sure to give them time to do so. Neither one of them had any idea what to say, but Sergeant Maczrakolski said that he would like to say something.

When the ceremony began, the maneuver brigade commander and command sergeant major were present, along with members of the brigade staff and representatives from each unit in the brigade. A pair of boots, a rifle, and a helmet were placed in front of the formation. The units were brought to attention, and the national anthem was played. The brigade chaplain said a prayer and talked about life and death. He was followed by Captain Pickett and First Sergeant Holman. When it was time for Sergeant Maczrakolski to speak, he was only able to make it through a few sentences of what he had planned before he was overcome with emotion. First Sergeant Holman conducted the Last Roll Call and called off the names of the soldiers from the unit roster. When he got to Staff Sergeant Feister's name, he called out twice, waiting for a response that he knew would never come. A recorded version of "Taps" was played, and when it had finished, the soldiers from the maintenance unit filed past the memorial to pay their last respects to their fallen comrade. The remainder of the soldiers representing the brigade stood at attention until the maintenance soldiers were finished. Afterward, the soldiers were dismissed, but the memorial stayed in place until nightfall.

Sara rode with Sergeant First Class Hermanson, and Wafiq rode with the second vehicle. Sergeant First Class Hermanson would be doing most of the lead work today, while the second vehicle would be in a support role. They were focusing on the ambush site and the village today, so it would not be as long as some of the other days. Sergeant First Class Hermanson wanted to be able to get back in time to check with Chief MacKenzie on the progress of getting additional linguists assigned to the teams. Once the operational tempo picked up, they would need extra personnel at the outpost.

When the vehicles got to the ambush site, Sergeant First Class Hermanson had everyone but the driver and Staff Sergeant Pederson get out. They would go up to the actual site on foot so they could look closer at the vantage points again. Sergeant First Class Hermanson glanced at the sketch they had made the first time they'd stopped at this location and started to position personnel at key points according to the sketch.

After thirty minutes of walking through the area and highlighting locations again, Sergeant First Class Hermanson had everyone get back into the vehicles. He made sure to put the grid coordinates in his notebook for the most probable enemy locations. He didn't want anyone getting surprised again, and if they did, he wanted to be able to focus fire missions on the expected locations as quickly as possible.

The two vehicles continued on to the village. Once again, Sergeant First Class Hermanson had his vehicle's personnel move out on a foot patrol through the village while the other vehicle provided cover, but this time, he had his vehicle slowly trailing behind him. He wanted to have a chance at stopping the small vehicle he thought was carrying the IED if it showed up again.

"Let's see if the elder will speak to us today," Sergeant First Class Hermanson said to Sara.

"Yes, Sergeant," Sara replied, walking behind him and to the left. She saw the elder standing near the electronics shop but did not move in that direction until Sergeant First Class Hermanson led the way.

"When we get to the elder, I want you to start out only interpreting for me. I am going to be very blunt with him," Sergeant First Class Hermanson said as they walked down the street. "If he is not being very talkative, I will tell you when I want you to speak directly with him."

"Yes, Sergeant, I understand," Sara nodded as they neared the electronics shop and the elder.

"Peace be with you," Sergeant First Class Hermanson greeted the elder who simply stood looking at the people on the street. "Is there a reason why you would ignore my greeting?"

"I have nothing to say to you," the elder responded, and Sara relayed that to Sergeant First Class Hermanson.

"Is it not customary in your culture to acknowledge and return a greeting?" Sergeant First Class Hermanson said, no longer smiling.

"It is part of my culture," the elder replied without looking toward Sergeant First Class Hermanson. Sara once again relayed what had been said. "Why do you do that? He can speak Arabic."

"She does it because I told her to do it," Sergeant First Class Hermanson said, moving closer to the elder.

"You do not frighten me with your actions," the elder declared, standing his ground. "I am an old man. If you have a desire to harm me or kill me, just be quick about it or move on."

"Maybe you can speak with him," Sergeant First Class Hermanson said to Sara as he stepped back onto the street.

"How can you be helping the Americans?" the elder asked Sara once Sergeant First Class Hermanson had moved away.

"I am a soldier," Sara said, "and it is my duty to obey orders."

"Obey orders," the elder repeated as he looked at Sara. "Where are you from?"

"I was born and raised in Iraq," Sara stated.

"The Americans invaded your country and are killing Iraqi people. How can you help them?" the elder inquired, trying to test Sara's loyalties.

"My family lived in the north, and I am accustomed to fighting against other Iraqis," Sara explained, trying to control her temper. "My family has defended our home for many years, long before I was even born, and you ask me how I can help the Americans."

"You are a traitor to your own people, and you will die just like the other Americans," the elder said in a raised voice. "If I were younger, I would kill you myself."

"I am an American, and if you were younger, I would love to see you try to kill me," Sara retorted with a hint of a smile. "And you would not be the first Iraqi for me to kill."

Sara turned and walked over to Sergeant First Class Hermanson.

"Sergeant," she said as she took her place next to him. "He is not ready to speak with me. Maybe it would be good to have Samir talk with him again."

"You know, that's probably not such a bad idea," Sergeant First Class Hermanson said as he turned and smiled. "Just don't shoot him before Samir has a chance to speak with him again."

"Yes, Sergeant," Sara said as they started to walk through the village again. When they reached the end of the village, they got back into their vehicle and headed back to the outpost.

Al Khafaji and Aisha spent the morning sitting through interviews with current and prospective local contractors. Their job was to do interpretation as needed and to provide any additional feedback. One of the things that Chief Provanski had told them to look for was the applicant's body language and how they reacted to questions. Al Khafaji believed this entire day would be a waste of time, but his chances of being able to go to the village tomorrow were much better now.

Aisha didn't really care what she was doing if it was inside the outpost. She knew some of the local people hated her for being there, and she just wanted to get through her deployment and go back home. If she had to sit and try to figure out whether someone crossed their arms or took a deep breath, then so be it. It was one less day for her to be in Iraq.

There was a total of six different people who came in for a meeting. None of them seemed especially noteworthy, and only two of them were individuals who did not already hold a contract with the military. There was no current work available for either one of them, so Chief Provanski thanked them for coming by and said that he would keep their information on file for ninety days in case something came up.

Al Khafaji recognized one of the contractors as the man who had given him his phone. He had almost forgotten about that. The man seemed nervous and kept looking at Al Khafaji, but he did not mention anything during the discussions. When all the interviews were done, Al Khafaji noticed the man speaking with Chief Provanski. Al Khafaji thought nothing of it at first. The contractor would risk losing his contract if he mentioned anything. Nevertheless, Al Khafaji would make a point of having a discussion with him again just to make sure.

Sergeant First Class Hermanson returned to the outpost early in the afternoon. He asked the other soldiers to take care of the vehicles and headed up to the operations building to find Master Sergeant Mandess.

"Top, we got a little problem brewing in the village," Sergeant First Class Hermanson said when he saw Master Sergeant Mandess sitting at his desk.

"What's going on, Herm?" Master Sergeant Mandess asked, turning in his chair to face Sergeant First Class Hermanson, who had taken a seat near his desk.

"Well, I checked out the electronics shop again but didn't see the little vehicle from last time," Sergeant First Class Hermanson said. "The interesting thing is there is now a larger vehicle parked near the electronics shop. Oh, and the elder was in a bad mood today. I think he was just showing where his support really lies. That's just another reason why I think there is something off about Al Khafaji. He seems to be the only one the elder will speak with."

"Maybe he just has taken a liking to Al Khafaji," Master Sergeant Mandess said, not wanting to jump to any conclusions.

"Maybe, but let me tell you the Paul Harvey on our trip today," Sergeant First Class Hermanson stated with a smile. "All the things we have been thinking about Sara are absolutely spot on. I had her speak with the elder after he was not interested in saying anything to me. They talked for a minute or two, and I think the elder called her a traitor and said something about killing her."

"Why didn't you zip-tie him and bring him in?" Master Sergeant Mandess asked.

"No need. Sara handled it just fine," Sergeant First Class Hermanson smirked. "She looked him in the eye and said she wished that he was younger and would try to kill her. She told him that he would just be one more Iraqi that she had killed. He was so mad he could have spit nails. It was classic."

"Damn," Master Sergeant Mandess said, now smiling as well. "Maybe we should bring her onto the team and make someone else go back to big Army as a medic."

"I would be happy to have her on my team," Sergeant First Class Hermanson said, "and I don't think what she said about just another Iraqi she has killed was just a line either."

"Well, maybe you would like to hear some really good news," Master Sergeant Mandess said. "The by-name request for Sergeant Abdullah was approved."

15

Sergeant First Class Hermanson wanted to get out on the road early. He told the specialists that another soldier was coming to work with them as an interpreter but did not tell them anything more. He had the other vehicle leave an hour earlier with Sara working as the linguist, while he took Al Khafaji with him. The plan was for both vehicles to meet up at the village and then return to the outpost. He hoped to be back from the daily mission by the early afternoon.

"We are going to the village, but I don't want you speaking with the elder today," Sergeant First Class Hermanson said to Al Khafaji as they got ready to depart the outpost. "I just want you to interpret for me today. Do not speak directly to him and do not answer any of his questions."

"Yes, Sergeant," Al Khafaji replied. He wondered what was going on but did not want to ask.

Sergeant First Class Hermanson had the driver slow down several times during the drive as he monitored the radio. The other vehicle provided progress reports while they moved along their route. This was a standard process, but it also let Sergeant First Class Hermanson track their progress. He had his vehicle stop one last time about one hundred yards from the village. He waited until the other vehicle was roughly ten minutes away from the village and then told his driver to slowly move forward. They were barely creeping along. He told the driver to stop again when they were fifty yards away. He wanted to make sure that people in the village saw his vehicle before moving forward. He hoped to have the attention of the people when the other vehicle came into the village at a quicker speed.

As Sergeant First Class Hermanson's vehicle slowly moved forward, the other vehicle came quickly toward the village from the other direction and then slowed as it got to the first building. It finally stopped about ten meters inside the village. Sergeant First Class Hermanson noticed someone looking down at the second vehicle from the top of one of the buildings. To his surprise, it was the small store and not the electronics shop.

"OK," Sergeant First Class Hermanson said as he turned to the other soldiers. "That's what we were looking for. Let's go see what we can find on top of that roof."

The soldiers exited the vehicle and moved toward the building where the market was located. When they got to the door, they changed to a stack formation as they entered.

"Where are the stairs to the roof?" Sergeant First Class Hermanson asked the only person working in the store.

"In the back," the scared clerk responded, pointing to the back of the store and then moving toward the front door to leave.

Sergeant First Class Hermanson quickly set up the five-person stack when they got to the door at the rear of the building. He instructed Al Khafaji to follow him through the door but to check the rear first to make sure nobody was coming up from behind them through the store.

Sergeant First Class Hermanson checked the door, and it didn't look as if there was any type of lock or dead bolt. He listened to see if he could hear anyone on the other side, but there were no sounds. He turned with his back to the door and gave it a kick. The door opened without an issue, and the first three soldiers went in without any problems or shots fired. Sergeant First Class Hermanson and Al Khafaji followed them.

The stack cautiously moved up the first flight of stairs, always looking as far up the staircase as they could, but there was no movement.

"Stay here and watch this door," Sergeant First Class Hermanson said to Al Khafaji when they reached the landing at the top of the first flight of stairs. "I'll let you know if I need you on the roof. In the meantime, once we go through that door, don't let anyone else come up these steps."

"Yes, Sergeant," Al Khafaji said, all the time thinking how easy it would be to shoot all of them when they started up the stairs.

The first two soldiers were on the second flight of stairs when they heard rifle fire coming from the roof. Shortly after the rifle fire started, one of the vehicles returned fire with their machine gun. The soldiers could hear people moving around on the roof, so they held their positions halfway up the steps. Within seconds, the door to the roof started to open, and a man with an AK-47 started down the stairs, followed by two others. Sergeant First Class Hermanson and the other three ahead of him opened fire. The three militants didn't get off a single shot.

"Moving to roof, hold fire," Sergeant First Class Hermanson called over his headset.

"Roger," came the reply.

The five soldiers continued to move up the stairs. The number one man went through the doorway, quickly followed by the second and third man. Sergeant First Class Hermanson didn't hear any more shots, so he also went through. The roof was clear.

The team came back down the stairs to the first landing. Al Khafaji was still there, looking at the three dead men. Staff Sergeant Pederson checked the bodies for papers or other weapons while Sergeant First Class Hermanson made his way around the bodies to check on Al Khafaji.

"Samir, are you OK?" Sergeant First Class Hermanson asked Al Khafaji, but he did not respond. Al Khafaji thought one of the men was one of the three he had seen earlier with the elder. "Did anyone come out of this door or enter the market downstairs?"

"No, Sergeant," Al Khafaji said.

"Come with me. We need to find the shop owner," Sergeant First Class Hermanson said as he continued down the stairs. Al Khafaji hesitated and then turned and followed Sergeant First Class Hermanson.

"Check around and see if you can find the shop owner," Sergeant First Class Hermanson said to Sergeant First Class Frederick and Staff Sergeant Perez. "Take Samir with you. I am going to talk with the other team."

Sergeant First Class Frederick and Staff Sergeant Perez took Al Khafaji and walked down the street while Sergeant First Class Hermanson moved over to the other vehicle. Sergeant First Class Richmond was standing alongside the vehicle with the rest of his team and Sara. Sergeant First Class Hermanson was glad to see that everyone looked fine.

"Everyone good, Jack?" Sergeant First Class Hermanson asked Sergeant First Class Richmond.

"We are all fine, but not sure why they would start firing at us in an armored vehicle with small arms," Sergeant First Class Richmond commented. "That was one of the dumbest things I have seen in a while."

"Won't happen again from that bunch," Sergeant First Class Hermanson replied. "They are all on the way to meet their maker, but I get your point."

Al Khafaji and the others from Sergeant First Class Hermanson's vehicle walked further down the road. He saw the elder standing next to a building on the other side of the small dirt road. Al Khafaji turned to see Sergeant First Class Hermanson still standing next to the other vehicle and thought this might be a good time to speak with the elder.

"Sergeant," Al Khafaji said to Sergeant First Class Frederick. "The village elder is there. Maybe he would know where the shopkeeper is."

"OK. We will be right here if you need us," Sergeant First Class Frederick replied. He thought it would be easier to speak with the elder if they were not all right on top of him. They were only about ten feet away and could easily help Al Khafaji if he needed it.

"My apologies, sir," Al Khafaji said as he neared the elder. "I have little time to talk. The Americans are very interested in the electronics shop, and they will be back. I also need to know where the shopkeeper went, as they want to ask him questions."

"Thank you," the elder said to Al Khafaji. "The shopkeeper is in the next building, and he is scared. I will speak with him and have him come out."

"Sergeant," Al Khafaji called as he walked back to Sergeant First Class Frederick while the elder went into the next building. "The elder is going to have the shopkeeper come out. He said that he is frightened from all the shooting."

"Good job, Samir," Sergeant First Class Frederick smiled when he saw the shopkeeper coming out of the other building.

Staff Sergeant Perez went over to the shopkeeper and zip-tied his hands behind his back just in case. He also checked him for any weapons but only found a small knife, which was not uncommon for a shopkeeper to have. They walked back toward his shop to meet up with Sergeant First Class Hermanson, who had Sara with him.

"Samir, go with Sergeant First Class Richmond in the other vehicle," Sergeant First Class Hermanson instructed as he and Sara walked past him. "You did a good job today."

"Thank you, Sergeant," Al Khafaji said before walking over to the other vehicle.

"Let's go back inside and see what Mr. Shopkeeper can tell us," Sergeant First Class Hermanson said as all the members of his team went back inside the market.

"I am not bad," the shopkeeper insisted as they guided him back inside the building.

Sergeant First Class Hermanson led the group through the shop and up to the second-floor landing.

"Do you know any of these men?" Sergeant First Class Herman-son asked the shopkeeper.

"No, I do not know them," the shopkeeper said nervously.

"Take another look," Sergeant First Class Hermanson said as he moved the storekeeper closer to the three dead bodies. "They were on top of your building. Are you sure you don't know any of them?"

"I do not know them. I am a good man, and I don't do anything wrong," the shopkeeper repeated.

"Who lives in this apartment?" Sergeant First Class Hermanson asked as he turned the shopkeeper to face the door.

"That is my home," the shopkeeper said. "I am the only one who lives here."

"So maybe we should go in and make sure everything is OK," Sergeant First Class Hermanson suggested. "We want to make sure that the three men that you don't know who were on your roof did not damage anything."

"I am sure everything is fine, so it will not be necessary to . . ." the shopkeeper started to say, but Sergeant First Class Hermanson had his back to the door. He looked at the shopkeeper and smiled while lifting his right leg and driving it back against the door. It swung open to reveal an empty room.

Sergeant First Class Hermanson moved the shopkeeper into the room ahead of him. The apartment did not look very lived in. Sergeant First Class Hermanson looked around and guided the shop-keeper toward a closed door.

"What's in there?" Sergeant First Class Hermanson inquired. He guessed it was likely the bedroom.

"That is my bedroom," the shopkeeper confirmed, eyes cast toward the ground.

Sergeant First Class Hermanson moved the shopkeeper close to the door and opened it. The bedroom had no people in it, but it had more than a dozen AK-47s, at least a dozen RPGs, and boxes of ammunition.

"Looks like we may need to take a ride to the base," Sergeant First Class Hermanson said as he contacted the other team and told them to send up a couple folks to help carry the weapons out to the vehicles. He had his team take the shopkeeper out to their vehicle. When they had gathered up all the weapons and ammunition, they headed back to the outpost.

Sergeant Abdullah was working on a vehicle in the maintenance bay when Sergeant First Class Broadmoor came over to talk with him. The pair went back into the maintenance building where Captain Pickett and First Sergeant Holman were waiting.

"Have a seat, Sergeant Abdullah," Captain Pickett said. Sergeant Abdullah did not know what was happening.

"Do you know why you are here, Sergeant?" First Sergeant Holman asked.

"No, First Sergeant," Sergeant Abdullah said.

"We received a by-name request from a Special Forces unit to have you reassigned to them for the entirety of their deployment, which should be about five months," Captain Pickett explained.

"Did you know anything about this?" First Sergeant Holman asked.

"No, First Sergeant. I did not have any idea," Sergeant Abdullah answered.

"Well, Carson," Sergeant First Class Broadmoor said. "We tried to keep you. There was a request that came out to identify all soldiers who could speak Arabic, and somehow, I forgot to add your name to the list."

"I would be happy to stay here with this unit," Sergeant Abdullah said.

"We believe you," Captain Pickett began, "but that just isn't possible."

"With what we have seen and heard of your other deployments," First Sergeant Holman said, "you will be a valuable asset to the Special Operations teams."

"You need to gather all your gear and be back here within the hour," Captain Pickett said. "I also want to let you know that I submitted you for an award for your actions the other day. I know that you feel bad about Staff Sergeant Feister, but your actions saved many lives."

"I am very proud to have served with this unit," Sergeant Abdullah replied.

"Let us know if you still feel the same way when you come back," Sergeant First Class Broadmoor responded, and Sergeant Abdullah looked a little startled. "Oh, yeah, that's the best part. When you are done with them, we will still have about six months left. So, you are just on loan."

"Thank you to all of you," Sergeant Abdullah smiled. "I came here with this unit, and this is the unit I want to go home with."

Sergeant Abdullah left the office and went to his quarters. He packed all his gear in his rucksack and duffel bag. When he was done, he opened the door again only to see a line formed by the mechanics. They clapped and patted him on the back as he walked past each one of them. Sergeant Maczrakolski came up and took his duffel bag.

"I got it, Carson," Sergeant Maczrakolski said. "It's the least I can do."

"Thanks, Ski," Sergeant Abdullah replied as he continued to walk down the line. When he got to the end, he turned and looked back. "I will miss each one of you, and I wish you all good luck."

Sergeant Abdullah got in the back of the vehicle, and it pulled away toward the front gate. He didn't realize it, but the crew in the vehicle was from the infantry unit in the brigade. Every member of the crew had volunteered to take him to the new location.

The drive took a little over an hour. By the time he got to the outpost, the teams were already out on their missions. One of the security personnel directed the vehicle to the operations building where Master Sergeant Mandess was waiting for him.

"Well, well, well," Master Sergeant Mandess said. "If it isn't Sergeant Carson. You are a sight for sore eyes."

"Hello, Sergeant," Sergeant Abdullah greeted him. "It is good to see you again."

"I'll show you where you will be staying, and then we can get some chow," Master Sergeant Mandess said. "The others should be back later this afternoon."

"Yes, Sergeant. That would be good," Sergeant Abdullah replied.

Master Sergeant Mandess and Sergeant Abdullah walked over to a sleeping quarters not far from Master Sergeant Mandess and Sergeant First Class Hermanson. It was a little farther away from the four specialists, but that was by choice. Master Sergeant Mandess wanted Carson to be monitoring all the specialists in addition to serving on the team. His experience would be important in trying to find out exactly where Al Khafaji stood with respect to loyalties and support. Both Master Sergeant Mandess and Sergeant First Class Hermanson still had concerns about Al Khafaji.

"I am very excited to be working with this unit again," Sergeant Abdullah said as he placed his duffel bag on the bunk. "I think I was always doing something important when I was with the Green Berets."

"Well, Carson, we are very happy to have you back with us as well," Master Sergeant Mandess replied. "It's a shame we could not have kept you with us from the last time, but that just isn't the way things work sometimes."

"Yes, Sergeant, but now I am back here where I feel like I belong," Sergeant Abdullah added.

Sergeant First Class Hermanson pulled up to the gate of the outpost at around 1500 hours. He had to stop by the operations building to bring the shopkeeper in to speak with the intelligence team and Chief Provanski. He released the other soldiers and made his way to the operations building with the shopkeeper.

Chief Provanski told Sergeant First Class Hermanson they would most likely transport the shopkeeper to the Green Zone once they were done. The weapons cache, along with the three dead Iraqis, tied him into the bigger picture. Every day, the pieces of the puzzle were starting to fall into place. Eventually, it would lead them to the center of the militant cell and the person they were looking for.

Chief Provanski also said that the intelligence folks in the Green Zone thought the leader was probably once a member of the Republican Guard due to the tactics that were being used in the attacks and ambushes. He told Sergeant First Class Hermanson that one of the dead Iraqis from the village looked like he could have been a match for one of the suspected leaders of a faction of the group.

"See, that's the part that's making me scratch my head a bit, Chief," Sergeant First Class Hermanson said. "Why would they fire at us with small arms when we were sitting inside an armored vehicle?"

"Good question, Herm," Chief Provanski said. "Maybe we can make him talk about it with us. If not, I am sure he will have something to say by the time he gets to Baghdad."

"You know, Chief," Sergeant First Class Hermanson said as he looked off into the distance. "I'm not sure, but this guy might just be telling the truth, and this is all just some type of a setup. It wouldn't be the first time that some of these folks gave their life for the cause."

"Well," Chief Provanski began, then paused for a second to think. "If he is telling the truth, then we will take him back to the village, but we must be sure first. I will let you know."

Sergeant First Class Hermanson walked over to the operations building to check in with Master Sergeant Mandess. He went through the door and saw Sergeant Abdullah talking with Master Sergeant Mandess.

"Carson! Boy, am I glad to see you," Sergeant First Class Hermanson said, reaching out to shake Carson's hand. Sergeant First Class Hermanson had been with the security team when Chief MacKenzie's team was ambushed. He had been a staff sergeant at that time and saw exactly what Sergeant Abdullah had done to protect his team leader.

"Hello, Sergeant. It is good to see you as well," Sergeant Abdullah replied as the two of them shook hands.

"If you are ready, we will be going back to the village tomorrow morning," Sergeant First Class Hermanson said.

"Top has not told me what I will be doing," Sergeant Abdullah said. Both of them turned toward Master Sergeant Mandess.

"Well, hell, don't look at me," Master Sergeant Mandess said. "Sounds like a great idea to me, but you might want to swing by the supply room and see if there is anything you need."

"Sure thing, Top. I'll make sure it gets squared away," Sergeant First Class Hermanson said before Sergeant Abdullah could respond.

Sergeant First Class Hermanson took Sergeant Abdullah back to the supply room and had him issued a complete set of gear. Sergeant Abdullah had brought much of what he was issued from the maintenance unit, but Sergeant First Class Hermanson looked at it and said it was crap. He told Sergeant Abdullah to just keep it secured, and they would bring him back to return it before they left.

Next stop was the arms room. Sergeant First Class Hermanson wanted Sergeant Abdullah to swap out his rifle, but Sergeant Abdullah wanted to keep it. Sergeant Abdullah did sign for a 9mm handgun as a backup to his rifle. The armorer also gave him a crate of rounds for the grenade launcher on his rifle.

"You can throw a regular grenade faster than you can shoot the rounds from your rifle," the armorer said as he handed Sergeant Abdullah the box.

"Yes, but I cannot throw them as far as I can shoot them," Sergeant Abdullah replied.

The two of them finished up and brought everything back to Sergeant Abdullah's quarters. Sergeant First Class Hermanson told him about the other linguists and discussed their strengths and weaknesses. Sergeant Abdullah was surprised to learn that Al Khafaji was there. *It is truly a small world*, he thought to himself. When they were finished, Sergeant First Class Hermanson took Sergeant Abdullah over to introduce him to the others.

"Folks, this is Sergeant Abdullah," Sergeant First Class Hermanson said once all four of the specialists were gathered outside of their quarters. "He will be working with us and providing immediate supervision of all four of you. If you have any questions, you can direct those to him."

"Thank you, Sergeant," Sergeant Abdullah said as he looked at the four specialists. "I know one of you, and I will work to get to know all of you very soon. Time will go past quickly here, and there is much to do in a short time, so I want to make sure we are all focused on those things that we must do. It is very good to see you again, Specialist Al Khafaji."

"Thank you, Sergeant," Al Khafaji replied, trying to figure out in his mind how this might affect his ability to work with his cousin.

"Sergeant, do you speak Arabic?" Aisha asked in English.

"Yes, I do. I was born and raised in Iraq before my parents immigrated to the United States," Sergeant Abdullah replied in Arabic. "I joined the Army as a uniformed interpreter/translator, but that MOS was discontinued, and I had to pick another to stay in the Army. That is where I met Specialist Al Khafaji."

Sergeant Abdullah's credibility immediately jumped several notches in Sara's and Wafiq's minds. They were both impressed that Sergeant Abdullah was a trained interpreter. Aisha didn't really care; she was more interested in what Sergeant Abdullah said about time going by quickly. Al Khafaji was trying to remember if he had said anything while in the mechanics course that Sergeant Abdullah might have heard that would give him reason to be concerned, but he couldn't think of anything.

"I want to make sure that the four of you sit down and talk about the mission we went on this morning," Sergeant First Class Hermanson said to the specialists. "Samir and Sara, I want each of you to discuss what happened in your vehicles so Aisha and Wafiq understand why we will be increasing our missions. If there are any questions that come up that neither Samir nor Sara can answer, feel free to ask Sergeant Abdullah. Any questions?"

"No, Sergeant," the specialists replied.

"We will be in the operations building," Sergeant First Class Hermanson said. "I will talk with all of you later about what the plans are for tomorrow."

Sergeant First Class Hermanson and Sergeant Abdullah walked back to the operations building to try to get Sergeant Abdullah an update on what had been happening in the area from the intelligence folks if they were done speaking with the shopkeeper. Sergeant First Class Hermanson checked their office, but they still were not in. He decided to go back to Master Sergeant Mandess's office and go over the action plans for the next couple of days with Sergeant Abdullah. He would circle back with the intelligence team later.

Master Sergeant Mandess wasn't in his office either, so Sergeant First Class Hermanson used the big map board on the wall to give Sergeant Abdullah an overview of what he knew. He explained the route the patrols usually took to cover the two cities and the village. He told him about the occasional disturbances in the cities and the attempted ambush. Sergeant First Class Hermanson spent most of his time discussing the village setup and the issues with the elder. He made sure to let Sergeant Abdullah know of the relationship that had developed between the elder and Al Khafaji. He also told him of his concerns with the electronics shop. Lastly, he told Sergeant Abdullah about the one rocket and mortar attack they'd had since they arrived.

"Herm, where have you been?" Master Sergeant Mandess said as he walked by his office. "Come on! The chief and the intel team are going to brief the old man on what they found out."

The three of them quickly walked down the hall to the large area they used for briefings. It looked like they had Major Palmer and Chief MacKenzie on the computer as well. Master Sergeant Mandess had a seat up at the table with Captain Starn, while Sergeant First Class Hermanson and Sergeant Abdullah sat in seats along the wall.

"Sir, we would like to begin by going over the actions from today," Chief Provanski stated as he walked everyone through what had happened earlier in the village. He then showed pictures of the three dead Iraqis and highlighted what they knew about each one. The first two were not known to be part of the leadership of the militant group, but there was a high probability that the third one was a high-value target. According to the intelligence team, they were able to say with better than a 90 percent surety that the individual was the leader of one of the factions of the larger group. The shopkeeper confirmed what they had believed. When it came to the shopkeeper, they believed he had been telling the truth about not being directly involved in the actions of the group. What he could not confirm was what was happening in the electronics shop.

"OK, here is what I want to do moving forward," Major Palmer said once the overview was complete. "Tell the shopkeeper that we will bring him to the Green Zone and protect him while we find a safe place for him to go. I'll make sure a vehicle gets down to you tomorrow to pick him up. We also need to get back down to the village and run through the electronics shop. See if we can catch them off guard by walking in dressed like locals. I'll have an EOD team sent down to the village to take care of any surprises. They can sit outside the village with the quick reaction team to not draw any extra attention. There is also a chance we may end up getting called on for assistance if the brigade working down in your area can get a good read on the location of the leader of this group. From what I understand, they have been hitting them pretty hard over the last month or so, and they plan on picking up the pace over the next couple of months."

"I heard the maneuver brigade took out one of their bomb factories in the city," Captain Starn said. "That probably took some momentum out of their plans."

"I heard the same thing," Major Palmer said, "but I also heard that someone from the maintenance unit took out their moving truck with a grenade launcher and made a big hole out in the desert."

"A mechanic with a grenade launcher," Sergeant First Class Hermanson said quietly to Sergeant Abdullah. "I wonder who that could have been."

"I like my grenade launcher," Sergeant Abdullah answered. "It is very effective."

"OK, Boss," Captain Starn said as he looked around the room. "I don't think there are any questions on this end. We'll head out at oh dark thirty tomorrow morning and get the quick reaction force settled in before our other folks move out and try to blend in with the regular foot traffic."

"Sounds like a plan," Major Palmer responded. "Be careful out there. These folks must feel that we are closing in on them, and they will probably be a little trigger happy."

"OK, folks, we have a lot to get done before tomorrow morning," Captain Starn said as he looked over to Chief Provanski. "Chief, I want you and Master Sergeant Mandess to lead the quick reaction force. I'll take the lead for the walking patrol. Herm, I want you to take two of your terps with you and leave the other two with the quick reaction force. I'll get a couple of drivers and weapons people from the other team. If there is anyone on the walking patrol that doesn't have clothes for the mission, get them back to supply and see what we can do. Any questions?"

"Boss, I have one of the linguists who might be better off to leave here on this one," Sergeant First Class Hermanson stated.

"That's fine, Herm," Captain Starn said. "We'll manage."

The room emptied as everyone left to get ready for the mission. Sergeant First Class Hermanson and Sergeant Abdullah went over to the specialists' quarters to let them know what was going to happen in the morning. Sara and Sergeant Abdullah would be on the walking patrol, while Al Khafaji and Wafiq would be in the quick reaction force. Aisha was not unhappy when she heard the news, but neither were the other three. It seemed like everyone was getting a chance to do what they wanted. Wafiq was the most excited of any of them, but he would rather have been in the walking patrol.

Sergeant First Class Hermanson brought everyone over to the supply room. He figured that now would be a good time to have everyone pick up some street clothes, even if they would not be using them in the morning. They also stopped at the arms room to get AK-47s for Sergeant Abdullah and Sara. When everyone was done drawing their equipment, Sergeant First Class Hermanson told them to get to dinner early and get some rest. They would be meeting up at the vehicles at 0400 hours.

Sergeant Abdullah walked with the specialists to their quarters to see if there was anything they needed help with to prepare for the mission. He didn't really know what level of support they had been providing with their language skills, so he would not be able to do much to prepare them as far as interpretation was concerned, but he could build their confidence in being a member of the team. He remembered how good it felt when the teams he had supported welcomed him as a member of the team, and he would try to do the same for these specialists.

"If there is anything that you have questions about or if you need any help getting your gear together, just let me know. I would be glad to give you a hand," Sergeant Abdullah said to the four specialists. "When you are ready to load your gear, let me know, and I will check to make sure you have everything. It never hurts to have another set of eyes when you are packing out—even old pros can miss something."

"Yes, Sergeant," the specialists said as they worked on laying out their gear.

When it looked like everyone was finished, Sergeant Abdullah went through the equipment that was laid out and gave advice on what to add and what could be left behind. The walking patrol would need to take less gear to fit in with the others walking into the village, while the quick reaction force was less limited in what they could take. Sergeant Abdullah made sure that Sara had more than two hundred rounds of ammunition in addition to the two thirty-round magazines. He also made sure she had a couple of energy bars from her MREs and put the rest of the meals in her rucksack, which would stay in the vehicle.

"You all have very important roles in this mission tomorrow," Sergeant Abdullah said to the specialists. "The Special Forces personnel are placing a great deal of trust in your ability to carry out your part of the mission. That includes you as well, Specialist Hassan. If the maneuver brigade requests support, you will be the only one that will be available to help them. Specialist Ghulam and Specialist Al Khafaji, you are both part of the support team that will save the members of the walking patrol if we come under fire. Your support will be crucial to the success of the mission if that happens. Specialist Rashidi and I are just going for a little hike."

"Yes, Sergeant," the specialists answered with smiles on their faces.

Following dinner, everyone double-checked their gear and went to sleep. They would all need to be up a little after 0300 hours to make sure they were at the vehicles by 0400 hours. Sergeant Abdullah knew it would be difficult for them to get much sleep, but it was a nice long ride out to the dismount point, so he wasn't worried. He was anxious as well to be back out on patrol.

When the others got ready to go to eat, Al Khafaji told them he would be there in a few minutes, and they should go without him. He said he wanted to see if he could check his email before dinner since it was his mother's birthday. Aisha commented on how nice that was as they left to eat. Once they had walked off, Al Khafaji took his phone out and dialed the number to contact his cousin.

"Is this important?" his cousin asked immediately upon answering the phone.

"Yes, there is much activity, and we will be going to the village in the morning to see the electronics shop," Al Khafaji said. The line went dead without a reply. Al Khafaji put the phone away and walked quickly off to the dining facility.

⌒

"Captain Taylor, I just got word that they have confirmed the one KIA from the village as the leader of the local faction of the group we are focused on," Chief MacKenzie said as he walked over to Captain Taylor's desk. "The whole thing sounds a little odd if you ask me. It's almost like the group gave this guy up, along with his two buddies. I mean, they pop up on top of a building, throw some small arms fire down at an armored vehicle, and then basically start walking down the stairs."

"I hear what you are saying, Chief," Captain Taylor replied, "but if they want to get taken out, what are we supposed to do?"

"No, it's not that," Chief MacKenzie answered. "It's just the way it all went down. It stinks like a setup. I just don't know who they are trying to set up. Is it our guys or is it the maneuver brigade folks?"

"What are you trying to get at, Chief?" Captain Taylor asked.

"Well, what if they want everyone to think that we have taken out the lead guy in the area when all along the real leader is trying to slip out under our noses?" Chief MacKenzie thought out loud. "Or better yet, what if they want to cover up what is really going on in that village by making it look like we took out the leader?

"Well, unfortunately for them, they'll find out differently in the morning," Captain Taylor said.

16

Sergeant Abdullah was up at 0315 hours. He checked his gear one more time and opened the door to walk over and check on the specialists. It was almost 0330 hours, and he was hoping they all were at least awake by now. To his surprise, the specialists were leaving their quarters as he walked up.

"Good job, soldiers," Sergeant Abdullah said when he caught up to them. "Did you have a chance to double-check your gear this morning?"

"Yes, Sergeant," they answered as they continued to walk.

Al Khafaji thought that Sergeant Abdullah must think they were all incompetent. He treated them like children. Oh, how Al Khafaji wished he could have been in the walking patrol instead of staying behind in the quick reaction force. It would be so easy to shoot the others during a firefight and return to his group as a hero.

Sergeant First Class Hermanson and a couple of other soldiers were already at the vehicles doing checks. Staff Sergeant Pederson was checking out the machine gun while Staff Sergeant Perez was going through the medical supplies, and Staff Sergeant Ivory was checking on the communications equipment. The other vehicle was being prepped in the same way by the other team, which would provide the bulk of the quick reaction force.

"Come on over, folks," Sergeant First Class Hermanson said when he saw Sergeant Abdullah and the three specialists approaching. "We should be ready to go shortly. Grab a seat. Sergeant Abdullah, if you didn't pick up any real grenades, there's some inside. You should probably grab a few for good measure and give Sara a couple. Better to have them and not need them than need them and not have them."

The two vehicles finished their checks and headed out of the gate. Sergeant First Class Hermanson's vehicle took the lead. The plan was to drive the same route and then go off-road about three kilometers south of the village and set up the quick reaction force about five hundred meters east of the village behind some small rolling hills. The walking patrol would march overland to intersect with the road about a kilometer north of the village. They would merge into the regular foot traffic heading into the village and try to keep ten meters between each one of them, with Captain Starn in the lead and Sara and Sergeant First Class Hermanson in the trail position.

As the lead vehicle approached the part of the road where the ambush had occurred weeks ago, a vehicle turned its lights on and passed in front of the lead vehicle and continued moving up the road. When the lead vehicle did not take up the chase, they started to fire at the lead vehicle with small arms.

"Really? I don't think so," Staff Sergeant Pederson said as he fired one burst from the machine gun at the vehicle. Then, he started to concentrate fire at the suspected firing positions from the previous ambush. The trail vehicle joined in by targeting other potential enemy positions further down the ambush route. One of the enemy fighters with an RPG came out from the side of the little hill that was expected to have been the sniper position in the first ambush. He was shot down by Staff Sergeant Pederson before he could even level the RPG at a target.

The two vehicles made the left turn as planned and continued on their route. They watched as the bait car caught fire and began to burn. The trail vehicle kept their machine gun oriented down the road behind them just in case, but nobody attempted to follow them.

"Don't think they will be trying that again anytime soon," Staff Sergeant Pederson commented.

Captain Starn decided to make a slight change in the route. He decided to go off-road earlier to avoid any additional surprises. He figured that the news had already been sent that they were on the way, and the enemy would have more than thirty minutes to prepare, so he plotted a course that would move them off-road ten kilometers sooner. This meant the walking patrol would have to move much faster on their hike to get to the road leading into the village.

"Our hike this morning to get to the road is going to be about two kilometers instead of one," Captain Starn explained to the members of the walking patrol. "Is everyone going to be OK with that? I need to know now because we are also going to have less time to get ready when we stop and leave the vehicles."

Sergeant First Class Hermanson checked the team to see if anyone was having issues, but he was particularly focused on Sara. He knew she had the will to get it done, but nobody had really tested her endurance yet. He was about to ask her outright if she thought she was able to do it when she spoke up.

"I will not fail this team," she said defiantly. "I will keep up."

That was all Sergeant First Class Hermanson needed to hear. He had no doubts she would do everything in her power to do exactly what she said; nevertheless, he would make sure that Sergeant Abdullah wasn't far away.

It took almost forty-five minutes to travel to the new location and get set up. The new location of the quick reaction force was farther northeast of the previous site. When they stopped, Captain Starn told Staff Sergeant Vincent to send a message to Captain Taylor and Chief MacKenzie to let them know of the modification to the timeline. The walking patrol was on the way less than five minutes after arrival at the site.

"OK, we're going to stay in a traveling formation until I give you the signal to stop near the road," Captain Starn said as they started out. "When we stop, just keep going. Each person stops about ten meters further down the road. One at a time, move out onto the road and mingle in with the foot traffic. Interact with the locals as little as possible, but don't lose sight of the person in front of you."

Captain Starn walked quickly, leading the small group toward the dirt road. Every so often, he would check his watch and walk a little quicker. Sara was managing to keep up with him but was hoping he wouldn't walk much faster.

"If we need to run, then I will run," Sara said as Captain Starn looked at his watch again.

"We are doing fine," Captain Starn replied. "The road is only a couple hundred meters ahead."

They continued walking for another three minutes before Captain Starn held his fist in the air and took a knee. All the others did the same. After another minute, Captain Starn and Sara got up and walked out to the road behind a small group of three other people. Sergeant Abdullah was next, but he had to move onto the road as soon as he was in position to stay ahead of a large group of eight or ten people. Staff Sergeant Perez and Staff Sergeant Ivory stepped out onto the road without anyone else around. Staff Sergeant Perez slowed down, and he and Staff Sergeant Ivory walked together. Sergeant First Class Hermanson walked out onto the road behind two older people whom he quickly passed and nodded his head at.

When they were less than eight hundred meters from the village, a truck came by on the road heading to the village. Captain Starn took a look as it went by, but the back end was closed up. It didn't seem to be riding low, so it probably wasn't carrying a full load. That's when Captain Starn spotted smoke coming from the village. The line of people stopped as others started working their way back out of the village on the dirt road. Captain Starn kept moving forward until he was about one hundred yards from the outskirts of the village.

The truck that had passed them earlier was backed into the opening next to the electronics shop with just the front end sticking out into the road. Captain Starn saw people running from the electronics shop with boxes and weapons. It looked like either the roof or the second floor of the electronics shop was on fire.

"Get up here ASAP and take up a blocking position on the road leaving the village on the north end," Captain Starn said to the quick reaction force on his headset. He then motioned for the rest of his team to move forward and take up positions on the sides of the buildings on each side of the road leaving the village. Captain Starn, Sergeant Abdullah, and Specialist Rashidi were next to the buildings on the left, while Sergeant First Class Hermanson, Staff Sergeant Perez, and Staff Sergeant Ivory were on the right side of the road.

"Don't engage until the truck starts moving in our direction," Captain Starn relayed to his team. "I don't want them to be able to turn that truck around and head in the opposite direction."

Captain Starn kept watch on the truck while it was being loaded. In the meantime, the two vehicles were making their way toward the northern end of the village. What Captain Starn did not know was there were more than thirty militant fighters on the southern end of the village waiting for the Americans to arrive, all thanks to the call from Al Khafaji.

"Alpha six, this is Alpha six one. We are fifty meters from position," the call on the headset said.

"Alpha six one, this is Alpha six. Hold and stand by, out," Captain Starn said. He still had not seen any movement from the truck.

Aisha was on security detail when the operations officer from the infantry battalion called to ask for linguist support. The operations sergeant from the other A Team came and told her that she would need to get her gear together to support another operation. She already had almost everything that she needed, so it took her only ten minutes to go back to the quarters and pick up her rucksack. She was standing at the gate ready to go when the unit vehicle showed up to get her. Aisha had no idea which unit required her support or what their mission was, but she was ready.

The maneuver brigade intelligence section had received information that the leader of the militant cell might be in the city near the northern sector of their area, so they were setting up a mission to move into the city with an infantry company supported by four towed howitzers, two Apache attack helicopters, and two Kiowa helicopters from an attack reconnaissance troop. They planned to enter the city from the south and secure the area block by block until they reached the expected location of the leader of the militant group.

When they arrived at the city, they had five blocks to clear before reaching their target area. They were able to stay in their vehicles for the first two blocks, but then the roads got much narrower, so they moved to using a foot patrol. The infantry unit detained six people and shot one in the first two blocks. While moving through the third block, they got into a brief firefight where they killed four more people and detained two others.

The lead squad of the infantry unit started walking down the fourth block, and Aisha could sense something was not right. She looked around, but all she saw was a group of kids in an open area on the right kicking a ball. She thought she heard a motorcycle, but then one of the kids kicked the ball to another. It rolled past him, and he took one step and stopped as it went out into the road. *The children kick a ball but don't go after it.* The sound of the motorcycle engine got louder as the engine revved.

"The kids kicked a ball but didn't go after it!" Aisha yelled, moving in front of the patrol leader and pushing him back. "It's a bomb!"

"Everybody, get down!" the patrol leader shouted, and the entire squad hit the ground.

The motorcycle kept coming as the driver cried, "God is great!"

The explosive vest the driver wore was loaded down with ball bearings, and it went off just like a large claymore mine when he was about twenty yards from the patrol. The explosion was made even louder as it echoed through the buildings on each side of the narrow road. When the smoke cleared, the next squad moved ahead quickly and began to exchange fire with the enemy while others moved the wounded from the first squad out of the way.

Most of the soldiers had minor wounds, as they had been able to get down before the explosion. Aisha was not that lucky. After she pushed the patrol leader, she was trying to regain her balance and the blast knocked her off her feet. As she went down, a couple of the projectiles smashed into her left arm, shattering her forearm and taking a large chunk out of her upper arm.

At first, she didn't feel much pain. All she knew was her arm felt wet and warm. She saw the other soldiers moving around her but had trouble hearing what they were saying. It seemed all muffled to her, and she didn't understand why.

When the next squad went forward to join in the fight, a medic that was attached to the company stopped and gave her first aid. He put a tourniquet on her arm just below her armpit and gave her morphine for the pain. He put a mark on her head, but she didn't know why.

Another soldier picked her up and carried her back to the vehicles where they had already called for a medevac helicopter. They drove her to the pickup site, which was only five minutes away, and the medevac helicopter landed shortly after.

The soldiers loaded the wounded onto the helicopter. Aisha was one of the last to be loaded on, which meant she would be one of the first to be off-loaded at the trauma center. Aisha's hearing was beginning to clear.

Aisha looked up at the flight nurse when they were loading her on the helicopter. She looked very familiar, but Aisha could not think clearly. She looked up at her and held her hand.

"You're going to be all right, honey," the flight nurse said with a southern accent. "We're going to take good care of you."

Aisha looked at her and a tear came down her cheek. "Can I go home now?"

"Sure, honey. We just need to make a stop first," the nurse said as she put in an IV and gave Aisha more painkillers. "Just rest now."

The helicopter had her to the trauma center in less than fifteen minutes. She was unconscious when they moved her from the helicopter to a surgical suite.

"They are all so young," the flight nurse whispered as the last patients were carried into the trauma center.

The truck started to pull out of the alley next to the electronics shop as several men jumped into the back of the vehicle.

"Now!" Captain Starn yelled into his headset microphone. He and the others began to fire down the road toward the truck as the two armored vehicles came out onto the road firing their machine guns. At some point, someone took the lucky shot that caused the stockpile of explosives on the truck to go off. It caused an unbelievable amount of damage to four of the buildings in the village. None of the people on the truck survived, and the electronics shop was nothing but a burning frame with the front wall almost completely destroyed.

As the smoke started to clear, an RPG round came out of the area behind the remains of the truck and just scraped the left side of one of the armored vehicles. Staff Sergeant Burleson fired several bursts from the machine gun in the direction the round came from. It seemed as if the entire village came alive with small arms fire all directed at the two vehicles. Captain Starn and the others were all firing back at the muzzle flashes, but it was still difficult to really see any true targets.

Captain Starn looked down along the side of the building for the two soldiers near him but did not see Sergeant Abdullah. He hoped that he had not been injured but could not move down to check. Captain Starn and Specialist Rashidi continued to fire rounds down the street. After a few minutes, they heard several explosions down the road followed by several rounds of AK-47 rifle fire.

What Captain Starn did not know was at the beginning of the firefight, Sergeant Abdullah had seen two armed men come out from a building in the village and move off to the east. He had moved over to an area that overlooked the only lower terrain running parallel to the village and seen the two men moving his way. He shot both of them and went down to finish them off with two shots. He then moved up to try to find out which building the men had come out of. Instead, he found a space between two buildings that was just wide enough to walk between if individuals went through the opening one person at a time. Instead of walking out onto the street, Sergeant Abdullah used the walls to inch his way up, putting his feet against one wall and his back against the other. When he got to the top, he pulled himself onto the roof.

When Sergeant Abdullah looked over the edge of the building, he could see more than twenty fighters in the road below him. They were standing in two groups behind two pickup trucks. He took out four hand grenades and pulled the pins on the first two, throwing one at each group. He immediately pulled the pins on the second two and threw them over the edge as well. As soon as the grenades went off, he looked over the edge of the building and emptied both of the thirty-round magazines into the group. Every one of the fighters was either dead or severely wounded. As Sergeant Abdullah was reloading his magazines, he saw another truck heading down the road near the south end of the village.

"Alpha six, this is Carson, over," Sergeant Abdullah said into his headset microphone.

"Carson, this is Alpha six. What is your location?" Captain Starn asked, sounding a little angry.

"I am at the top of a building in the village," Sergeant Abdullah said. "It is clear to advance vehicles now."

"Roger, out," Captain Starn replied with a big smile on his face. "I should have never doubted that guy."

Sergeant Abdullah waited until he saw the two armored vehicles moving in his direction to go back down the wall. He wanted to make sure he had help in case one of the fighters was still able to fire a weapon. He heard the teams getting out of the vehicles and begin searching the area.

"Carson," Captain Starn called out. "Where the hell are you?"

"I am coming out on your left front, sir," Sergeant Abdullah said, inching along the final few feet before getting to the road.

"All right, let's see if Carson left us anything that we can take back to have the intel guys look at," Captain Starn said, and everyone started to check the wounded and dead who were laying on the road. "Make sure to get me a count of KIA and WIA so I can send it up to Captain Taylor. I want to be out of here in fifteen mikes."

It was extremely difficult to get an accurate count of the KIAs in the big truck that blew up, but Sergeant Abdullah totaled eighteen KIAs and five WIAs. Two of the wounded fighters would probably not survive the ride back to the outpost as a result of the wounds they had received. As far as documents went, there was very little that survived the fire and explosions; however, there were several cellular phones found on the fighters and a computer that was found in the rubble of the electronics shop. The soldiers looked around but could not find the village elder anywhere.

Captain Starn gathered all the information he needed to provide a Situation Report to Captain Taylor. When he finished relaying the information, Captain Taylor told him what had happened to Specialist Hassan. She would survive, but the surgeons were not sure she would be able to keep her arm. Only time would tell, but she would be moved to Germany and then on to Walter Reed in the United States. She had finally got her wish and would eventually be heading back home. Captain Starn decided to wait until they all got

back to the outpost to break the news to the others about Specialist
Hassan.

The infantry company fought a running battle through the entire
fourth block of the city. It turned out to be a very bloody encounter,
but they made it through to the final block by calling in a second
company from the battalion. They overwhelmed the enemy fighters
with sheer numbers. Along the way, there were several more IEDs
and suicide bombers. That was one way the intelligence personnel
knew they were getting close to the final objective.

The infantry companies lost a total of more than two platoons of
casualties with most being WIA. The enemy wasn't nearly as lucky.
The estimate was more than forty KIA and at least that many WIA.
The infantry units took twenty-eight wounded prisoners off the field
of battle. The enemy had taken a huge loss, but as the infantry units
prepared to go inside the target building, they realized that trip wire
had been strung across every entrance.

The brigade headquarters ordered the infantry companies to secure
the area and clear the surrounding buildings. The reconnaissance and
attack helicopters flew around the building to see if they could confirm whether it was still occupied. They saw no signs of activity. The
attack helicopters used their guns and fired into the top two floors.
There was no response from inside the building.

The infantry company brought up five of their soldiers with
grenade launchers. The remainder of the soldiers stood well behind
the other five as they started to fire grenades into the building through
windows and doors. Three of the grenades found their way through
the openings, while the other two hit the building and went off outside. When the three grenades went off inside the building there were
multiple follow-on explosions of a larger magnitude, which caused
debris and smoke to pour out of the building.

The infantrymen were eventually able to enter the building once all the smoke cleared. The building was empty. There were no bodies, papers, computers, or cell phones to be found. If the leader of the group had been there, he was long gone, and it looked like he probably knew they were coming well before the fighting even started.

Major Palmer informed Captain Starn that the prisoners needed to be transferred to him outside the city northeast of the village. The intelligence personnel in the Green Zone wanted to question them before putting them in the jail that was being used to hold prisoners of war. They also wanted to have all the cell phones and the laptop as well.

Captain Starn had the team get back into their vehicle, and they headed down the road toward the city. One of the wounded fighters died during the drive, and another was barely hanging on when Major Palmer arrived with another vehicle traveling behind him. The soldiers transferred the prisoners to the new vehicles and continued down the road to the other city. They drove as quickly as possible but still were pummeled with anything that could be thrown in their direction. The locals were really upset this time, and Captain Starn was surprised that nobody was shooting at them.

The two vehicles didn't reach the outpost gate until late afternoon. It had been a long day, but Captain Starn told everyone to be at the dining facility in twenty minutes. He said he wanted to go over the mission and give them news of other operations that were conducted earlier in the day.

The soldiers washed out the back of the vehicles in an attempt to get most of the blood off the floors from the enemy wounded. It took almost fifteen minutes to finish, so they had to hustle over to the dining facility. When everyone arrived, Captain Starn was there with another captain they had not seen before.

"This is Captain Graham," Captain Starn said, motioning to the other captain. "He is a chaplain from another unit, but I asked him to be here because I have some difficult news to tell you. Specialist Hassan was wounded today while supporting a mission with an infantry unit in the city. She has serious injuries and was transported to the trauma center where they operated on her left arm. She is going to be OK but will be going back to the States for further care."

"What happened, sir?" Sara asked. "I thought she was supposed to be here while we were gone."

"The brigade called asking for support, and Specialist Hassan was sent to assist," Captain Starn said and then quickly added more details. "Specialist Hassan saved many lives today when she alerted the infantry unit of a possible bomb. Her actions gave the soldiers time to hit the ground before the explosion, but she was injured."

Are you sure they are talking about the same person? Al Khafaji thought to himself. *The little princess saved someone's life?*

"I am proud of her," Sara said as she focused on keeping her emotions in check. "Can we see her?"

"I don't think that will be possible," Captain Starn said, "but I'll make sure we are notified of everything that happens with her and where she is. If the doctors agree, we may be able to set up a video call with her once she is back in the States."

"Thank you, sir," Sara said.

"The infantry unit was able to reach the building where the suspected leader of the militant cell was located," Captain Starn continued. "But when they got to the building, it was empty, so we are all still actively trying to locate him."

The leader has beaten the infidels once again, Al Khafaji said to himself, but he did smile. He looked up and saw Sergeant Abdullah looking directly at him.

"That is good news that we are getting close to him," Al Khafaji quickly said. "Hopefully they were able to kill many fighters."

"The enemy lost a significant number of fighters," Captain Starn said. "Eventually, we will also catch or kill the leader. It's just a matter of time."

"But we lost Aisha," Wafiq said sadly.

"We have not lost Aisha, Wafiq," Sara said. "She has been wounded, but she is not gone. You can lose her if that is your choice, but when we are back in the United States, I will find her and see her again."

The chaplain said a prayer for Aisha's recovery. The dining facility brought out food from lunch if anyone was hungry, and the soldiers all ate very quietly. The chaplain went from table to table asking if anyone would like to talk about what happened, but nobody was interested in sharing anything with him.

Sergeant Abdullah and the three specialists walked back to their quarters. They all wanted to help pack Aisha's things, but Sara wouldn't hear of it. She said that she could handle it and didn't need any help. She was told to pack everything she could into the duffel bag and make sure it was clearly marked with Aisha's name. Master Sergeant Mandess said that someone would be by the next day to make sure it got shipped back to the United States. If there was anything that she might need or want, like personal items, it was to be put into a small shipping box, and the medical personnel would determine where it would be sent.

Captain Starn and Master Sergeant Mandess went back to the operations building for a video conference with key leaders in the maneuver brigade. The units had done damage in the village and one of the cities, so it wasn't hard to guess where the focus would be next, but the thought had to go through the planners' heads that the enemy was probably thinking the same thing. It was also possible that the group had taken serious enough losses to make them go dormant for a while, allowing them to recruit and rebuild their organization. Captain Starn was happy to see that Major Palmer and Captain Taylor had joined the video conference. That meant that he wouldn't have to join in the conversation unless Major Palmer told him to do so.

The brigade commander started out by talking about what the goal of the operation was and what units were engaged with the enemy. He then turned the briefing over to the brigade operations officer who walked through the timeline of what had actually happened during the day. He did not mention anything about the actions in the village, but Captain Starn figured it was because it was solely a Special Operations mission. He covered friendly and enemy losses and identified the number KIA and WIA for both sides. What he did not discuss was the status of the militant group's leader.

"Yeah, that's great, Mike," the brigade commander said, cutting the operations officer short in his brief. "Can you tell everyone what happened to the leader of the group?"

"Sir," the operations officer said, taking a breath. "We believe he was able to depart the area prior to our forces arriving at the building he was occupying."

"So he fucking got away!" the brigade commander yelled, slamming his hand down on the table. "Look, I don't really give a shit about how many of these bastards we killed. I want this son of a bitch dead or wishing he was lucky enough to be dead. We are going to pull out all stops on this effort. I want to flush him out and fucking squash him like a bug. Is that clear?"

"Yes, sir!" the room shouted. All the unit commanders felt terrible for the operations officer, but there wasn't anyone who would say a word once the brigade commander was in one of his moods. They all knew the old man was probably catching a lot of flak from his superiors, but to a man, they all thought there was a better way to go about motivating them to do a better job.

"Major Palmer, are you online?" the brigade commander asked without looking at the attendee list.

"Yes, sir," Major Palmer answered.

"Great. Can you tell everyone what happened in the village today?" the brigade commander said.

"Sure thing, sir," Major Palmer responded and began to go over what his teams had detailed in their mission reports. He also highlighted the actions of Sergeant Abdullah and said that he was going to put him in for an award. Major Palmer decided to leave out the part about one vehicle getting away.

"That's out-fucking-standing!" the brigade commander exclaimed. He looked less annoyed after hearing the details of Sergeant Abdullah's actions. "How long has this soldier been in your unit?"

"Sir, Sergeant Abdullah has worked with us on several deployments starting out as a specialist," Major Palmer said. "He was just recently transferred to us from the maintenance unit he was assigned to under your command."

"Whoa, wait a minute," the brigade commander said. Everyone in the room expected another outburst. "This soldier is a mechanic?"

"Yes, sir, but that isn't what he originally did," Major Palmer explained. "He joined as an interpreter, and when his MOS was disbanded, he chose to stay in as a mechanic. His actions probably saved Chief MacKenzie's life on a previous deployment."

"Sir," the brigade adjutant said quietly from her chair along the wall of the room. "I believe this is the same soldier who has been recommended for an award by the maintenance company for blowing up a truck from the bomb factory."

"No shit," the brigade commander said. "Well, if I get the chance, I want to meet this warrior and pin his medal on myself."

"Yes, sir," the adjutant said as she wrote herself a note.

The brigade commander also heard updates from the logistics officer and the intelligence section before the meeting came to a close. He told his staff to put their heads together and develop courses of action for the next operation. He wanted to make sure that the plan had considered possible contingencies and included options. The brigade executive officer was tasked with coordinating additional resources if needed to finally bring the militant leader's group to an end. In the brigade commander's mind, that also meant finding a new brigade operations officer.

<h1 style="text-align:center">17</h1>

When Al Khafaji got back to his quarters, he checked the phone and saw that his cousin had tried to call three times. The last call was only an hour ago. He was glad to see that his cousin was OK but didn't know how he would be able to call him back. He decided to try to get on the computer to check his email. Maybe he could send his cousin an email instead of calling him.

Al Khafaji walked into the building where the computer was located, but someone else was using it. He was hoping the other soldier would not be long but had no idea how long he would have to wait. Al Khafaji kept looking at his watch, and the other soldier finally saw him standing there.

"Sorry, I'll be done in a second," the soldier said as he finished up looking through his email and sending replies. "There you go."

"Thank you," Al Khafaji said as he sat down at the computer. He quickly opened his email but didn't see any new messages. He was about to check his junk mail when Staff Sergeant Pederson walked into the room.

"Samir, do you still have that phone the village elder gave you?" Staff Sergeant Pederson asked.

"Yes, Sergeant," Al Khafaji replied as, touching his side just to make sure the phone was still there. "The elder tried to call me three times today. When I tried to return the call, there was no answer."

"Well, Captain Starn wants to try to call the elder to speak about what happened today in his village," Staff Sergeant Pederson explained. "Where is the phone?"

"It is in my quarters," Al Khafaji said. "I will go find it and bring it to the captain."

"OK, but make it quick," Staff Sergeant Pederson said. "Captain Starn is in his office."

"Yes, Sergeant," Al Khafaji said. His mind raced to try to figure out what to do.

Al Khafaji was walking across the open area near the logistics building when he spotted the contractor who had lent him his phone. He walked quickly over to the contractor's vehicle. The contractor was unloading supplies that he had brought in as part of his government contract.

"I never repaid you for allowing me to use your phone," Al Khafaji said to the contractor. "Can I help you unload your vehicle?"

"That is very kind of you, but I am done," the contractor answered. "I will be leaving now."

"I need you to take me with you," Al Khafaji said as he slowly raised the barrel of his rifle. "I cannot tell you anything else until we are away from this place."

"I cannot take you with me," the contractor protested as he began to walk toward the driver's side door.

"Please, I beg you to help," Al Khafaji replied, lowering his rifle. "I cannot help the Americans fight against our own people any longer."

"I know it must be difficult, but it is your job as a soldier," the contractor said as he moved closer to Al Khafaji. "That is the choice you made. I cannot fix that for you."

Al Khafaji thought this might be his only chance, so he waited for the contractor to come a little closer. He swung his rifle up and struck the contractor on the side of his head. Al Khafaji then took the sling from his rifle and wrapped it around the man's neck, twisting the sling tighter and tighter until the man fell limp at his feet. Al Khafaji picked him up and put him in the passenger's seat of the truck. Then, he hurried around to the other side and started the truck. He wanted to step on the gas and go as fast as he could, but he slowly drove toward the front gate to avoid attracting attention.

The guards did not recognize him and thought the contractor was asleep. They checked the back of the vehicle, and when they saw that it was empty, they waved him through the gate. Al Khafaji drove off toward the village and stopped at the ambush site to see if he could contact his cousin again. He called the number, and this time, his cousin answered.

"Hello. Why are you calling?" his cousin asked.

"I am not worried about speaking with you, cousin. I am no longer with the infidels," Al Khafaji proudly said to his cousin. "I want to join you and the leader to fight for our people."

"I almost did not make it out of the village today," his cousin said in a quiet voice. "Are you sure that you want to be a fighter?"

"Of course," Al Khafaji said without hesitation. "That was always the plan. That is why I was sent to school in the United States, and that is why I joined the Army."

"Yes, but things are different now," his cousin said. "We lost many fighters and are not as strong as we were before. The leader is trying to bring in other fighters, but right now, we have less than one hundred left."

"I am still ready to give my life for our cause," Al Khafaji stated defiantly. "I am not afraid to die. If you have lost your will, just give me fighters, and I will find a way to make the infidels suffer."

"It is so easy for you," his cousin said, sounding tired. "You have not had to look death in the face yet."

"Can you meet me in the village?" Al Khafaji asked his cousin.

"I am already there," his cousin replied. "We came back after the Americans left. I had something that the leader wanted me to do."

"I will be there in less than an hour," Al Khafaji responded, glancing over at the contractor.

Al Khafaji got out of the truck and walked over to the passenger's side of the vehicle. When he opened the door, the contractor fell out of the truck. Al Khafaji knew the contractor was dead, but he took his rifle and shot him once in the head just to make sure. That would be his second mistake. The first was taking the phone with him.

$$\backsim$$

"Where the hell is Al Khafaji?" Captain Starn groused as he waited for the phone. "It's been almost a half hour waiting for him to bring that phone. I hope to hell he didn't lose it."

"I'll go see what is going on," Staff Sergeant Pederson said. "He should have been here by now. He said that the elder tried to call him three times today. Al Khafaji said he had tried to call the elder, but there was no answer."

"OK, let's try to find Al Khafaji and get that phone," Captain Starn said, trying to keep calm. "I think the elder may have more to do with everything than we imagined. Hell, it wouldn't surprise me if he was the leader of the group everyone is trying to find."

When Staff Sergeant Pederson stopped by the computer room, Al Khafaji wasn't there, so he went over to the dining facility. Al Khafaji wasn't there either. Staff Sergeant Pederson walked over to Al Khafaji's quarters, but Specialist Ghulam was the only one there.

"Wafiq, have you seen Samir?" Staff Sergeant Pederson asked. "I need to find him. Captain Starn wants to talk with him."

"No, Sergeant," Wafiq replied. "I thought he was going to check his email."

"Yep, he isn't there either," Staff Sergeant Pederson said. "Do you know where he put the phone that the village elder gave him?"

"I think it was in his rucksack," Wafiq said.

Staff Sergeant Pederson found Al Khafaji's rucksack and looked through all the pockets but couldn't find anything. He also checked Al Khafaji's duffel bag and his bed with no success.

"Is there any other place you think he might have gone?" Staff Sergeant Pederson asked.

"No, Sergeant," Wafiq answered. "Have you spoken with Sara? She may know where he is."

Staff Sergeant Pederson hastened over to Sara's quarters and knocked on the door. When nobody answered, he went in, but Sara was not there. He strode out of the quarters and saw Sara walking by the operations building.

"Sara, have you seen Samir?" Staff Sergeant Pederson called out.

"No, Sergeant," Sara replied. "I have not seen him since we left the dining facility."

"OK, thanks," Staff Sergeant Pederson said. "Where the hell did he go."

He figured he would head back to the operations building to see if Al Khafaji went straight there with the phone to give it to Captain Starn. He wasn't surprised when he got there, and Al Khafaji wasn't there either. Staff Sergeant Pederson felt it was time to break the bad news to Captain Starn and the others. Al Khafaji was gone.

Al Khafaji drove the truck as fast as it would go on the dirt road. The only times he slowed down were when he came to a turn or when there was a dip in the road. He was making really good time. He had to slow down as he neared the village to make sure he didn't alarm anyone. The last thing he wanted to do was get in a firefight with the people he was hoping to fight alongside, and he knew the fighters must be on edge after what had happened.

As the truck slowed down, two armed men walked out into the road. They motioned for him to stop. One of the fighters walked toward the driver's side of the vehicle, and the other walked toward the back.

"What are you doing here?" the man asked Al Khafaji as he got closer to the driver's door.

"I am here to help my cousin," Al Khafaji answered. "Can you tell him that I am here?"

"So, you must be Samir," the man said as he lowered his rifle. "Peace be with you."

"And may peace be unto you," Al Khafaji replied.

"Samir!" a voice called out from the building. His cousin Abdurrahim came running out into the street. "It is good to see you. Come in and let's talk. Move this truck behind the buildings so it cannot be seen from the road."

One of the fighters stepped up into the truck cab and drove it away, while the other fighter moved back to his position inside the building. Al Khafaji and his cousin went inside the building where a table was set up in the back room with two glasses of tea already poured for them. As Al Khafaji looked around, he could see only one more person with a rifle.

"It is good to see you again, Samir," Abdurrahim said as he sat down. "So why are you here now? What has happened?"

"The Americans wanted the phone the elder gave me," Al Khafaji explained. "They would have seen the calls we made and figured out what I was doing. The infidels I worked with are very smart, and they would have tortured me to make me tell them about you and the leader."

"Then it is good that you were able to come here," Abdurrahim said as he drank his tea. "But how did you get a truck?"

"It belonged to the contractor that I killed," Al Khafaji said, starting to feel a little uncomfortable about all the questions. "Do you not believe that I have come to join you in the fight?"

"Of course, I believe you," Abdurrahim replied. "I would never doubt you, Samir. I just need to be able to explain everything to the leader when I speak with him. I must be able to give him all the details. I do not want him to have any doubts because I think you should be considered for one of the leader positions in our group. I am sure the leader will agree with me when we speak."

"Thank you, cousin," Al Khafaji said. "I would be honored to help lead our people to victory against the infidels. I have dreamed of this for years."

❧

"What do you mean he is gone?" Captain Starn demanded. He couldn't believe what he had just heard.

"I checked everywhere, and he isn't anywhere on this outpost, Boss," Staff Sergeant Pederson said. "It looks like he may have taken the phone with him."

"All right, get with the security folks and close down the outpost. Nobody comes in or goes out without 100 percent identification checks. That also includes full inspections of every vehicle. If he is still here, I don't want him getting out of this post. I also want you to find out how many vehicles left in the last two hours," Captain Starn commanded as he laid out a plan to figure out where Al Khafaji could have gone. "We need to ask them if they remember which direction the vehicles went when they left. I also want three vehicles ready to move out as soon as we collect any intel on his most likely route."

"Roger that, Boss," Staff Sergeant Pederson said. "I'll head down to the gate and see what they can tell me."

Staff Sergeant Pederson ran out of the building and headed toward the front gate. He wanted to get answers as soon as possible so his team might have a chance at catching Al Khafaji. He didn't really know why Al Khafaji chose today to leave, but it must have had something to do with the phone. Staff Sergeant Pederson reached the gate and told the guards to write down all the information they could remember from the last two hours.

"Sir, do you want me to check the cameras?" Chief Provanski asked.

"What cameras are you talking about, Chief?" Captain Starn asked.

"I was trying to check on spies and put out some trail cameras last week," Chief Provanski explained. "When they record, they send video to my computer."

"Yes, Chief," Captain Starn replied. "That would be great. Let me know if anything comes up."

Chief Provanski checked the computer feed from the two cameras over the last two hours. He ran everything fast-forward to try to pinpoint any recordings of Al Khafaji.

Staff Sergeant Pederson got the list of vehicles from the guards after they worked on it for five minutes. It looked like there were either three or four vehicles that went through the gate. One of the lines was scratched out. When Staff Sergeant Pederson asked about it, they said that was the same military vehicle that left and came back.

So, there were only two civilian vehicles that left the outpost. Both were trucks, and both were empty except for drivers and passengers in the front. The guards said that one of the passengers seemed to be asleep as they waved the truck through the gate. Staff Sergeant Pederson asked which way they turned, and the guards said that one turned left, and one turned right. The truck with the sleeping passenger turned left.

That's got to be it, Staff Sergeant Pederson thought. *He is headed back to the village.*

"Boss, I think I found something on the camera near the logistics building," Chief Provanski said to Captain Starn. "There is only the front of a truck, but it looks like someone is putting another person into the front seat, and then they get into the driver's seat. It's a little hard to tell, but I think that looks like Al Khafaji."

Captain Starn took a look at the still picture from the video clip, and although he could not be 100 percent sure, it looked close enough for him. Shortly after Captain Starn looked at the picture, Staff Sergeant Pederson came running back inside the building.

"Boss, it looks like Al Khafaji might have left the outpost in a contractor's truck and could be headed toward the village," Staff Sergeant Pederson announced, trying to catch his breath.

"OK, time to head out and see what we can find," Captain Starn said, and the three of them headed toward the waiting vehicles.

"We're heading to the village," Captain Starn called out to the other vehicle commanders. "I'll take lead."

"How many fighters are here?" Al Khafaji asked his cousin.

"We have seven including the two of us," Abdurrahim said, "but this village is very well protected."

Abdurrahim took Al Khafaji down the hall to the back of the building and showed him a hidden entrance to a tunnel system that ran between the buildings. He explained to him that the tunnel ran under both sides of the village. There were also connector tunnels that went from one side of the road to the other.

"Through these tunnels, our seven fighters can look like many more," Abdurrahim said to Al Khafaji. "We can even cross from side to side in two places, so when they go to one side, we can shoot them from the other side of the street."

"That sounds like a good plan, but why don't we do this as well?" Al Khafaji drew a small diagram on the dirt floor.

"Yes, I think that will work well," Abdurrahim agreed as he looked down at the symbols.

"We should start getting everything in place," Al Khafaji suggested as he looked around. "The Americans will not take long to realize what has happened, and they will come to find me."

The other fighters were called into the building. Abdurrahim explained what the plan of attack would be. Each of them was given a location to start and another one to move to. They all had several hundred rounds of ammunition and four thirty-round magazines. Everything was set—now all they had to do was wait for the infidels to arrive.

245

"Everyone, stop!" Captain Starn called over the radio. Looking out to the right, he saw a body lying near the side of the road. "Carson, go out and take a look. See if he is still alive."

"Roger," Sergeant Abdullah said as he exited the vehicle and walked over to the body. He checked for any visible booby traps but didn't see anything. He saw the entry wound in the man's forehead and the large pool of blood on the ground behind him. There was no need to check for a pulse; he was dead.

"He is dead, sir," Sergeant Abdullah said as he reentered the vehicle. "I did not recognize him, but he was an older man."

"Most likely he was the contractor," Captain Starn sighed, wondering why the contractor had been shot and left on the side of the road. "All right, let's get out of here and head toward the village."

The three vehicles drove off down the road. Captain Starn was hoping to not have to stop again. It was getting late into the day, and he wanted to be heading back to the outpost before dark.

"I want to run this similar to what we did the last time we were out this way," Captain Starn called out on the radio when they were about ten kilometers from the village. "Trail vehicle, I want you to pull off and head northeast. The other two vehicles will continue to the southern end of the village."

"Roger," the reply came from the other two vehicle commanders. The trail vehicle pulled off the road and proceeded to head northeast.

"All right, take it down to about half speed," Captain Starn told the driver. "I want to give the trail vehicle time to get into place."

The vehicles continued to slow down as they waited for a report from the third vehicle. Finally, when they were roughly one kilometer from the village, the third vehicle called in to let Captain Starn know they were in place. When they were within two hundred meters of the village, they were able to see that the street was empty of vehicles and people.

"Can you see any people on the road heading into the village from your direction?" Captain Starn asked the third vehicle's commander, now positioned on the northern end of the city.

"There isn't anyone on the street right now, but there are a lot of folks heading north on the road about two hundred meters away," the vehicle commander reported. "There isn't anyone heading south on the road."

"OK, folks, I think we found our man and his friends," Captain Starn said. "Take it slow and watch for any movement."

"Why are they just sitting in place?" Abdurrahim asked Al Khafaji as they watched the two vehicles sitting just outside the village.

"I think they are expecting something to happen," Al Khafaji replied as he continued to scan the road for any targets. "We should be patient and let them move toward us. They do not want to leave the safety of their vehicles."

Al Khafaji was partially right. Captain Starn had no plans to commit his men until he had an idea of what they were facing. He had no idea if Al Khafaji was in the village, and if he was, Captain Starn did not know if he was by himself or if there were fifty other fighters with him. He couldn't engage any of the buildings unless there was a threat, and he had no idea if there were any civilians still in the buildings. Captain Starn had to be patient and see how things played out.

"Staff Sergeant Burleson, do you have any type of a shot at the rubble that used to be the electronics shop?" Captain Starn asked over his headset on the internal communications line.

"I can see the pile, but not sure what I am looking for," Staff Sergeant Burleson said.

"If you can see it and hit it, fire off a few bursts," Captain Starn said.

Staff Sergeant Burleson lined the machine gun up on the pile of rubble and fired a few short bursts. A few rounds ricocheted off into the distance but most just impacted into the pile. There was no response from anyone.

"That's it. Everyone must stay calm," Al Khafaji said as he watched the two vehicles. "They are afraid to come in and find us. The infidels are cowards."

"OK, so wherever they are, that wasn't close enough," Captain Starn said as he looked out at the other buildings, hoping to see something that didn't look right. "What about the top portion of the market building? Can you hit that?"

"Sure thing, Boss," Staff Sergeant Burleson responded, moving the machine gun around toward the roof of the building where the market was and fired off a short burst. There once again was no noticeable movement or response.

"Are we going to just let them continue to fire at different buildings without shooting back?" Abdurrahim asked Al Khafaji.

"Yes, for now," Al Khafaji replied. He was enjoying playing with the infidels. "When the time is right, they will know we are here."

Captain Starn directed the other vehicle to pull up closer to him, and he had his driver move a little more to the right side of the road. Now both vehicles' machine guns were pointing down the road and scanning the area for targets. The machine guns being moved as they traversed from side to side was definitely noticeable both by sight and by sound, but there still was no response from inside the village.

"Carson, do you think you can get a round from your grenade launcher on the roof of the market building?" Captain Starn asked.

"Yes, sir," Sergeant Abdullah answered as he exited the back of the vehicle with his rifle.

Sergeant Abdullah carefully peered around the corner of the vehicle and looked down the street at the market building. He loaded a grenade in the grenade launcher, took a breath, and then stepped into the narrow space between the two vehicles. When Sergeant Abdullah raised his rifle to fire the grenade, he noticed a person looking out of one of the other buildings. Sergeant Abdullah pulled the trigger and the grenade headed down the street toward its target. The round exploded on top of the building as Sergeant Abdullah moved back inside the vehicle and closed the door again.

"Sir, it looked like there was a person in the third building on the left," Sergeant Abdullah said to Captain Starn.

"OK, can we put a couple rounds right near the base of the building?" Captain Starn said to Staff Sergeant Pederson.

"Sure thing, Boss," Staff Sergeant Pederson said as he squeezed off a short burst from the machine gun that hit less than a foot from the base of the building.

"Now is the time to pull them into the trap," Al Khafaji said. "Begin firing and move after firing ten rounds."

Five fighters began to shoot at the armored vehicles from the houses on the west side of the street. They stopped firing after ten rounds and then moved into the tunnels and made their way to the other side of the road. When they got to the other side, they moved into position while Al Khafaji and Abdurrahim continued to fire from the west side of the street. Now they just had to wait until the Americans got out of their vehicles to try to enter the buildings on the western side of the street.

"Something stinks, Boss," Master Sergeant Mandess said over the radio. "Every time they want us to do something, they fire at the armored vehicles with small arms. I'm just not sure what they want us to do."

"I hear you, Top," Captain Starn replied, looking out at the buildings on the west side of the street. "Empty the gun on the west side of the street."

Staff Sergeant Pederson began firing into the buildings and moving the machine gun from south to north along the road. Big chunks were flying off the exterior walls of the buildings. When the machine gun finally went silent, Al Khafaji and Abdurrahim started firing again at the vehicles.

"The only way we are going to get them out of there is to dismount and go in," Master Sergeant Mandess said to Captain Starn. "I'll have Staff Sergeant Burleson lay into them with our machine gun while Staff Sergeant Pederson is reloading. I can take my team around the corner while the gun is firing and then inch our way along the wall until we get to their building. Throw some grenades in and go through the front door."

"OK, Top," Captain Starn said. "I'll have my team ready to go at the back of the vehicle in case something comes up."

"Roger that," Master Sergeant Mandess said as he moved his team out of the vehicle under the sound of the machine gun fire.

The team formed up along the wall with Chief Provanski as the number one man and Staff Sergeant Vincent as the number two. Master Sergeant Mandess followed as the number three and Specialist Ghulam took the trail position as number four. They moved past the first building and were hugging the wall of the second building when the five fighters now on the east side of the street opened fire. The team made for an easy target, and many of the rounds fired by the enemy hit their mark. The machine guns from the two vehicles traversed to the east side of the street as quickly as they could and started to fire into the buildings. The fighters were forced to take cover.

Captain Starn and his team rushed out to move the wounded off the street while the machine guns kept the fighters pinned down. It was almost impossible for Captain Starn to direct the team with anything other than hand signals over the sound of the machine guns firing. Captain Starn and Sergeant Abdullah provided overwatch while Sergeant First Class Hermanson, Sergeant First Class Wichman, and Staff Sergeant Ivory helped move the wounded. Most of the team had been shot in the legs, but Chief Provanski also had a gunshot wound on the side of his neck. Specialist Ghulam was shot in the shoulder and the side of his helmet but was able to still stay in the fight.

Sergeant Abdullah took aim at the third building on the east side of the road and fired a grenade into it. He immediately put in a new round and fired another grenade into the next building and continued down the line until he had fired six grenades. There was no additional firing or movement from inside the buildings.

"Alpha three two, this is Alpha six, over," Captain Starn said as they moved back toward the vehicles.

"Alpha three two, over," the voice said.

"I want you to pull up next to the road but don't pull onto the road," Captain Starn said as he continued to look for movement from either side of the road through the village.

"Roger that," the voice said. Captain Starn heard the vehicle's engine revving as it pulled up through the brush.

"We should go down the road and kill them all," Abdurrahim said to Al Khafaji as they headed through the tunnel. "You will be a great leader of our group. The leader will be very pleased with you."

"I want them all dead so we can put their heads on stakes outside of the village," Al Khafaji said as his anger continued to build. "They killed our families, and now they also will die."

Al Khafaji and Abdurrahim continued until they came to a turn in the tunnel. That's when they heard the explosions going off from Sergeant Abdullah's grenade launcher. Shortly after the last explosion, their men started moving into the tunnel that crossed under the road. There were only four fighters.

"Where is your brother?" Abdurrahim said to one of the fighters.

"He was in the building where the first explosion happened," the fighter muttered as tears welled up in his eyes. "I did not see him enter the tunnel."

"He is a brave man and will enjoy all of the gifts of a true believer," Al Khafaji said, putting his hand on the shoulder of the fighter. "We are all brothers."

"What does it look like, Doc?" Captain Starn asked Sergeant First Class Wichman.

"No arterial bleeding but a lot of blood loss on a couple of them," Sergeant First Class Wichman stated. "We would be safe to call for a bird. I can go with them and set up a landing zone, and then we can turn around and get back into the fight."

"OK, why don't you head out northeast of the village and about three clicks out?" Captain Starn suggested, thinking out loud. "I want them to think we are calling in the cavalry. We are just going to sit tight and see if we can rattle their cage."

"Roger that," Sergeant First Class Wichman replied, and he called in the medevac request. The medevac radioman told Sergeant First Class Wichman the ETA would be fifteen minutes. "I'll blow the bugle when we are on our way back, Boss."

The vehicle backed out of position and headed off around the buildings on the east side of the street. They moved along the same path that had been used on another mission, staying in a shallow depression that ran all the way to the northern end of the village. Sergeant First Class Wichman planned to use a panel to mark the landing zone, but Captain Starn instructed him to use smoke. He also said to make sure to throw two or three extra canisters downwind of the landing zone once the helicopter landed to pick up the wounded.

Sergeant First Class Wichman made sure the landing zone was clear of any obstacles and waited for the helicopter to get within sight of his position. When he heard the helicopter coming into range, he threw a canister out for visual recognition by the pilot. The pilot verified the color of the smoke and proceeded to land.

Sergeant First Class Wichman assisted the crew in loading the patients and explaining what he had already done in the way of treatment. He took the other canisters, walked about twenty meters downwind, and began tossing them further downwind. Once he was done, he got back in his vehicle and returned to the side of the building. Captain Starn had also asked him to pull behind the building so the vehicle would not be visible to anyone in the village.

Al Khafaji and Abdurrahim made their way back into their original positions on the west side of the street in the two buildings next to the remains of the electronics shop. Al Khafaji looked out to the south and was surprised to see only one vehicle parked at the southern end of the village. That was when he noticed the smoke behind the buildings on the east side of the road. The smoke was blowing to the south, so he had no idea where it was actually set off.

When Al Khafaji looked back at the vehicle, he saw soldiers moving toward the buildings on the west side of the road, with Captain Starn in the lead. Al Khafaji and Abdurrahim tried to fire at the soldiers, but they could not hit them without leaning out the window. The fighters on the east side of the road must not have been in position yet.

"Now, Carson!" Captain Starn yelled out.

Sergeant Abdullah turned toward the buildings on the east side of the road and started to fire grenades through the windows once again. Two of the fighters attempted to fire back, but the other two were not as lucky. They had just come up from the tunnel when the grenades came through the window. Captain Starn and Sergeant First Class Hermanson engaged the two fighters in the other buildings, and the shooting stopped.

"OK, bring your vehicle up onto the street," Captain Starn said over his headset. "Pull up near us and have your team check out the buildings on the east side of the road."

"Roger, on the way," the voice responded. The vehicle came quickly over the little hill and turned onto the street.

Abdurrahim stepped out from the building he was in and started shooting at Captain Starn and his men. He hit Captain Starn in his hand and vest, knocking him back into Sergeant Abdullah. Sergeant First Class Hermanson squeezed off a burst from his rifle and caught Abdurrahim in the chest. Al Khafaji saw what happened and wanted to go to his cousin, but he knew there was nothing he could do for him. He turned his back to his cousin and went back down into the tunnel.

The other team found the five dead fighters in the buildings on the east side of the street. While they were looking through the building that was near the center of the village, they saw a dim light coming from the back of the building on the floor.

"What is that?" Sara asked one of the soldiers.

"I'm not sure," he said. "Maybe it is a storage cellar."

Sara walked over for a closer look and noticed the light was coming from under a large rug that was moved to the side. She took her hand and felt around the side of the rug for any trip wires or mines but didn't feel anything. She slowly folded the edge of the rug back until she could see the hole and steps leading to the tunnel.

"We got some kind of tunnel over here!" the soldier yelled out to the other team members.

"We found one in the other building too," someone else called out.

Specialist Rashidi went down inside the tunnel to see if there were any more of the fighters hiding. She stayed as close to the wall as she could get just in case someone came out from a hiding place. When she came to a part of the tunnel that turned to the left, she stopped to see if she could hear anyone else. She heard someone moving through the tunnel, but she thought it must have been a good distance away as the sounds were very faint.

Sergeant Abdullah made sure that Captain Starn was OK and then moved forward toward the building where Abdurrahim had appeared from. He nudged Abdurrahim's body as he walked by just to make sure he was dead. Sergeant Abdullah pushed through the door and fell onto the floor, looking around the room for Al Khafaji, but he wasn't there.

Sergeant Abdullah got up and saw a wooden box near the back of the room with a hole right next to it. The end of a ladder was barely visible sticking out of the top of the hole. Sergeant Abdullah looked over the edge of the hole and could see the bottom, as there seemed to be a light in the tunnel. He could hear something in the tunnel but had no idea who it was.

"Samir!" Sergeant Abdullah yelled down into the hole. "You must come out and surrender. You cannot survive."

"I will die avenging my people," Al Khafaji retorted as he tried to think of a way to get out of the tunnel. "What greater honor is there than that?"

Specialist Rashidi could hear Al Khafaji speaking with Sergeant Abdullah. She lay down on the ground and peered around the corner. She saw Al Khafaji standing at the other end of the tunnel, looking down to his left with his rifle held up in front of him.

"You are wrong," Sergeant Abdullah said. "There is no great honor by dying in a hole in the ground. The people that you think you are fighting for will never know what happened to you."

"How can you tell me what is right or what is wrong?" Al Khafaji said. "You are a traitor to your people. You will not be looked upon kindly when your time comes."

"I live my life as a good person doing what I believe is right," Sergeant Abdullah said. "I do not kill the innocent like you have done. How will you explain that when your time comes?"

"If death is for the greater good, then it is acceptable," Al Khafaji replied. "I am a warrior for my people."

"Do you realize that you are the only one of your group who is still alive?" Sergeant Abdullah asked.

"I do not believe you," Al Khafaji said. "You are a liar and no better than the other infidels. If you come down here, I will kill you."

"Oh, shut the fuck up!" Sara shouted to Al Khafaji. A burst of gunfire followed. She knew that he was dead as soon as she pulled the trigger. It was impossible to miss from such a short distance.

"Samir, what is going on?" Sergeant Abdullah yelled into the tunnel.

"It is Specialist Rashidi, Sergeant," Sara responded as she worked her way through the tunnel. "Samir is dead."

Sergeant Abdullah went down into the tunnel to make sure that Al Khafaji was indeed dead. He had managed to get away once, and Sergeant Abdullah wasn't going to let that happen again. Al Khafaji was not moving when he reached him, but he was still breathing.

"So, you have done it," Al Khafaji said quietly once he saw Sergeant Abdullah. "I am ready to die, but there is much more to the plans the leader has. He will bring the fight to the very den of the beast, and all will understand just how powerful he is."

Al Khafaji's last words were difficult to hear or understand as he struggled to breathe. Sergeant Abdullah searched Al Khafaji and found the phone. He also found a small notebook with several pages of notes. He put both the items in his pocket so he could turn them over to the intelligence personnel for review.

Sergeant Abdullah noticed that the tunnel, which looked like it only had one possible turn where Al Khafaji died, actually had another tunnel that went in the opposite direction. The turn was immediately across from Al Khafaji. There was no light, and it looked like it was just a depression in the wall, but once Sergeant Abdullah walked over, he noticed that another section of the tunnel went off to the right.

"There is another section to the tunnel down here, but I need a light to go any further," Sergeant Abdullah said over his headset.

"Roger, Sergeant," Specialist Rashidi replied. "I will find some lights and bring them down to you."

Specialist Rashidi returned to the tunnel after a few minutes. She came down the steps so fast Sergeant Abdullah thought she was going to fall. She was carrying two large headlamps with her rifle strapped over her shoulder. She handed Sergeant Abdullah one of the headlamps and put one on as well. She started to move toward the opening.

"Nope, I will take the lead," Sergeant Abdullah said. "Keep the barrel of your rifle over my left shoulder and keep your focus to the front. We have no idea what we are walking into."

Sergeant Abdullah cautiously moved forward, checking for any booby traps or trip wires. They only had to walk about ten meters before they came to a large opening. When the light from their headlamps illuminated the opening, they saw they were entering a large room. They were even more surprised when they saw what was in it.

The room must have been about fifteen feet wide and twenty feet long. There were stacks of mines and explosives five feet high. Along one wall were boxes of ball bearings and nails. One box had Velcro vests of all different sizes, some of them small enough to fit a child.

Another wall had cases of ammunition for AK-47s, rocket-propelled grenade rounds, and launchers.

"We found a large room full of ammunition and explosives," Sergeant Abdullah relayed to the team members on the ground.

"Roger. I'll see if we can get an explosives ordnance disposal team out here," Captain Starn said. "Is there anything else down there?"

"It looks like there may be another ladder leading up to another building," Sergeant Abdullah said. "Do you want us to check it out?"

"Negative. Just head back our way," Captain Starn instructed as he looked down the road. "I'm thinking that you are probably near the electronics shop judging from the layout of the tunnels. I don't think that is much of a surprise to anyone."

"Roger. We are headed back up," Sergeant Abdullah said. He and Specialist Rashidi began to move back to the main tunnel. Sergeant Abdullah looked at Specialist Rashidi and waved her forward. "Now you can lead."

Specialist Rashidi walked down the tunnel until they arrived at the opening that had been used to get into the tunnel system. She went up the ladder with Sergeant Abdullah following her. They were both happy to be above ground again. Sergeant First Class Hermanson was waiting for them at the top of the ladder.

"Excellent job. That is an amazing find, Carson. Nice work," Sergeant First Class Hermanson congratulated Sergeant Abdullah. "That will be a huge hit against that group's ability to cause any more damage in this area. Captain Starn wants to see both of you."

"Thanks, Herm, but it was Specialist Rashidi who found the room," Sergeant Abdullah said. Specialist Rashidi looked at him with a surprised look on her face.

"Great job, Sara," Sergeant First Class Hermanson said as they all walked over to the vehicle to speak with Captain Starn.

"That was some damn fine work," Captain Starn commented, adjusting the bandage on his hand. He must have lost quite a bit of blood as the gauze bandage was almost completely dark.

"Boss, maybe we should take a trip to the field hospital and let them take a look at your hand," Sergeant First Class Wichman suggested to Captain Starn.

"Probably not a bad idea, Doc," Captain Starn replied. "Herm, make sure you wrap things up here with the other team. I need you all to stick around until the EOD crew gets here. We also need to get Al Khafaji out of that tunnel. Traitor or not, he was still an American when he died."

"We got it covered, Boss," Sergeant First Class Hermanson said. "Hey, Doc, do you want to take Wafiq with you just in case?"

"Yep, good idea," Sergeant First Class Wichman said and then motioned to Specialist Ghulam. "Come on, soldier. We're going to take Captain Starn into the medical treatment center, and we need you to help us out."

"Yes, Sergeant," Specialist Ghulam responded, hurrying over to the vehicle. He felt very proud to be called a soldier. "What can I do?"

"I'm going to ride back here with the boss," Sergeant First Class Wichman replied as he looked at Sergeant Nichols. "I want you to ride up front with this guy to make sure he doesn't get lost."

Sergeant Nichols just smiled as Specialist Ghulam got into the passenger seat of the vehicle, which was normally reserved for the vehicle commander. When everyone was ready to go, Sergeant Nichols pulled forward and headed north on the road through the village. Sergeant First Class Wichman radioed ahead to the field hospital to let them know he was bringing in a patient.

"OK, folks, let's figure out how to get Al Khafaji out of the tunnel," Sergeant First Class Hermanson said once the other vehicle had left the village. "I think we are going to have to carry him to the tunnel opening and use the winch on the vehicle to get him out."

"Why don't we bring him up through the electronics shop?" Sergeant Abdullah suggested. "I think the ladder near the explosives room was for the electronics shop."

"If you are right, we'll save a lot of time," Sergeant First Class Hermanson said. "Head back down there and see where it leads."

Sergeant Abdullah and Sara went back down the tunnel. "Sergeant, why did you tell them that I found the explosives?" Specialist Rashidi asked as they walked.

"You were there with me," Sergeant Abdullah explained. "I am getting medals for doing things. I think there are plenty of medals to go around."

"Yes, Sergeant, but it was still not my doing," Specialist Rashidi countered. However, she understood Sergeant Abdullah's position.

"Well, then, just think of it as an award for making Al Khafaji shut up," Sergeant Abdullah replied.

"Yes, Sergeant," Specialist Rashidi said. "I am sorry for losing my temper with him."

"You have nothing to be sorry for, Sara," Sergeant Abdullah said. "You are a good soldier, and I am proud to serve with you."

They found the ladder, and Sergeant Abdullah went up to find out where it led. When he got to the top, he tried to make enough room to get out, but something was blocking the way. He tried again and felt it give a little. He heard someone walking above him.

"Carson, where are you?" Sergeant First Class Hermanson said.

"We are right here," Sergeant Abdullah answered as he pushed up on whatever was covering the opening one more time.

"Keep talking. I need to clear away some of this mess to get you out," Sergeant First Class Hermanson said as he started moving boards and pieces of the wall. He eventually moved enough of the debris out of the way so Sergeant Abdullah could squeeze through. Once Specialist Rashidi got out, they all started working on clearing the area around the hole so they could pull Al Khafaji out.

Sergeant First Class Hermanson had one of the vehicles pull up as close as possible to the back of the building where the hole was located. They carried Al Khafaji's body over to the bottom of the hole and wrapped the winch around his chest. When they started to reel in the line to the winch, Al Khafaji began to move up through the hole. Sergeant Abdullah came up the ladder once Al Khafaji started to move to make sure his body did not get stuck. Once he was out of the hole, they put Al Khafaji into a body bag so they could transport him back to the outpost.

The EOD team arrived thirty minutes later. Sergeant Abdullah brought them into the tunnel and showed them where the explosives room was located. They were told to take pictures and send them back to the headquarters in the Green Zone before taking any action.

When the headquarters reviewed the pictures, they contacted the EOD personnel and asked them what the options would be for the stockpile of explosives. The EOD specialist explained to them where the explosives were located and the proximity to other structures. He also mentioned that since the stockpile of explosives was underground there would be less damage to the village if they blew it up in place. The only other thing that he mentioned was that it might create a huge crater that could affect traffic on the road through the village.

"Clear the village out as much as possible and blow the stockpile up where it stands," the headquarters personnel said after ten min-utes of debate. There were some in the Green Zone who wanted to remove all the explosives to minimize the impact on the village. One picture was able to convince them that it was wiser to just blow up the stockpile in place. The picture showed a small receiver attached to a wire near the stack of mines. The entire room could be set off with a remote transmitter or code from a cell phone.

The family of the village elder insisted that he come with them when the group of fighters came into their village to meet the man in the truck. He had driven into the town, and then the truck was parked behind the buildings by another fighter. They were worried that there would be another fight with the Americans in their city. Before leaving, one of the fighters talked with the elder and gave him a phone. He reluctantly accompanied his family when they left the village a short while later.

They kept walking toward the city and didn't stop until the buildings of the village were almost out of sight. The elder kept complaining that they were going too far, and he didn't want to go any further. Eventually, his family stopped to appease him, but they planned to pause only for a short time before continuing down the road.

When the elder heard the explosions from the grenades, shortly after seeing the helicopter land, he took the phone from his pocket and entered the code he had been given, but nothing happened. He tried over and over again until he was in tears.

"I have failed," the elder said quietly as he looked down at the phone.

The elder's family could not understand why he was so depressed, but they convinced him to continue on with them to the city where other members of the family lived. They hoped to be able to get away from all the violence they had seen over the last year. When they moved to the village years ago, they wanted to be left in peace, but that was not possible in their country. They hoped and prayed that all the fighting would end, and they really did not care who eventually won. They just wanted the fighting to stop.

Sergeant First Class Hermanson had the soldiers go from door to door, checking to see if anyone was left in the village. When his team told him that everybody was gone, he told the EOD team that the village was clear. One of the EOD specialists set a charge on top of the mines and then ran a line out to the armored vehicles they had driven to the site. They carefully connected the line to a detonator and visually checked the area one more time.

"OK, folks," the EOD specialist said over the radio net. "This is going to be really loud in three, two, one!"

He activated the detonator, and there was a huge explosion that sent dirt and smoke up into the air and shook the ground. When the smoke cleared, there was a massive crater where the electronics shop used to be that extended out into the road. The small alley next to the electronics shop was also gone, as was the building immediately next to the shop. Thankfully the other buildings in the village were still standing.

"Damn, that will wake you up in the morning!" Staff Sergeant Pederson shouted.

"OK, well, it's time for us to head back to the house," the EOD team leader said.

"Thanks. You guys be careful," Sergeant First Class Hermanson said as he shook their hands. "Round up everyone and let's head back to the outpost," he told the other vehicle commander. "I think that's about enough for one day."

The two vehicles started out back to the outpost. Everyone was ready for a meal and a rest. Sergeant First Class Hermanson notified the post of the whereabouts of the contractor's vehicle, so the family would be able to go retrieve it if they wanted to do so.

The drive back was uneventful and a break from the action earlier in the day. Little was said on the trip home, and there was only one radio message. Sergeant First Class Wichman contacted Sergeant First Class Hermanson to let him know that Captain Starn needed surgery on his hand. He was transported to the trauma center, and they would notify the unit if he needed to be sent to Germany or back to the United States. He also let him know that they'd stitched Specialist Ghulam up and were sending him back with the rest of them. He hadn't heard anything else about the other members of the team who'd been evacuated earlier. Sergeant First Class Wichman was happy to say that he was on his way back to the outpost with the remainder of the crew.

When the two vehicles returned to the outpost, Major Palmer and Chief MacKenzie were waiting for them. He thanked all of them for what they were able to do and told them he wanted to speak with all of them in the operations building in an hour. They parked the vehicles, leaving Al Khafaji's body in the back of Sergeant First Class Hermanson's. He would ask Major Palmer where to put the remains when he spoke to him. Everyone walked over to the dining facility to try to get some coffee and a meal.

"Specialist Rashidi, are you OK with what happened to Al Khafaji today?" Sergeant First Class Hermanson asked, trying to evaluate her emotional status.

"Yes, Sergeant," Specialist Rashidi replied. "The only thing I am sad about is that he did not turn and face me when I shot him."

OK, Sergeant First Class Hermanson thought to himself. *I should have known.*

The dining facility was about to close, but they gladly stayed open to feed Sergeant First Class Hermanson and the team. Word had already gotten out about what had happened that day in the village, and they were all happy. Not just because the team was successful but also because the person who had killed one of the other contractors had been killed as well. The man that Al Khafaji murdered was very well liked.

Sergeant Abdullah ate his meal without saying a word. It was nice to not have to think about anything but eating. He was physically OK, but he was mentally drained. He knew this was not the end of the fighting, but he was very relieved that at least this part of it was finished. Sergeant Abdullah really felt like he fit in with the Special Operations people, but he didn't think that he could do what they did on a regular basis anymore. Sergeant Abdullah smiled when he thought that maybe he could be an on-call mechanic for the Special Forces. He was looking forward to hearing what Major Palmer had to tell all of them.

Sergeant First Class Wichman pulled up to the gate of the outpost while the others were at the dining facility. The security guard told him that Major Palmer wanted to meet with everybody at the operations building. He had the driver pull up in front of the building, and then he went inside.

"Sir, the gate guard said you wanted to meet with us," Sergeant First Class Wichman said when he saw Major Palmer standing near Captain Starn's desk.

"Yep. Why don't you have your folks come in and grab a seat?" Major Palmer said. "The others should be here in about five minutes."

"Roger, sir," Sergeant First Class Wichman said, then turned to get the others.

Sergeant First Class Hermanson was walking toward the operations building from the dining facility when Sergeant First Class Wichman came outside and waved at him.

"Hey, Herm. I just went in to talk with the boss, and he says he wants to talk with all of us," Sergeant First Class Wichman said. "Any idea what's up?"

"Nope. We got the same message when we rolled through the gate earlier," Sergeant First Class Hermanson replied. "I told the folks at the dining facility that you were on your way in. He said he would hold some meals aside for you, but they needed to cut the help loose in forty-five minutes."

"Thanks, Herm. Much appreciated," Sergeant First Class Wichman said. "It sure would be nice to get a good meal after today."

"Well, at least we didn't lose anyone today," Sergeant First Class Hermanson said. "It could have been a lot worse."

"I think they were gunning for Wafiq and chief today," Sergeant First Class Wichman stated, sharing what Specialist Ghulam had told him. "Seems like the reason why Wafiq got hit in the shoulder was because he was trying to get a good look down his hard sights when he got hit. I think those guys were trying to hit him in the neck."

"Aren't you giving them too much credit, Doc?" Sergeant First Class Hermanson asked. "Heck, most of these fighters barely even aim. It's mostly just pray and spray."

"Keep going. You'll get there," Sergeant First Class Wichman said.

"But they were all firing on semi," Sergeant First Class Hermanson commented. "They didn't switch to automatic until the second time we engaged them."

"Did you ever think that they wanted to take the number one and number four man out and purposely just wound two and three?" Sergeant First Class Wichman speculated. "They saw two vehicles. What would happen if all four men were down? Wouldn't the personnel in the second vehicle come out to help them?"

"Well, yeah, that's what happened," Sergeant First Class Hermanson said. "Except Carson had the grenade launcher."

"They were not expecting that, and that is why the second team is still around," Sergeant First Class Wichman said as he looked over at Sergeant Abdullah. "I'm not sure he even realizes what he did today."

"If you asked him, he would probably say he was just doing what anyone would do," Sergeant First Class Hermanson smiled. "Good thing he is on our side."

"Seems like I have heard that before," Sergeant First Class Wichman said as they walked into the operations building.

"All right, folks, come on in and take a seat," Chief MacKenzie said. "The boss has a few things he wants to talk with you about, but first, I just want to say thanks for the outstanding effort you all put forth today. I can't even begin to tell you how important that was, and a lot of folks took notice, including the bastard who is the leader of this group. May he rot in hell."

"Thanks, Chief, for stealing my opening," Major Palmer said with a smile. "Before we get started, I want to give all of you an update on the list of injuries. Of course, you already know what is happening with Specialist Hassan, but the good news is they are trying to save her arm, and she will be flying to Walter Reed for additional care and surgical procedures. Captain Starn will also be out of action for a while, as he will require surgery to repair his left hand. Chief Provanski is in intensive care where they are monitoring his wounds. He should have a full recovery, God willing, without any additional surgeries required. Staff Sergeant Vincent has a wound to his lower leg that should see him back here with us in less than a week. Master Sergeant Mandess will also be out for a while, as he was wounded in his upper leg, but the bullet shattered his bone, and he will require follow-on surgery in the States. Specialist Ghulam, as you can see, should have a full recovery very soon."

"Yes, sir," Specialist Ghulam said with pride.

"As you can see, we've been banged up a bit," Major Palmer stated, looking across the room. "That leaves me with a difficult decision to make. Do I bring in replacements for your team, or do I send the entire team back to the States and send another team in? Since we are having this talk, most of you have probably already figured out what I have decided to do."

"Come on, Boss. We can make it work," Sergeant First Class Hermanson insisted.

"I know that you would give it everything you have, but it's just not the right thing for me to do," Major Palmer said. He knew that his soldiers didn't want to go, but having a completely fresh team that had been training together was a better call for him to make.

"What about us, sir?" Specialist Rashidi asked.

"I want you to stay until the next team leaves," Major Palmer said as he looked at the two specialists. "Sergeant Abdullah, your brigade commander asked that you return to your unit if the team is no longer deployed."

"Yes, sir," Sergeant Abdullah said with mixed emotions even though he'd known all along that was the plan. It was just going to be earlier than he had expected.

"Does anyone have any questions?" Major Palmer asked, gazing out over the group. "OK, I just want to say that I am very proud of all of you. I hope to have all of you heading back to the States in three or four weeks."

"Sir, one last thing," Sergeant First Class Hermanson said. "What about Al Khafaji?"

"Put him in my vehicle, and we will take him back to the Green Zone," Major Palmer said. "Folks are still talking about what the best thing is to do with his body. He was an American citizen, but there are some that want to revoke his citizenship and leave his body in Iraq. Not my circus, not my monkeys, to quote an old Polish saying. Someone from intel will be out to look through his things tomorrow."

"Roger, sir," Sergeant First Class Hermanson said. He and Sergeant Abdullah took care of moving Al Khafaji to Major Palmer's vehicle. It seemed like such a waste to Sergeant Abdullah for someone to die at such a young age, but that was how this war was being fought. Young people on each side were paying the ultimate price. When he thought about it, it was much like any other war with young people going off to fight for governments run by older politicians.

"So, what do you think about going back to your unit?" Sergeant First Class Hermanson asked Sergeant Abdullah after they put Al Khafaji's body in the back of the vehicle.

"I would rather stay here with your unit," Sergeant Abdullah said. "But it doesn't look like your unit will be here very long. I chose to be a mechanic, so that is what I will do."

"I just want to say that it has been an honor to serve alongside you," Sergeant First Class Hermanson said. "Watching what you did for Chief MacKenzie back in the day, I thought it was just a one-time thing. Now that I have worked with you, I can honestly say that you are one brave individual. You are the definition of selfless service, and your unit will be much better with you back on the roster."

"Thank you for the kind words," Sergeant Abdullah replied. "But I am just a soldier. I am also very impressed with you and the Special Operations units. I am not sure I could do what all of you do on a regular basis. The Army taught me to do what is right, and that is always my focus. I am just happy to be able to help."

"Well, it does wear on a person after a while," Sergeant First Class Hermanson admitted. He looked at Sergeant Abdullah and began to smile. "We need to get one of those big lights to flash a sign up in the sky when we need you, just like Batman."

"I watched Batman on the channel that plays the old shows," Sergeant Abdullah said. "They had strange-looking uniforms."

"Yes, they did," Sergeant First Class Hermanson agreed. "But you wouldn't have to worry. We would never expect you to turn up in tights."

Major Palmer and Chief MacKenzie were walking back to the vehicle as Sergeant First Class Hermanson and Sergeant Abdullah were leaving. "Carson, I just wanted to give you another chance to change your mind about going back to the maintenance unit," he said as he reached them. "I would like to find a way to have you permanently assigned to us."

"Sir, I am not sure that is something that would be able to happen," Sergeant Abdullah said. "I am a mechanic now, and I need to finish my work with them."

"OK, I understand," Major Palmer replied. "But don't be surprised if you get new orders someday that has you reporting for duty with the Special Forces."

"I do not think anything is impossible when the Special Forces are involved," Sergeant Abdullah smiled, shaking hands with Major Palmer.

"Carson, I'm not even going to say goodbye," Chief MacKenzie said, "because I know that somehow down the line, I am going to run into you again. It most definitely is a very small Army. Take care, and I wish you all the best."

"Thank you, Mister Mac," Sergeant Abdullah said. He knew he would miss Chief MacKenzie most of all, but he was very happy for him. "May God bless you."

Over the next five days, everyone returned to the outpost except Captain Starn and Master Sergeant Mandess. They were still recovering from their wounds. Chief Provanski was released from intensive care once they determined that his neck injury would not require additional surgical procedures. He assumed command of the team and made sure everyone was staying busy until their departure, which was set for twenty days later. He was not interested in finding any more spies.

The unit tried to keep Sergeant Abdullah as long as they could, but the brigade was getting adamant about his return, so they reluctantly decided to have him turn in his gear and scheduled a return date that would put him back in his unit in a couple of days. Realistically, Sergeant Abdullah had already turned in all the things he had been issued days earlier. He did not want to be a burden to his Special Operations friends.

The day before he was scheduled to depart, Sergeant Abdullah spent the morning packing all his personal gear and checking to make sure he had not forgotten anything. He was excited to be going on to something new. The time he had spent with the Special Operations soldiers and the linguists had affected his thoughts of what he wanted to do. He was seriously considering moving on to something outside of the military. Maybe it was time for him to hang up his uniform. He knew that he could get a position as a linguist with several companies, and he was still getting messages asking if he would be available for contract work. He was just undecided on what he really wanted to do. Maybe his time back with the maintenance company would give him time to figure that out.

Sergeant Abdullah decided that he needed to do something other than sit in his quarters. He looked at his watch, and it was about time for lunch, so he finished with his bags and headed over to the dining facility.

"Sergeant Abdullah," Specialist Ghulam called out when he and Specialist Rashidi saw him heading to the dining facility. "Would it be OK if we shared a meal with you?"

"Of course, Wafiq," Sergeant Abdullah agreed, and they all continued to walk toward the dining facility.

The line was short. Sergeant Abdullah thought it was because there were many folks out on patrol, but he had no idea what was really happening. When he walked in the door of the dining facility, he was completely surprised. Major Palmer, Chief MacKenzie, and all the other soldiers from the Special Operations teams were there, and they all started clapping.

Sergeant Abdullah was very embarrassed and didn't know what to say. He looked at Specialist Ghulam and Specialist Rashidi, and they were also clapping and smiling.

"So, you knew about this," Sergeant Abdullah said to both of them.

"Yes, Sergeant. It was our job to bring you here," Specialist Rashidi said.

"Sergeant Abdullah, front and center," Major Palmer said. The clapping quickly died down.

Sergeant Abdullah walked over to Major Palmer and Sergeant Major Wagner. The sergeant major had to redirect Sergeant Abdullah to the correct place for his ceremony. It was not something Sergeant Abdullah was accustomed to. He was not well trained in drill and ceremony.

"Sergeant Abdullah," Major Palmer began, "you have been recommended for an award, but unfortunately, it will take time to get processed. In the meantime, everybody wanted to make sure that you didn't leave here empty-handed, so here are just a few tokens of our appreciation for what you have done."

Sergeant Major Wagner turned to the small table behind him and gave Major Palmer a United States flag that was stored in a wooden presentation case.

"We flew this flag over the outpost two days ago in your honor," Major Palmer said. "We want you to have it to remember how much this unit has appreciated your service with us."

"Thank you, sir," Sergeant Abdullah said as he held the case in his hands.

The sergeant major turned and took another item off the table. It was a paper bag with something wrapped inside of it.

"We can't officially make you one of us," Major Palmer stated, "but we all feel that you have earned this." He handed Sergeant Abdullah the bag and had him open it.

"Sir, this is very kind of all of you," Sergeant Abdullah said as he held a green beret in his hands. "This is a great honor for me, and I will do my best to try to live up to what this beret stands for."

"Group, attention!" Sergeant Major Wagner called out as the door to the dining facility opened and a lieutenant general and his entourage walked in. The lieutenant general, Major General Fisher, was the commanding general of the United States Army Special Operations Command (USASOC).

Lieutenant General Fisher made a point of trying to drop in on his soldiers when they were deployed. He was part of the reason for the going away recognition for Sergeant Abdullah. He was already in the country when he spoke with Major Palmer about the award recommendation that had been submitted for Sergeant Abdullah. After reviewing the award recommendation, he told his aide to set up a meeting with Sergeant Abdullah.

"Carry on," Lieutenant General Fisher said as he walked up to the center of the room.

"Sir, we were just congratulating Sergeant Abdullah for all the hard work he has done in supporting our unit," Major Palmer said.

"Oh, is that so?" Lieutenant General Fisher asked. "Well, I guess I am in the right place. Sergeant Abdullah, I understand you have been awfully busy working with this bunch of guys."

"It has been an honor for me, sir," Sergeant Abdullah said.

"Well, I don't give many of these out," Lieutenant General Fisher said as he turned to his aide, who handed him something. "The first coin is my personal memento as the commanding general of USASOC, which I give to individuals who have performed in an exceptional manner." He handed Sergeant Abdullah the coin as they shook hands. Someone in his entourage was taking pictures.

"The next coin I am giving you is even more special to me," Lieutenant General Fisher explained as his aide handed him a larger coin, which came in a special presentation box. "This coin is only for a few very special individuals who I consider to be part of my Team of Heroes. After reading your recommendation for award, I think you are extremely well deserving of this honor. You are also the only individual who is not technically a member of Special Operations who I have given this to. Thank you for all you have done."

Once again, Lieutenant General Fisher extended his hand, and as they shook hands, he passed the coin to Sergeant Abdullah. There was also once again the obligatory photo.

Lieutenant General Fisher had everyone in his group come through and shake hands with Sergeant Abdullah. When the last person in line was finished, the room was once again called to attention as Lieutenant General Fisher prepared to leave.

"Sorry I can't stay longer, folks, but I have some helicopter pilots outside the compound who get a little antsy if they have to stay on the ground too long," Lieutenant General Fisher said. Then, he turned and headed toward the door. Before he exited, he turned and looked at Sergeant Abdullah and said, "I wish you all the best, young soldier. Here is your first salute."

Sergeant Abdullah saluted but didn't really understand why.

"Carry on," Sergeant Major Wagner said as the commanding general left the building.

Next, all the soldiers in the room filed by and shook Sergeant Abdullah's hand and wished him all the best. Sergeant Abdullah was completely overwhelmed by the entire event. He could not find the words to express his gratitude.

Chief MacKenzie came by after the room was starting to clear and handed Sergeant Abdullah a book. It was about Kit Carson.

"I just thought you might want to read a little about the guy your nickname comes from," Chief MacKenzie said as he handed Sergeant Abdullah the book.

"Thank you, Mister Mac," Sergeant Abdullah said.

Sergeant Abdullah put the book with the other things he had been given and walked to his quarters. When he got inside, he laid everything on his bed and said a prayer to thank God for his life and all the good fortune that had been bestowed upon him.

18

Sergeant Abdullah checked his messages after dinner and found a couple from his parents that he had not answered. They had heard that there were problems in Iraq and were worried about him. He tried to never tell his parents what he was doing or had done. The last thing that he had told them was that he was working as a mechanic, which made his father very proud. He sent them a quick message to let them know everything was well with him and not to worry. He apologized for not responding earlier and explained that sometimes it was difficult to use the computer. Sergeant Abdullah told them he would be better at answering their messages because he did not want them to worry.

The next morning, Sergeant Abdullah woke up and stacked all of his gear on the bunk. He walked over to the dining facility for breakfast and watched everyone else as they moved about getting ready for another day. He knew that all the soldiers would stay busy until their departure, but just like leaving any unit, it was hard to accept that everyone would be able to just go about their business without him. The Army was very good at making you feel like a superstar one day and then moving right along without you and not missing a beat the next. It's just the way the big machine ran.

Sergeant Abdullah went back to his quarters and put on his rucksack. He had his duffel bag in one hand and his rifle in the other. As he closed the door, he looked back and thought of how nice it was to have a place of his own, but Sergeant Maczrakolski was a good person, and it would also be nice to have someone to speak with at the end of the day. He felt like he was finally ready to go back to the maintenance unit.

Sergeant First Class Hermanson saw Sergeant Abdullah leaving his quarters and walked over to help him carry his gear up to the front gate.

"Here, Carson," Sergeant First Class Hermanson said as he reached out to take Sergeant Abdullah's duffel bag. "Let me help you with that."

"Thank you, Herm," Sergeant Abdullah replied, gladly releasing the duffel bag.

The two soldiers walked over to the front gate, with the others wishing Sergeant Abdullah good luck along the way. When they reached the small building next to the gate, Sergeant First Class Hermanson set the duffel bag down next to Sergeant Abdullah.

"Stay in touch, Sergeant," Sergeant First Class Hermanson said as he turned to leave.

"Will do, Herm," Sergeant Abdullah replied.

Sergeant Abdullah took a seat on his duffel bag and waited for the infantry unit's vehicle to show up. He'd been told they would arrive before noon but figured it was easier to wait at the gate just in case they were early. Sergeant Abdullah didn't want anyone to have to come looking for him.

He passed the time by watching the vehicles come and go through the gate. The other team was doing most of the missions now as everyone waited for the other team to arrive. Most of what they were doing was foot patrols in the city as they went out in local dress in support of the regular units. Sergeant Abdullah had heard there were also other agencies looking for the leader as well, but it seemed as if he had disappeared for the time being.

It was almost 1100 hours when the vehicle arrived. Sergeant Abdullah wanted to just go outside the gate and meet them, but the security guards insisted on having the vehicle go through a regular inspection and then move inside the gate to pick him up. He picked up his gear as the vehicle went through the gate and pulled up beside him. The back door opened up, and a tall soldier stepped out.

"Are you Sergeant Abdullah?" the soldier asked, moving toward him.

"Yes, Sergeant," Sergeant Abdullah said. "I am sorry that you had to come inside the gate."

"Well, don't be," the sergeant said. "That's the right thing to do. My name is Staff Sergeant Gentry. I've heard a lot about you."

"Thank you, Sergeant," Sergeant Abdullah responded, picking up his gear.

"Let's get you on the road," Staff Sergeant Gentry said. "We can talk some more on the way back to your unit."

"Yes, Sergeant," Sergeant Abdullah replied. Staff Sergeant Gentry turned and got back inside of the vehicle.

The door closed, and the vehicle pulled around and waited for the security guard to wave them back through the gate. The security guard motioned for them to proceed, and as he did, he saluted the vehicle. The driver laughed as Staff Sergeant Gentry returned the salute.

"What the hell are you laughing at?" Staff Sergeant Gentry said to the driver, who immediately stopped laughing.

"I just thought it was funny that they would be saluting our vehicle," the driver said. "I mean, who do they think we have in here anyways? The president?"

"We should have you back with your unit in about an hour or so, Mr. President," Staff Sergeant Gentry said, smiling at Sergeant Abdullah. "Kick back and relax. We got this, Sergeant."

The vehicle carrying Sergeant Abdullah made its way down the dirt road toward the city. There was very little traffic. Just the occasional small group of people walking. As they neared the improved road, the vehicle traffic got heavier as people drove into the city to do business.

"It seems quiet on the streets," Sergeant Abdullah observed.

"I figure they are still trying to recover from the beating they took over the last two months," Staff Sergeant Gentry said. "I heard tell that you were involved in blowing up the truck full of explosives. Is it really true that you blew up the truck with a grenade launcher?"

"Yes," Sergeant Abdullah said. "It was the only thing I could think of to stop the truck."

"Wait," one of the other soldiers said. "You blew up a truck with a grenade launcher?"

"Oh, that's not the half of it," Staff Sergeant Gentry explained. "It was a moving truck that was heading toward him."

"Hell no," the soldier said in disbelief. "I'm going to have to throw the BS flag on that one. Is that true, Sergeant?"

"Yes," Sergeant Abdullah said, "but sadly it took me two shots to hit it."

"Yeah, but there's more," Staff Sergeant Gentry continued. "I heard something about you blowing up a village."

"OK, Sarge, now you are pulling my leg," the soldier said. "Don't tell me that is true."

"No, that is not true," Sergeant Abdullah began.

"See, I knew it," the soldier proudly said.

"It was the explosive ordnance experts who blew it up," Sergeant Abdullah continued. "But it wasn't the entire village. It was just a big underground room with a lot of explosives in it."

The two soldiers asked Sergeant Abdullah to tell them the whole story, and he reluctantly agreed to do so. He made sure to include all the heroic acts by the other members of the team and was especially proud to tell the story of Specialist Rashidi killing the traitor in the underground tunnel. Neither one of them asked about the previous trip to the village, so Sergeant Abdullah cut his story short. Even though he had killed seventeen and wounded five others, he still thought it was a team effort. He didn't enjoy killing; for him, it was just part of a soldier's duty during a time of war.

"That's one heck of a story," Staff Sergeant Gentry commented.

Sergeant Abdullah just nodded his head. He was hoping that he would get back to the maintenance unit and spend the remainder of the deployment just working on vehicles, but he was reminded of a saying his drill sergeant used to tell him during Basic Training: "Abdullah, hope is not a method!"

Sneak a Peek at Book Two:
Defending the Eagle

The meeting between the remaining leaders of the jihadi movement against the infidels was to be held in the Anbar Province west of Baghdad late in the evening. The leaders had agreed upon the location based upon where the fight was still actively being fought. Anbar Province was an area the Americans were not trying to currently occupy.

While most of the leaders believed a meeting was necessary, many of them who had survived were not happy that they were asked to travel outside of their area. Traveling was not safe, and many of the leaders were known to the enemy. The fight was not going well for them, and the Americans had become more determined of late. The victories the American forces had enjoyed over the last two months were bolstering their resolve. Many of the jihadi leaders did not want to have a meeting, but some of them had lost so many fighters that they had little room to disagree.

The leader of the groups in the south of Baghdad was particularly annoyed. He had been a senior officer in the Iraqi Special Republican Guard. His name was Abdulaziz Mahmoud, but all of his fighters just referred to him as the leader. He was very cautious not to share names outside of his inner circle to avoid anyone providing information to the infidels if captured.

The meeting began with the usual customary small talk as the leaders talked with each other about everything except the fight that was at hand. Several of the leaders had been in the Iraqi Army and would rather get to the point, but they were not the majority and went along with the others, trying to act like they were really interested in the welfare of everyone's families. The leader from the Anbar Province, as the host of the meeting, finally asked everyone to take a seat.

"I would like to thank all of you for agreeing to come to this location for our meeting," the Anbar leader said as he looked around the room. "We must talk of our strategy as we move forward. It is important that we all work together and do not become entangled in separate fights against the Americans."

"I agree," the leader from the areas north of Baghdad said, but that was understandable since he was more concerned about fighting the Kurds than the Americans.

"So, are you proposing we fight with the same tactics or that we are all supporting an effort to rid our country of the infidels?" another leader from the east asked.

"We need to make sure everyone has all the weapons and supplies they need before we go forward with any more fighting," the leader from Baghdad said.

"I believe that we should find a way to bring the infidels to their knees," one of the leaders declared, and all the others nodded their heads in agreement. That is, all of them except Abdulaziz Mahmoud. "And what of you, Abdulaziz? I did not see you agreeing to my point."

"Well, I believe that all of you should determine whether you want to actually fight or just hold meetings and talk," Abdulaziz said, trying to remain calm.

"You are just upset because your fight is not going well," one of the other leaders responded. "My region has not lost a single fighter in the last month."

"That is because your fighters do not fight. They sit and hide like scared animals," Abdulaziz replied, remaining relatively calm.

"Come now, brother. You do not have any more fighters to die for you. Maybe you should reconsider the way you fight against the Americans," the leader from the west suggested. "Our methods in the west are showing good results. The Americans try to avoid coming here."

"The Americans do not come here because your area is a wasteland," Abdulaziz retorted, his voice rising. "I will not be preached to about tactics by someone who had his unit surrender en masse to the Americans in the war. You have the leadership skills of a camel spider."

"You have failed in this fight just like you failed to protect the capital in the war!" the western leader exclaimed.

"I am done with these discussions," Abdulaziz spat. He took out his pistol and shot the leader from the west in the forehead.

As soon as the leader raised his pistol, his men raised their rifles but did not fire. They were waiting to see what the others would do. Thankfully for the others, nobody reached for a weapon.

"Now," Abdulaziz began as he wiped some blood from his forehead, "I will need men from all of you. You will make sure that they arrive in my area in the next four days."

The four leaders in the room all nodded their heads. They were still in disbelief at what had just happened. One of them slowly raised his hand.

"I do not have many fighters," he said. "How many do you require us to send to you?"

"I need thirty fighters from each of you," Abdulaziz commanded, looking around the room. "I will make sure to find a way to keep track of how many you send. If you do not have that many fighters, then kidnap the rest and send them with your fighters. Do not fail me in this request.

"Find me the person who was second-in-command to this dog," Abdulaziz said to his senior security officer.

"Yes, leader," he replied. Then, he went out the door with one of the security guards for the fallen leader from the west.

There was a discussion outside of the room followed by a gunshot. The security officer for Abdulaziz walked back into the room and strode over to the other security guard.

"Would you like to tell me who the person is that my leader is looking for?" the security officer asked the individual who was almost shaking.

"I can take you to him," the security guard said.

"Good, but if there are any tricks, I will kill you and your family," the security officer warned.

The security officer left the room with the security guard while Abdulaziz called the others back to the table. The other leaders sat down to listen to Abdulaziz tell them of his plan to drive the infidels out of their country. It would require actions from all the leaders and even some areas that were not represented in the room.

"The first thing I want to do is place a bounty on the head of the American commander who has been attacking us in the southern region," Abdulaziz said and then proceeded to go through his plans with the others. "I will pay one hundred thousand American dollars to the individual who kills him."

The security officer returned to the room with a middle-aged man after about thirty minutes. He looked like he was still half asleep. The other leaders had already departed.

"You are now the leader of the western region," Abdulaziz said to the man before telling him about the plan and the need to send him fighters.

"Our fighters are ready to help when you need them," the new leader said as he glanced over at the body of his predecessor. "We can send more if there is a need. We have many men here who would like to fight against the infidels."

"That is good to know," Abdulaziz said. "But for now, thirty will be good. If you can recruit more, just continue what you have been doing in your area."

"We will continue to bloody the infidels," the man declared.

"You will be a good leader, brother," Abdulaziz said to him with a small smile.

When the vehicle bringing Sergeant Abdullah back to his unit finally arrived at the base of the maneuver brigade, all the members of the crew had a deep admiration for Sergeant Abdullah. The driver pulled through the gate and drove to the maintenance area. When the vehicle came to a stop, Staff Sergeant Gentry picked up Sergeant Abdullah's duffel bag while the other soldier carried his rucksack. The two of them followed Sergeant Abdullah over to the quarters he had shared with Sergeant Maczrakolski.

"It was great to meet you," Staff Sergeant Gentry said to Sergeant Abdullah.

"Yep, same here, Sergeant," the other soldier added.

"Well, I am very pleased to meet you as well," Sergeant Abdullah replied as the two headed back to their vehicle.

"I'll be damned. Look who is back in town," Sergeant First Class Broadmoor commented when he saw Sergeant Abdullah standing near the building. "Boy, have I got a surprise for you."

9 781962 202169